THE HELIX TWISTS

Sequel to The Helix Blink

By

Jeanette Appel Cave

THE HELIX TWISTS

Sequel to The Helix Blink

By

Jeanette Appel Cave

Copyright 2016

Outside Parameters Press

Sacramento, CA

ISBN-13:978-1523917051

ISBN-10:1523917059

Cover designs: Matt Musselman, www.invokedesign.us

This is fiction. Any places, people, or events are imagined and any resemblance to real places and people is fictitious. No part of this book may be used, except for excerpts for reviews, or copied in print or digital formats, without the permission of the author.

Author of

The Helix Blink

Dark Continents: Survival Instinct

Crystal Vision

The stars were so bright and beautiful above him, the constellations so clear and distinguishable that he stared up in amazement, loving the memories it stirred looking at them. Dale would have been using this as a teaching moment, pointing out where to find each constellation. Dale made everything about science take on a magical sense of wonder and awe. Gavin felt he was high enough in the tower to reach out and touch the heavens, and the night was so clear that it was a canopy of twinkling magic above his head. He certainly preferred looking at the sky tonight to watching the ground below him. He could recall pleasant memories in the past when he and his brother Dale would lie in an open field, risking gators near his Florida home and look up at the stars; Dale could name nearly every constellation from the time he was ten, and Gavin thought his brother brilliant for having memorized so many. Fortunately, looking up didn't make him sick to his stomach, it was looking down that made the world spin. His fear of heights was a lifelong phobia, even stepladders bothered him and made him insecure and nauseated. He had tried everything under the sun to conquer his phobia but had never really succeeded. However, he could not afford to allow anyone in this village to know that he had any weakness that might make him "expendable."

Gavin sat alone in the tower, watching over the newly-founded village of Hades, where El Paso, Texas, once stood. He balanced on the stool that they had given him, the only comfort in the six- foot-by-six-foot platform, his rifle cradled in his lap. He, along with many of the other guards, those brave enough to express it, felt that the "watch" was nothing more than a huge waste of time. However, since he only had to serve two consecutive days every other week, according to the camp assignment charts, he was willing to go along with this, however unfruitful and overly cautious it seemed.

They hadn't seen other humans for a very long time. The last had been months ago and that had been a small group of wanderers who were almost demented enough to have been accepted into the Hades group, had they only had the sense not to surrender so eagerly. Had they fought back, even a little, according to Casto, they would have won the respect of the council. But as Casto contended, who could respect a group of fully grown men who would bend knee just because they were outnumbered? At least that was Casto's warped reasoning and his vote was the one everyone waited to see. Casto had given the thumbs down as soon as their knees had touched the dust on the ground and the rest of the council followed; the slaughter had been extremely short lived. The celebration feast lasted for days. Gavin didn't even want to think about that. Since he had never been forced to join the cannibalism, he managed to steer clear of such "celebrations."

Casto was becoming the undisputed leader of Hades. Even the other council members deferred all decisions to him, everyone could see it. Gavin knew that it was more that nearly everyone feared his wrath than anything else. He was stone cold crazy. It was easy to see that there was little he wouldn't do and the man was fearless in his intent to do anything he wanted. Gavin avoided him when he could, keeping the lowest profile he could possibly keep, even though it had been Casto who had brought him here. There were times when Gavin thought that the fact that he had come here with Casto's group was the reason he was afforded autonomy that few enjoyed here. He'd been a member of this group for almost two years now and did not want to do anything that would jeopardize his position. He had watched enough death to know that you didn't stand up to the council; whatever they ordered you to do, you just did. He was considered one of their hardest workers.

He had seen Casto order murders, he had even seen him commit murders. No one was ever brave enough to call his decisions anything but "justice." To this despot, "justice" was anything he wanted it to be. With Casto, murders were the easy way out. He leaned more toward slow, painful torture. Gavin tried to be absent from those public punishments, choosing a work detail so that he could avoid the "trials" and administered punishments. It made him feel like a coward and like he was living in denial, but he simply could not witness any more atrocity, there had already been too much. He knew that he needed to ignore such things if only to keep his sanity.

Gavin was wise enough to follow the rules to the letter so tonight he was sitting watch in a tower that gave him vertigo, the tower facing north. It wasn't that only the north tower affected him, it's that he'd only ever been assigned the north tower because the line boss used the same assignment sheets over and over again, not wanting the extra work of reworking them, so he always drew the north tower. He didn't even know what the view was like from the other towers. It was probably going to be like this forever, since the line boss showed no inclination to change things up and everyone now just went to their "usual" tower when arriving for duty. The line boss, called "Pit Bull" by everyone, possibly because his face did resemble the dog by the same name, was an older man who seemed very unhappy about having to face anything out of the ordinary, including changes. He liked predictability, so everyone knew that, so long as Pit Bull was in charge, things would remain the way they were.

Even the guard house was a testament to Pit Bull's resistance to change. If one of the other line bosses rearranged the central guard house, Pit would have it back to his way before the end of the first hour: he wanted to rely on the fact that the megaphone was hanging on the wall just to the left of the clipboard with the assignment sheets, the desk would always be arranged so that when Pit was in his office chair, he was directly across from the door, with the charts, megaphone and guns on the wall to his right. The door was off center to leave room in the eight-foot wall for a small window beside it and each of the remaining three walls of the building had a window in the center and Pit kept his chair off center so that he could move a half revolution in his chair to see out the window behind him. A pile of what might be conceived as riot gear was in the far corner opposite the doorway. Gavin had never been shown what to do with the "riot gear" so he assumed that it would only be used by the mobile guards on retrieval duty in their jeeps and trucks.

There were twelve towers in all, surrounding the gated and walled camp. Each was situated almost a hundred yards or more from one another. His was the most northern, almost two miles from the center of Hades, straddling the wall with ladders on either side leading up to the platform. It sat right at the foot of the hills. The pattern of the towers was laid out like a clock, completely by accident, nobody really gave it much thought, they just wanted towers when they began building them, so they could see a great distance if someone were daring to approach the camp. Not that he could see anything in the dark, but he would be here in the daytime, too. The "watch" was a full 48-hour duty. How he wished he would have been assigned a post at the gate, but that just wasn't his luck. His assignment would always be the north tower. Even if he became sick from looking down, he knew that he didn't have the courage to do anything but tough it out.

It would take more courage than he could find within himself to complain, even if he could have complained, even if speech were possible. Those who shirked their duties or complained were among the last group of public crucifixions. However, the most courageous thing he was capable of to date was to keep his dreams secret and he knew that nothing would make him give them up, perhaps because the dreams gave him hope of escape, of getting away from Hades and finding a different life, a life more in tune with his moral code. He wanted to believe in those dreams, he sincerely wanted to believe that somewhere close those who visited him in his dreams lived and played free and happy. He NEEDED to believe it. He knew that it was probably his own fantasy that created the dreams, but they gave him something to cling to. SHE was something to cling to.

Gavin had witnessed too much horror to allow himself to think back over the last two years, but he simply had no idea what to do about it. He was a muscular, tall man for his age, nearly sixteen, and strong as an ox, which was what the council liked about him. But, what they didn't know was that he thought them evil, he hated all of them and was happy that they thought him too witless to befriend. The acts they committed were wrong, the killings, the rapes, and, above all, the cannibalism. It was wrong and nothing could have ever have made him join them had he a choice. He hid and he kept that low profile and, when asked, he simply shrugged and let them go on thinking he was simple-minded. It had worked, this ruse of playing deaf and dumb. He knew that some of them considered him a harmless but strong and useful pet. A very strong and hard-working pet.

So, he took his turns gardening and cleaning, digging and working on machinery, which was something he had always been good at, doing the work of three men, and allowed them to assign him watch in this dreadful tower. Let them laugh at his feeble-mindedness, let them chuckle behind his back, believing him to be half-witted and innocent. The dream sustained him. The horror had taken his voice, a voice that he had once had in the long ago time before the world ended, so he knew that he would not slip and use it.

He had tried to use it, when he was out in the field where no one could hear him, but no sound came, try as he might to regain his voice. That was what gave him the idea to play a deaf mute, he actually had lost the use of his voice and wasn't sure it would ever return. Pulling himself into his shell made it easy to pretend that he heard nothing said or done. He could even ignore loud, threatening, sudden noises. He had become expert at ignoring even the loud report of a gun fired over his shoulder.

He was allowed three hours of sleep each night in the tower. He had only to signal the other towers that he was going down for his break once they flashed him to let him know it was his turn, then they would signal when his three hours were up. The bright lights (they also used the air horn but believed he couldn't hear that) never failed to wake him even when he was asleep on the floor of the platform. He had a sleeping bag for comfort although it made his skin crawl to think about how many others had used that same sleeping bag when taking their turns at watch. So many unwashed bodies in Hades, so few with interest in personal hygiene. Actually, Casto was one of the cleanest, aside from himself. He found that he could only work up the courage to sleep on top of the bag, and only then when he threw his own blanket down on top of it; nothing could get him to sleep inside of it. Besides, it never seemed cold enough to need a down sleeping bag, anyway.

He allowed himself to think about last night's dream, while watching his assigned perimeter. Another of the guards was enjoying his sleep shift. Gavin's would be next, in only two more hours. He had come to anticipate this sleep like none other because, when he worked the tower, the dreams were the strongest. The bells would let the other watcher know when the hours passed and the other watcher would signal for Gavin's sleep time to begin, and then, and then...

In the dream, there were many children. Happy children, children running free and certain that they were protected and safe. In his dream, they welcomed him, they ran toward him as if happy to see him, their hands out, their smiles friendly and inviting. He wanted to join those children more than anything, especially the one they called Laurel. She was one of the oldest of the children and she was prettier than any girl that Gavin had ever seen. Laurel, with her blond hair and bright blue eyes, smiling and laughing and making his dream seem so real, he wanted to reach out and touch her. He never wanted the men in Hades to see Laurel or any of the children. He never wanted to see those children murdered, torn apart, eaten. He knew that he would kill for Laurel, to keep her safe, even from Casto. The children showed him kindness and it brought tears to his eyes just thinking about it. It had been too long since anyone had shown him kindness. Just the way they looked into his eyes and smiled at him made him feel human again, made him FEEL again.

Last night Laurel had caught his eye and smiled directly at him. The smile made him warm from the tip of his head to his toes. Not even his old girlfriend in junior high, in the long ago just before the world ended, made him feel so appreciated, so cozy. He winced at the way it made him feel, thinking about Sandy and Laurel at the same time; Sandy had been real, had been flawed because she was human, real, Laurel had the advantage of being so perfect because she was dream material, he had created her in his fantasy. He had thought himself in love with Sandy in the long ago, but Sandy could never even begin to hold a candle to Laurel. It still made him feel disloyal to Sandy even to think about how pretty Laurel was. He knew that he didn't have to feel this guilt, that it was silly to feel disloyal, he was a single man. Besides, Sandy was long dead, he had seen her body after the first wave of bombing, and he had left everyone he loved behind, unburied, back there in his home town of Ocala, Florida.

To leave Ocala, he had hotwired a pick-up truck, just like his older brother Dale Jr. had taught him to do when they wanted to go joy-riding in their folks' truck. Dale was another body left behind in Ocala, and their parents, as well.

Gavin had been at school and, for some strange reason, the building collapsed around him, leaving him standing under a conjunction of steel girders, the only survivor. He had been able to walk home after digging his way out of the rubble of the school and surrounding buildings. His home had been hard to recognize. In actuality, there was little left of his entire neighborhood. His parents were dead, but he at least got to see their bodies. He buried them in the garden. Some of their neighbors' homes had completely vaporized. Dale had been working in the garage when the bombs hit and the garage was a smoking cairn of ash and stone, there was nothing left to bury.

Gavin sat on the ground outside of the house for a long time, mourning his loss and wondering what to do and where to go.

He walked around Ocala for almost a week afterward, looking for survivors. What he saw in Ocala and the shock of finding what had happened to Dale took his voice, it happened all at once, one moment he was screaming, the next he was unable to bring forth any sound at all, but he continued to search, hoping to find another living soul. When he found none, he found a pick-up truck with giant tires that would be able to leave the highway to detour around the cars left abandoned on the tarmacs. It was one of those monster trucks that required the driver and passengers to climb up into it, hoisting themselves from treads in the tires to a rod hanging below the door, while using the handholds on the inside of the door. He chose it because it challenged his phobia of heights; he consistently tried to overcome the phobia. And he chose it because it was a truck Dale would have chosen to own, had they had the money to afford it. Dale would have loved this truck like he loved his dog, and that was a whole lot of love.

The truck was a beautiful shiny deep red, one of the best paint jobs he had ever seen, it drew him like a moth to flame. It was a rich shade of red, not flashy, not cheap looking, it was the red of ripe, luscious cherries. Someone had poured a lot of money into this truck. He winced when he realized that poor someone was probably now just vapor or ashes, like Dale. He felt like he was driving from the sky when he sat in the cab and he hurried to leave Ocala. He drove as far from Florida as he could get, siphoning gas when he ran low and working his way against a tide of people heading for the coasts. Why were people going toward such desolation and pain? The truck was really cool and, even though he was afraid of heights, he was happy to have something that could maneuver around or even over some of the obstructions in his way. He drove with that fear of heights in the pit of his stomach, embracing his fear, letting it drive him forward. Many people had tried to steal the truck from him and he had narrowly escaped those willing to harm him to take it by force. Eventually he found a loaded gun on the body of a man in a gas station. He taught himself how to use it and, when he reached Atlanta, he found a gun shop that had almost been looted bare, but he was able to find a box of ammunition for his revolver. He stopped worrying so much about thieves, he had his own personal tower on wheels.

For some reason, he had never even wanted to head toward a coast where it seemed everyone on the road was heading. He wanted mountains, he wanted away from humans, he wanted to find trees and animals. He had always trusted animals far more than humans, anyway. He nearly settled in the Blue Ridge, after passing through

Georgia and the Carolinas, planning to build a cabin and live off the land, if necessary, but met up with a sweet and defenseless old couple in Virginia who asked him to drive them to St. Louis, where their daughter and her four children lived. He didn't have the heart, nor the means, to tell them that it was unlikely that they actually "lived" from what he had heard from others on the road, so he had just nodded and complied. They had no one else, and neither did he. He had seen a lot of death and destruction in his travels but couldn't bring himself to break their ancient and optimistic hearts. Besides, they were very patient with the fact that he was mute. The old man would write him notes and had even begun carrying a notepad and pencil in the front pocket of his flannel shirt. They treated him so good that he came to love them, against his own will, since it seemed that nothing he loved could survive.

They both had died on the way to St. Louis. Friendly and wise old Alfred Gray and his wife who he called Hildy, a woman Gavin would have loved to have for his own grandmother, she was so sweet and comforting. He found he missed their voices for weeks afterward, slow-talking storyteller Alfred and his Hildy, whose voice was mouse-like and squeaky and who rattled on about how things "used to be" and how her pappy had said this or that. His own grandparents were long dead, but had never been warm and comforting, they had been too involved in their golf games and their socials. He was shocked at how quickly the Grays had gone from having some flu symptoms to just dropping over dead. Hildy had gotten it first and Alfred tried so hard to nurse her to health, then, the day before she died, he was almost too sick to tend her at all and Gavin fed and cared for them both. Alfred only outlived Hildy by three days. Gavin did the best he could for them, but they went downhill so fast, and he knew nothing about medicine, even though he stopped at nearly empty and looted drug stores and got what they had told him to find.

The loneliness was a burden. By the time they had died, he had seen too much ugliness out on the road, and was beginning to question his sanity. People were a constant flow of movement, walking or riding toward the coast, but the crowds were starting to thin some. He felt so strange being one of the only people heading west. He actually stopped in Kentucky and buried Hildy and Alfred, since they had told him they had both been born in "Kan-tuck." He laid them in a grave together in the woods along a lonely stretch of highway. Hildy was already wrapped in a shroud of blankets and had been dead a week, since Alfred would not part with Hildy's body when he became sick. Gavin's tears were all used up, he simply couldn't find any left to shed but he stood over their grave and hoped they were happy to be together in the warm "bosom of the earth," as Alfred was fond of saying, "Oh, Gavin, boy, I just need to lay her in the warm bosom of the earth like she deserves. She was a good woman, sturdy, capable and kind and I loved her. I know you can't hear me, but I shore loved her, indeedy I did."

He was armed, but still wasn't sure that he could bring himself to kill. He had shot above the heads of potential thieves to warn them to leave him and the Grays alone but had not killed anyone. He just wanted to stop someplace and live a hermit's life. He picked up some tough looking kids on the way to St. Louis, more for mutual protection than loneliness. He caught himself wondering why he continued to head that way since there was no real reason for him to go there except it had been a "destination" and he had none other in mind. Even when they passed St. Louis, he kept on going west, though the kids had tried to talk him into going south to the ocean, even plotting to head south when he slept, so he seldom did. That was when he realized that they assumed that, since he was mute, he was also deaf. He heard them talking about taking the truck while he slept and leaving him along the highway. He allowed them to embrace the deception but was careful where he put the keys from that point on.

The kids, three guys and a girl, helped him put mattresses in the back of the pick-up and they traveled together until they met up with a small group of men, headed by Casto, who had, at first, seemed friendly enough and helpful. When Casto and his friends had shared drugs with the three guys and the girl, Gavin declined with a shake of his head. Drugs had never been his thing. Looking back on those days, he tried everything he could to forget what Casto and his friends did to those kids. Only the girl survived, but she probably had wished many times that she hadn't. She was now the "old lady" of one of Casto's lieutenants. Gavin would never understand why they had spared him but, since they seemed to think him "simple"; and as that seemed to amuse them enough to allow him to live, he stayed "simple." Casto and his friends headed for Texas after killing the boys; taking him, the truck, and the battered girl with them.

He shook his head and wondered why he had allowed unpleasant memories to occupy his time, when he could be remembering his dream. Reality had been a nightmare. The dream had been pleasant. He felt he could even smell the clean air and feel the cool breezes on his face when he spent time with the kids in the dream. The children were all nationalities, like some kind of commercial for world peace; not just pale and ugly, brutish white guys, and their "old ladies" like those who made up the population of Hades. The children showed him their huge garden. prepared for a growing season. It was early spring where they were, he could see the trees budding. He could almost smell the loamy earth. He dreamed about helping those children in that garden instead of the barren, dusty excuse for agriculture in Hades, where they grew mostly mealy potatoes and root vegetables to add to stew that was usually made up of canned goods that were so old that the expiration dates were no longer visible.

Laurel had taken his hand during the dream, he could feel the softness of her skin against his, and told him not to worry, that magic would protect them from any evil, that he would be safe, too, if he could only join them. She put a cool hand to his fevered brow and looked concerned. Then she turned to a boy nearly their age, a boy who looked to be Native American, or maybe Latino. Gavin was never good at knowing such things; he found he didn't really care what someone's background was, so long as they were good and kind. The boy smiled a welcome at him as well and asked him his name. He struggled so hard to tell them but he couldn't. The boy and Laurel smiled, "It doesn't matter, your secret is safe with us," they told him. "We can hear your thoughts, you don't have to use your voice. Ah, your name is Gavin, thank you for thinking it for us."

They could hear his thoughts, and yet, Laurel still smiled at him, even though she had to be aware that he was thinking how beautiful she was and how much he wanted to touch her.

Oh, how he looked forward to his sleep, how he hoped to dream again. The only thing pleasant about his life were those few hours of sleep and those wonderful dreams.

Even if they were only dreams, they revived a hope in him that he thought had died a long time ago.

*

"Did you see him again?" Yellow Feather asked. "I could see him so clearly this time."

Laurel nodded, blushing, and told him, "Wherever he is, he's very scared and unhappy. The people around him, his thoughts kept calling them evil and I could feel it, they truly are. Even though I knew in my mind that I was really here and safe, they frightened me. Some of the things he has witnessed came through into my own memories, and I nearly made myself awaken. They were too much for me, they were nightmares! The people he's with are very much like some of the ones we encountered on the way here, the ones our gatherers protected us from. He is nearly imprisoned by fear, no, he IS imprisoned by fear. I feel so sorry, so sad for him."

"So do I. I tried to get him to look around, to get a look at the camp but it is very difficult for him. He was in a tower, a really high tower and he is afraid of heights, he's nauseated and miserable. Maybe it was a punishment, maybe there is good reason for him to be so afraid. All I could see was a big camp. It looked really haphazard, they don't seem very organized, or maybe they don't care about organization, brute force seldom does. I hope we don't have to wait for the next time he's in the tower to communicate with him."

Cody nodded, "So far, he's our best chance to find out what their camp is like. We don't dare enter the minds of any of the others, they might see something that would lead them to our camp. We have to keep our defenses up, if any of them are 'travelers', we don't want them aware of us, we don't want them to 'visit' someone here; something they see might give away our location. Even a glance at the mountains can be iconic enough for some Americans to pinpoint our approximate location."

"I wonder if he realizes how powerful he is," Raven added. "Imagine, his mind is strong enough to have connected to us in a dream! He didn't even have Travis to teach him how to do that! I don't think that even Path or Gwen, with their minds open to magic, would be able to do that, project into another's dream just out of the wish to witness something pleasant and soothing, a mental search for comfort. I'm not sure if he even realizes that's how he connected with us."

Yellow Feather nodded in agreement, "When we are connected to him, I can feel his power. It makes me wonder who he was before, in his other lives, and why he is so shy and reclusive now. He must have had a hard life to allow himself to be so withdrawn. Even his memories of his hometown show him to be a bit of a loner, shy, noninvasive. He must have felt very isolated, being as brilliant and talented as he is, mentally."

"Maybe we should tell Pathogent," Laurel wondered.

"No, not yet," Travis said, softly. "We need to find out more before we talk to the adults about this. They may try to stop us from contacting other camps, you know how fearful they are that the wrong kind of people will find their way here."

Yellow Feather nodded in agreement. The adults were certainly paranoid about such things, but he also felt a twinge of guilt. It was hard for him to hide anything from Pathogent or Gwen; they were his closest friends in several of his former lives.

Raven bit her lip, feeling guilt. Her encounter with Gwen the other day had already revealed a lot. She wondered if she should admit her mistake and decided to come clean about it with the other children. If Gwen told Pathogent, it was already too late to change anything anyway. She stood to tell them, apologetically, ready to take their disappointment.

*

Gwen had noticed the little girl, Raven, one of the youngest of the children, sitting alone on an outcropping just a short way up the mountain behind the cabins. She slowly walked up, taking care to pace herself along the way. Age was so unkind, putting a limitation on things that once came so easily to her body. It seemed to take a very long time to reach her, perhaps the better part of an hour. Gwen smiled, apologetically, as she approached Raven, out of breath from the exertion, returning the smile that the child gave her.

It must have been difficult for the child to watch the elder climb all that long, long way. Regardless, she greeted Gwen with a warm smile and sat back, letting the sun warm her face. Raven was growing into a very secure and happy little girl. What was she now, Gwen tried to remember, could she be five? Raven was one of the original five children that she and Path had rescued upon arrival in Denver. Little as she was, she was always eager to learn and to help, especially helpful when chores were assigned, and was always willing to do more than her share. She seemed to be smiling throughout the toughest chores, and finding the brighter perspective on things. She was always a delightful child to be around. When with other adults, she spoke like a toddler. Gwen knew there was another side to Raven that she so seldom got to talk with.

"It's a beautiful place to sit and take it all in, isn't it?" Gwen asked, trying to catch her breath, putting her hands on her hips and leaning back and arching her spine to take the stress out of it, as she turned to face the sunrise, and realized that, not only did Raven have a wonderful view of the camp from this vantage point, but she also could see foothills stretching out for miles, the blue sky above them filled with puffs of snow white, fluffy, cumulus clouds, the green grasses and forests just now giving up the mist of morning that had settled on them overnight. Morning in the mountains was ethereally beautiful to observe and Raven had picked a perfect vantage point. Gwen wondered if she came here often. This was an ideal spot to greet the day and well worth the climb.

"I can't stop looking at this beautiful world," Raven told her, a touch of another smile at the corners of her still childlike, angel-bowed mouth. "In my other life, I could neither see nor hear and this beauty is just something that I will never find anything but entirely captivating."

Gwen was becoming accustomed to the children using adult terminology when talking to her without other adults around. Though they were entirely children when they were within earshot of any of the other adults, it was when they were with one another, or with Gwen or Pathogent, that they could do so and seemed to enjoy relaxing and allowing former memories to come through. The child was physically only about four or five, but she was very small for her age, a delicate child who had been raised by other children from the time she was just an infant, possibly not getting the nutrition she had needed but tough enough to survive.

She had been living in a mall with other children who had survived the flu that had taken much of the population of Denver after the bombings and other disasters ended. She was Tyler's younger sister and the two of them had narrowly escaped being murdered.

Gwen and Pathogent had just arrived in western Denver and were resting on a bench when they heard a man's voice and children screaming. The tableau they found after following the sound was both frightening and surreal. A man, in the grasp of religious zeal, stood over two small children and a dead woman, waving a knife and shouting Bible passages about the sacrifice of Isaac. Pathogent had stopped the zealot from killing them in a religious frenzy, in the very moment the knife was being thrust to slaughter them. He had no choice but to kill the zealot at the time, and the children had grown to love him for saving them, and for being a fun, grown-up "kid." Gwen smiled at the thought that all the children loved Path for his inner child.

The little girl smiled up at Gwen and knew that she was wondering what former life she referred to but Gwen had decided long ago to allow the children to share that information only when they were ready. Raven patted the ground beside her in invitation, looking up and filling her in, "My name was once Helen Keller, Gwen. I struggled with blindness, muteness, and deafness in complete isolation from the world until Anne Sullivan came into my life and helped me develop my other senses to the point where I could communicate with people outside of my family members. She opened a gateway for me and gave me freedom. I will never stop appreciating the senses I once did not have. They gave me a strong perspective, when it comes to sight and sound."

"She was an amazing person," Gwen said, nodding, "but then, so were you! I've read some of your writings, you were a courageous inspiration to so many struggling with disabilities."

"That is too kind, I was more fortunate than most," Raven smiled and admitted, "First, I had memory of sight and sound. I had memory of other lives, but that life taught me to appreciate so much of the world around me. One doesn't know how much you can miss the simple perfection of something like a sunrise until you live so many years without ever seeing one. Besides, as Helen, I had influential friends who helped me. Not all handicapped have so much going for them. It takes a strong web of support to be able to accomplish what Helen..." she stopped and smiled, embarrassed to be talking about herself in third person, then finished the thought, "what I accomplished."

Gwen smiled and nodded, completely understanding what Raven meant. In all the lives she had lived, mental scars from other lives carried forward with her, helping her to appreciate such things as the freedom of childhood and innocence. They both took in the beauty of the vista surrounding them. Gwen sensed that Raven wanted to talk to her about something that was on her mind, so she let the moments pass in silence. It wasn't hard to do, considering the beauty she could simply allow to comfort them both as they sat in the morning sun and it warmed them.

The village had grown strong and self-sufficient. They had made it through their second winter in Golden now and she knew that the group was growing in trust, the children happy and free and able to develop the skills they needed at their own pace. Many of them were finding the strength to cope with some of the horrible things that had happened to them or the people they had loved in their past. There were still emotional and mental scars from the loss of family, the treacherous trip from their homes to Colorado, and the fear of those who stalked them on the way. Now that they had learned to trust the adults in Golden, many of them were starting to feel free to laugh and behave like children again. For some it came easy. Others were still reticent and had to be drawn out by the other children and the thoughtful and educated adults who were teaching and counseling the young ones.

The adults were enjoying their own freedom and happiness, now that the village was stable and everyone had less to do to maintain the progress they had made. The mountains were teeming with wildlife, so that those who decided to eat meat had plenty when they hunted, but most of the village remained vegetarian or, at the least, pescatarians, since the mountain streams and lakes were teeming with healthy fish.

"You must have wondered why some of us came back to be together now, revealing our former lives to one another. I know that we do...wonder, that is. I mean, Gwen, there have been thousands upon thousands of good and heroic people who have lived on this earth. Why does it only seem to be those of us who were time-travelers who've survived to come back at this particular time, all in one place, all together?" Raven mused.

"Well, that's not entirely the case. All the 'gatherers' were not time-travelers, not a single one of them, aside from Path, Dave, Layla and me, that is. Their only links seem to have been almost genetic. Lincoln now contends that we leave some kind of genetic implant in the lives of those we have *blinked* into, which is as good an explanation as I can conceive. As for the fact that all of you children were time-travelers, I think it was necessary that you have recall of past lives so that, eventually, this world can be moved forward with memory of what was done before that led up to the failure of mankind. Perhaps this is an attempt to put the world back to 'right' so that the same mistakes aren't made and a better world can be accomplished." Gwen wondered aloud. "Maybe that was the reason for time traveling to exist in the first place, to give a chance for 'rebirth' in other ways than just personally."

"Do you really think so? Do you honestly think that a better world is the end goal? Obviously we will have to repopulate. Your 'descendants' and the children will all need to become parents or at least some of them will. Will we give birth to other time-travelers? Will your descendants have perfectly normal human children who have no past life memories? I sit and wonder if this is some 'design' or if there is some great mystery we have to solve to move things forward. Will we see that 'design' or is this just another random role of the dice?" Raven obviously didn't expect Gwen to answer those questions. This was just something that was discussed among the children in their most introspective moments.

"Now you sound like me!" Gwen laughed. "Path has always thought this was a carefully thought out plan for the future of mankind, for the saving of the planet. I leaned more toward your 'roll of the dice' theory. I have to admit, it really can't be simply 'coincidence' that our lives and the lives of the 'gatherers', as we've come to call them, were so intertwined, but I don't know what we do or where we go from here. Will we continue to *Blink* while we live here? Will some of this begin to make sense?"

"Gwen, there are already several *Blinks* happening, didn't anyone tell you?" Raven said, smiling at her friend. She leaned back to allow the sun to warm her face again, and said, calmly, "A couple of the children have had *Blinks* that took them somewhere in this time, but elsewhere, while others have actually entered into other lives in other times, it's almost as if they were sent to gather information we may need. We're just trying to piece it all together when it happens."

"Were they gone long?" Gwen asked, wondering at the fact that none of the children had seemed to have been missing for any length of time. Were they *blinking* into other lives to only return just a few moments later, as she did when she was able to visit the lives of her descendants in their struggles toward Golden?

"That's the strangest thing, Gwen, it seems that during our sleep here, we can live another lifetime elsewhere. I never had realized it before, but we seem to be returning shortly after leaving and yet, we have still spent a great deal of time in other hosts."

"Have you?" Gwen asked her.

"No, but Tyler has," she said, referring to her brother, "I know that Coyote lived a few years as a writer in California. You probably heard of Jack London...he enjoyed that but can't figure out what it might mean for us in this time and place," she smiled. "There doesn't seem to be any accounting for who is going to time travel, why or where they go. We're all trying to figure out why we are still traveling and what we are learning during these *Blinks* that might be important to our plight today. Well, I mean, aside from those who can control it and travel at will. I find that I am hoping that I don't travel, I very much like it here and I sincerely love the life I am living right now. "

Gwen could completely relate to Raven's last statement. That was exactly how she felt during several of her lives, the ones she spent with Pathogent. It was a blessing to be able to spend a good life in quiet repose, with no real sense of responsibility or stress. One of her favorite lives had been when she had been the ancestor of one of the "gatherers", Shawnee, when she and Path had been Little Moon and Siginak, respectively, members of an Ohio Shawnee tribe. "But if it is only a few hours of our time here..." Gwen began, then shook her head. "I don't even want to think about it, it never did make any sense."

"I don't know, Gwen, what if you could go back and actually experience having the children you say that you didn't get to experience having?"

Gwen lifted a brow at that temptation. If there were a way to control it, she could think of many lives she'd lived that she would like to revisit, to touch again. The romantic in her longed to relive long lives with a young, happy

Pathogent, like when he was Jacob Coen, the brilliant musician, in another life. However, wouldn't it be a temptation to change things, just a little, to keep him from driving on that fateful day, and, if that had been inevitable, would she then be tempted to have helped Harmony to see what she had done to her own child? And, if she changed Harmony's life, even a little, would that perhaps have changed things just enough so that Melody's memories would be affected, IF Melody would now exist at all? No, that would actually be too tempting and too risky in her estimation. For some reason, it seemed to her that it would be a danger to her descendants, if she or Path were to alter something in their past.

"You said that some of them are traveling in this time. Are you saying that they are finding other groups?" Gwen asked, realizing that the children spent a lot of time together, exchanging this information, information that they could not possibly share with their teachers and protectors, other than the four adult "travelers."

Raven winced, not sure if she should share this information since it seemed too vital to Travis and Yellow Feather, but relented and nodded, "Yes, there are other groups alive, some of them not pleasant at all. They have witnessed a few in this hemisphere. There is one in South America, near Rio de Janeiro that is very much like us, peaceful and trying to start over the 'right way'. There are two on the continent of Africa, Africa was not as fortunate as you adults seemed to have thought, it was terrible, the things that happened there, but those seem of little concern as well. There are only two groups discovered so far that are a great concern to those who visited them, but one is in India and very primitive, it seems."

"And the other?" Gwen asked, feeling a chill going down her spine.

Raven's dark eyes met Gwen's and held, "That group is the one we're watching more closely. They are here, on this continent. We have finally determined that they are near a place once called El Paso, Texas. They seem to be cannibals and other, for lack of a better word, troglodytes who gathered together to increase their strength. They have already attacked and wiped out weaker groups much like themselves. Poor Laurel is traveling there every chance she gets. She found a boy who doesn't belong there and she's very worried about him. She and others visit him to try to encourage him to escape to come to us. Yellow Feather has met him, too. I've seen him in one of our 'joint' dreams, he's a big, strong, handsome guy, I think that's another reason Laurel visits so often," she smiled, mentioning Laurel, who was a romantic poetess in many of her other lives.

"Do they know we're here?" Gwen asked, finding herself barely able to breathe.

"We have no way of knowing that, yet, Gwen. We don't know if there are other time-travelers that might be among them. Though it never seemed to be so, might it be possible that there are travelers with more evil intent?" Raven shook her head, not wanting to think about time-travelers who might represent the more evil side of humanity, the Jack the Rippers, the Marquis de Sade, or the Ted Bundys of the world. Could there be sociopathic travelers, juxtaposed against those whose intent was to save the world, intent on destroying it once and for all? Raven allowed room for Gwen's own thoughts, trying to push away what she and the other children had speculated, then added, "There is still plenty of food in all of the big cities. Most of the population died out too fast to use it all. Of course, that would be canned and processed food, nothing fresh, no meat..." she let that thought fade slowly, then added, "I hope there is a lot of game around El Paso."

She continued, "We do know that they've been killing any survivors they found, so there really is little chance that there are many other groups. I think we would have sensed them by now or that there will be others coming to us. Most of us feel that we would know, that we would be able to travel into them, were there any. But we still hold out hope. As you know, we still send patrols to Denver, to the New Hope meeting place. We are much more careful now, though, since we know that 'they' might be waiting there to attack us."

"How can we use this information to make ourselves ready? Is it time to let the 'gatherers' know about the travelers among us?" Gwen asked.

"Talk to Tecumseh and Crazy Horse about that, but I don't think so," Raven said, referring to the children, Yellow Feather and Coyote, in their former lives' names. "Though we know that you and Pathogent still maintain the magic shield to protect us, we are preparing for breaches or any magic that they may have up their own sleeves. Our leaders are working with all the children to build our skills. You may be aware but do you know that you have a massive group of small children who are very skilled at archery and knives."

"Every trip to the city sees the older children bringing back more weapons, more arrows and weapons for close combat. We are also learning to make weapons and cache them throughout the forest. We know that Pathogent, Dave, and Clint have supplied us with a strong arsenal of guns and ammunition and have destroyed or buried many other arsenals so that an attacking force would not have access to replenishment of their own weapons. None of us think that they would come at us full force; they will be sending small parties to hunt, if at all. It may not come until we are all grown and far more capable. But they will expect us to be weak and clueless. That is not what they will find."

"What we do know, Gwen, is that we cannot allow this to steal our happiness. We will be diligent and watchful, but we will not allow ourselves to dwell on what may never come. But, thanks to having so many among us who could lead armies, we will be prepared. Please know that we are watching this carefully and still don't want it to steal the childhood we are enjoying. Please don't allow anyone to overreact. Gwen, I am trusting you to take this information and use it wisely," she repeated, "don't allow anyone to overreact."

"Are you telling me that there are some among you who can travel at will and can control where you are able to go?" Gwen asked, incredulous at the possibilities.

"You didn't know?" Raven stated, equally surprised. "Yes, we have some very talented and powerful travelers among us. Travis, who was Alan Turing in one of his more famous lives, was capable of doing that many lives ago. His travels into the future gave birth to some of his inventions. He is working with others to develop their skills. He contends that we all have it in us to do so, we just didn't tap into that part of our minds. Just as we realize that you and Pathogent found a way to tap into the segments of your minds that allow you to work magic, to use nature and the elements at will. Alan and Galileo...working with Da Vinci...."

She had finally learned all the children's names and faces, how was she ever going to learn all their other identities? Which of the children was Galileo? Who on earth had been De Vinci? Gwen spent a long passage of time in silence as she absorbed the information that Raven had given her. This was a lot to take in. The names of the former lives the children occupied had never been fully revealed to her. She had never pushed them to reveal themselves. Now she sat in awe as she began to realize the full scope of what powers were brought to this place and time. It had been an unspoken agreement to let the children reveal their past lives at their own speed and she often felt that she had barely scratched the surface of what they could reveal. How would she be able to relay all this to Path without blurting it all out in a jumble of excitement and panic?

How could she, like Raven, sit so calmly and recite these discoveries? And, selfishly, she hoped that there would be time for her to get to meet and talk to each of the former personalities, heart to heart, like this. What an amazing and daunting opportunity to be in the company of such greatness and be able to converse with people whose past lives were beyond extraordinary! Over the last two years, she had met many of their former personalities, but there were obviously so many more. She felt her fear decreasing as she realized that such people, with the full sum of their pasts, were here, planning and taking control.

She mused, "Your collective skills with bows and arrows, is that why Haylie became such a force to be reckoned with at the archery range?"

Raven smiled and winced, "Oh, that girl! She has such an edge in the competitions. You see, in one of her lives, she was Boudicca, the fierce leader of the Britons; in a more recent life, her name was Annie Oakley. How can any of us compete with that? She won't mind that I've told you that, she considers it an unfair advantage in competitions so has told nearly everyone who competes against her. Now they compete just to test their skill against her superior and amazing talents."

On that lighter note, Gwen laughed and relaxed. She and Raven leaned back and enjoyed a game of finding shapes in the clouds over their heads, just as one would tend to do with a child Raven's age. Raven pointed out a perfectly formed elephant, with tusks and uplifted trunk. Gwen showed her a pony that drifted and transformed into a cat. They both saw the stern face and crown of Lady Liberty in the clouds. They spent a long time enjoying this relaxing occupation and clearing their heads of the concerns of the future, before heading down to help the camp with breakfast.

*

She found a way to tell him that very afternoon, as they lounged on their bed talking and relaxing. Pathogent was massaging her right hand. It had been giving her trouble. They both suspected it to be a touch of carpal tunnel syndrome or, perhaps, arthritis. It was hours before they normally would retire, before they would go for the nightly campfire meeting that had become tradition with the adults. She told him of her conversation with Raven, of the skills of the travelers, and the discoveries of other groups of survivors.

He listened carefully, never given to reacting with anything but calm and open acceptance. What had she been worried about? She recited it all in depth and his calm questions prompted all the information she had thought she would forget. Pathogent was the more accepting and calm and thoughtful of the two of them, she admitted to herself; he would know how to process the information and pass it on to David and Layla. She could see that he would also probably seek out Tecumseh, known to the camp as Yellow Feather, to discuss what intelligence the recognition of the travelers had gathered. He smiled as she told him about the efforts to become warriors that all the children were engaged in.

"We have several children who could be generals, strategically planning everything. I don't think we have to worry, my love," he assured her. "I think this is one time that we can safely put our futures into the hands of these children and relax. Of course we will be diligent, of course we will be cautious, but not so much that it alters our lives.

We've faced harder battles with fewer weapons at our disposal. Look at the joy and happiness we have found here, look at the growing families..." he was referring to the fact that Conner, an Englishman who came from the east coast where he had been teaching before the bombing and destruction, and Shawnee, born and raised on the Pine Ridge reservation in South Dakota, who had been visiting relatives in Oklahoma before the world went crazy, were expecting a child together at any moment. Equally thrilling was the news that Declan, a sweet-talking Irish actor, and Melody, whose family gave her a legacy of skilled and famous musicians, had just announced that Melody was also pregnant. That happy news had greeted them at last night's campfire. "We already voted that we won't 'court' war, but we will defend ourselves, if necessary. Besides, I, for one, am not going to allow anything to dampen the fact that I have you back again now, your health and your memories all intact, and that we are being allowed to grow old together. Even if I knew that it would only be a few more months, a few more days, it doesn't matter, I've been given the gift of these past two years with you, nothing will take that from me."

She lay facing him and cupped his face in her hands and smiled, "You always know just what to say to make every moment with you so perfect."

There were many things that Pathogent might never be too old to do, her young at heart magician and fellow time-traveler.

*

Lincoln, a skilled physician who had walked his group across the deep south to Colorado, had sent Layla, another of Gwen's and Path's fellow time-travelers, to awaken them from their nap. They were both refreshed from the two-hour sleep and he wanted their presence, knowing that they would want to know that Shawnee was now in active second stage labor. With all that she had gone through before coming to Golden, everyone knew that she was strong and in good shape now. She had been eating good, nutritious food, and they knew that the baby would have the best hands tending the birth; but they still hurried to join the group outside the Sommerville cabin, arriving at the same time as Declan and Melody. Conner greeted them, hugging them and accepting kisses from Gwen. He smiled over at Declan and said, "You next...are you ready for this, old man?"

Declan laughed and hugged Melody close to his side and nodded, "So ready. All the children are growing too fast, we need some babies around here to keep things balanced! A new generation to welcome. Eh, Gwen, Path?"

Pathogent smiled and nodded, but remembered to ask Conner, "How is she doing?"

"Shawnee is so much stronger than I am, Path, you know that!" Conner told him, smiling with confidence, "She's making this look so easy and I've seen so many descriptions and diagrams of births, I KNOW she's just stronger than most. I can't get over how happy she is, she's taking me to the moon and back with this, I'm on a cloud right now! Go on in, Gwen, I'm sure that Lincoln and Stephanie will be happy to have you at their elbow, in all the lives that you've been a physician, you've probably birthed more babies than anyone here!" He followed her in the door but held back to give her time with Shawnee.

Gwen entered the cabin and washed her hands in a basin of hot water, applied the mask, gloves, and gown that were laid out on the table and smiled at Lincoln and Stephanie, as attending obstetrics nurse, who were on opposite sides of Shawnee. Lincoln gave a thumbs up and said, "She's doing great! Her labor started this morning and she's dilated and ready, but seems to have been stubbornly waiting for you."

Shawnee smiled up at Gwen. A sheen of sweat on her forehead was quickly tended by Stephanie's tender touch. "Grandmother!" she said, her favorite greeting for Gwen, referring to the fact that Gwen was once her ancestor in another of her lives. She nodded at Lincoln and, at her signal, began to breathe through her strong contraction. Gwen moved forward and watched as Lincoln examined the positioning of the baby in the birth canal. At his smile and nod, they helped Shawnee to a squatting position on the mattress, Lincoln talked to Gwen during the entire procedure, "This brave young hero wants the best position for the safety of her baby and told me that she wants to deliver this way, as her ancestors did. I think she's right, letting gravity help. She refused even a local anesthetic and has been doing a very good job keeping her breathing strong and steady, with the help of her coach. Conner, it's time, come in here now."

As if on cue, Conner appeared at Shawnee's side and smiled with his eyes above his mask, "Ready, beautiful?" he asked. At Shawnee's nod, his concentration joined into the contraction with her, watching her closely, and he coached her to breathe at the right times, breathing with her and feeling part of the entire process. "Do you want to stand?" he would ask her between contractions, rubbing the small of her back. Sometimes she stood on the bed, with their help, just to relieve the cramps in her legs.

"You can tell these two have not only read everything they could get their hands on, thank goodness, but they have actually practiced!" Lincoln told Gwen, proudly. "They are going to be great parents, and this healthy little…" he caught the tiny little body as it slipped from the birth canal, now that the head had been freed, working quickly to clear the air passages and do a perfunctory examination, "…GIRL…is strong and healthy, and here you are, princess, say hello to your momma and daddy!"

It was the easiest birth that Gwen had ever witnessed. Lincoln quickly examined the robust little girl and handed her to Gwen so that he could help Shawnee with the placenta expulsion, then they eased her back onto the bed so that Gwen could put the baby on Shawnee's chest for bonding. Stephanie looked like she could hardly contain herself, wanting to clean and hold and cuddle the baby. Conner could not hold back tears and he put his forehead against Shawnee's and told her that he loved her and was so proud of her as they both looked into the tiny face of their new daughter. He put his face close to the infant's and looked into her eyes and fell madly in love with his daughter immediately. Then he moved to hug Lincoln, Stephanie, and Gwen, celebrating with them.

Lincoln asked them if others could come in now and they both nodded so he turned and motioned Pathogent and those waiting at the doorway.

"She's perfect," Stephanie told them, as her eyes examined the baby, "have you chosen a name?"

Shawnee smiled and looked at Conner who smiled back and, looking at Gwen, told them, "Her Native American name will be Matchsquathi Tebethto. Gwen or Path can tell you all what that means."

Pathogent smiled and spoke for Gwen who was fighting tears and unable to reply past the lump in her throat, burying her face against his shoulder to contain herself.

He grinned at her and hugged her tightly, "Little Moon," he pronounced it again, as a prayer, "'Matchsquathi Tebethto', Little Moon, which was Gwen's Shawnee name."

"And we will probably be calling her Little Moon," Shawnee added, kissing the tiny little head. "Her English name will be Gwenyth Anne, the Anne, coincidentally was both Conner's mother's and my grandmother's English name."

"Can I get little Gwennie Anne Little Moon cleaned up so that she can show everyone how pretty she really is?" Stephanie asked. "Come on, little child of many names, let's get that vemix off of you and make you as beautiful as your name!"

Gayle, a scientist and physician from the west coast, moved beside her, anxious to give the newborn a thorough examination as well. There were so many skills at hand to make certain that their new arrival had the best they could bring to bear. Everyone wanted to ascertain that Conner and Shawnee's baby was given the best start in life.

Shawnee handed the baby to her trusted nurse and smiled at Stephanie, thanking her, then accepted a hug from Gayle. Conner linked his hand in Shawnee's, still glowing over the fact that they were now a family.

Declan handed Conner a package. "Mel and I worked on this for you and hope you like it!" he said, grinning so that Conner, knowing Declan so well, expected the package to be something amusing. He unwrapped a small bunch of cords and leather and looked puzzled.

"It's her first set of climbing ropes and harness!" Declan laughed, "You don't think any daughter of Shawnee's is going to let you leave her behind when the two of you go rock climbing and rappelling, do you?" Nearly everyone in camp had gone climbing with Conner and Shawnee and were amazed by their ability to scale any rock fearlessly, finding handholds where none seemed to exist.

Conner laughed and nodded, admiring the effort put into assembling tiny harnesses just the right size for a small toddler. "I think I've just become a lot more careful about where I climb now," he said, referring to his newfound protectiveness. "But we probably ARE going to need these, knowing my Shawnee!"

The entire village celebrated with the couple and then, realizing that it was getting late and no longer early evening, left them to rest and feed their newborn. No one worried that they weren't capable, both of them so educated by the books they had read and the preparations they had made, not to mention the children they had worked with in the camp. But they practically had to pry

Layla and Stephanie away from Little Moon. Tonight's "campfire" was pre-empted by Little Moon's appearance.

Once outside, Lincoln told Gwen, "I tried to talk them into letting us do this in the hospital, where we would have equipment and be able to run tests, but they wanted 'the old ways' and this lovely simplicity. I can't say I disagree with them. This was nice. The coziest, most relaxed birth I've witnessed in many, many years, it was probably more like my own grandparents' births than I want to admit to myself."

Path patted Lincoln's shoulder, "At least they had the best doctor, and nurse, with them. Your grandmother probably didn't have that luxury! I think a lot of the young ones will want to go back to a more natural and relaxed birth. We'll just watch them carefully, if they show any signs of distress, we'll have the guys rev up those generators again."

Gwen was still feeling very emotional over the beautiful experience of being part of her descendant's special event. She leaned back to embrace the breeze and looked up at the sky and smiled at the full moon. Oh, the wolves would be singing tonight. She looked around to catch Yellow Feather's eye and signaled for him to look up, and he did and smiled. Little Moon had been born under a good sign; a full, spring moon. Together with Path and several of the others, they worked their way to a quiet place at the forest's edge and stood, waiting. It didn't take long before a long, breath-taking howl came from a distant hillside. Joined by others from horizon to horizon, the chorus was beautiful and haunting.

"They've probably been singing all night, and now they are saying, 'Welcome to the world, Little Moon.'" Path said, softly, his arms around Gwen as she leaned back into his warmth.

*

The moon had been full tonight and Casto had spent a few moments just looking up at the bright globe in the sky before going to his private quarters for sleep. Casto leaned back into the cushions that made up his bed, his mood dark and surly. He was getting so tired of this boring, senseless life: nightly orgies, drunken fools wandering everywhere outside looking for a fight. There was always some altercation to break up, always some need for him to assert leadership. This was not the community he had planned when he first envisioned a city of strength. There was an overload of testosterone, more than enough brute strength to move mountains but nothing productive was being done. Even the council he had formed would rather sit back and let him make decisions so that they could return to their own debaucheries. There were so few among these Neanderthals with the wit to awaken in the morning and tie their shoes, let alone build something or produce something to enhance their community.

Casto stood and paced his cabin. He was compact and small. He was almost painfully thin but wiry and those who thought his small stature a sign of weakness soon found out how dangerous a former Marine could be. Casto was an odd looking man, with eyes almost too big for his small head and a large, thin, crooked nose; he kept his head bald and shaved, like the rest of him. He even had no eyebrows or lashes. There was no hair on his entire body; he hated hair, it repulsed him. Hair invited pests like lice. He had once seen a magnification of an insect that lived in the human eyelashes. On that day, he plucked them out, however painful that had been, not stopping with the lashes but removing the brows as well. He had insisted that his old lady shaved, completely, every day so there was no stubble. Thankfully, she was pretty and thin and her baldness was actually attractive, and he wasn't the only one who found her to be so. He had no idea when his fetish about being hairless began, but it wasn't something he gave much thought. Hairlessness seemed cleaner, more in touch with "self". Fur was for dumb animals, in his estimation.

His last tour of duty had been in the Middle East and he had killed so many people with his bare hands that he often felt that using a weapon was a "cheat" of some sort. Skilled with almost any kind of artillery, he had been trained to infiltrate, observe, and neutralize. When the word "neutralize" had actually been part of the order, he would smile, slowly planning his way through the mission so that he could have a chance to neutralize individuals with silent and most assuredly deadly force. Mercilessly, he left no survivors, no witnesses, even civilians. He had taught himself that the word fear would never be part of his vocabulary. No one would ever make him show fear, for he was far more deadly and capable than even the biggest foe. And Hades had given him many chances to prove that to the point where he was unquestionably feared and respected; there would be no challenge from any quarter since nearly every single citizen of Hades had witnessed his ferociousness when forced to kill.

He washed his hands thoroughly for several hours after a kill, washing off the dirtiness of the opponent, and the feeling of touching their "fur." He shivered at the memory. He could wear their blood, though, blood was clean, and he often walked around for hours with blood all over his face and clothing. Something about the smell of it, the heavy iron smell of blood, made him feel strong and invincible. Besides, it impressed upon others that they did not want to question his leadership. Few lived to do so.

Hades was a mess. No one but Casto could see that they needed to organize, that this ramshackle excuse for a town was becoming a landfill, trash strewn everywhere, latrines stinking to high heaven. Yes, he would have to foster a sense of community if he had to make them all suffer.

Community! There wasn't even the hint of that in this raggedy place. Had he not moved early on to assert his alpha male position, he wouldn't even be capable of getting these worthless idiots to do their current assigned duties. He was fully aware that most of them only accomplished those duties out of fear, not a sense of building something here that would last. It disgusted him to move through the haphazard mess that loosely formed their "city." It looked more like a dump, like the refuse piles of many generations. It was disgusting to him to realize that they had been here for two years and, instead of getting better, it was getting rapidly worse. No one picked up after themselves, there was garbage everywhere, coyotes moving boldly through the camp, since it was much easier to find scraps than to hunt for rabbits or other game.

His lip curled as he looked around his own spotless, meticulously organized tent. How could they be happy to live like that? Should he let the rest of them live like pigs in their squalid shanties? Any attempt to change the status quo would be met with lazy and grumbling resistance but that might build to a mutiny among those who would say that they never did come here to get bossed around and told what to do. Not that he feared a mutiny, he would relish "neutralizing" any leaders of such an effort.

There was already enough grumbling about doing the sentry duties and following those rules. He had punished those who had overslept on their three hours down and that, too, was met with hostility. It would require him to, once again, assemble his loyal lieutenants to suppress any uprising with force and that would only mean more dead. Could they afford that? What if they were attacked by a larger force?

He groaned at the thought. If they were attacked, it would be a fiasco, there was no organized resistance in all of Hades. What was he even thinking?

That did it! The realization that they might be overtaken by a stronger, more organized force was evident. He was determined to begin today. Many of the men here were former military and he would appoint them generals, give them conscripted "troops" and have them begin to organize and train many militias. It was time to change things up around here. Anyone who resisted the training would be made an instant example of why it would be unwise to think that anyone would be getting a free ride now.

Not the women, though. They would continue to be the cooks and give the comforts expected of them. He smiled lasciviously. No, the women would simply be expected to step it up and keep their tents cleaner. Maybe he could make several of them "madams" and organize the sexual favors they now so freely gave out. If he had a handle on that, he had a handle on controlling the men, as well. He amazed himself, coming up with such great ideas. Weren't they lucky to have his brilliance in control?

He grinned, now THIS was thinking! He would call a council meeting first thing this morning. He hurried to find a paper and pen to write it all down. Once he began organizing it, other ideas would come. He would definitely enact change and it would begin this day! After Connie's visit, that was, AFTER his own woman came to give him some much needed release from all this pent-up anger. Connie, with skin as smooth and soft as a baby's behind, Connie, who made an art out of her naked, hairless skin. He shook his head as his body began to respond to his thoughts. As always, he gave himself a timeline. Within a month, this place would look like the most shipshape camp ever witnessed; it would shine. Or there would be bodies to attest the reason why. Right now he just wanted to rest.

*

Leland Casto had been orphaned at a very early age. They told him that his dad had died in an alcoholic stupor, and his mother, Maybeth, survived him by only a few years. She had a sudden heart attack at the tender age of only thirty, her body worn out and abused by drugs and a hard life. Leland had been only eight when she died, and could only remember a mother so worn out from working two jobs to make ends meet that she barely spoke, except to tell him to eat and when to wake up, when to bathe and when to go to bed. They lived in a shanty on the outskirts of a small Alabama company town called Chickasaw, in the northern part of Mobile. The only claim to fame this place had was that it was the birthplace of Ray Sawyer, the singer of Dr. Hook and the Medicine Show. Best known for their song, "The Cover of the Rolling Stone" which made them a name in the early seventies. They were basically what was known as a "one hit wonder." Leland didn't know anything about Ray Sawyer but that his mother had records that she played over and over, talking about the rock star that her mother had dated. Rumor had it that the "Cocaine Katy" in the song was his grandmother. And people of Chickasaw believed that rumor, having known the wild woman who raised his poor ma.

A scrawny little seven-year-old boy would get up in the morning and be sent off to school before his mother would leave for work. He would sometimes go to school but almost as often, he would run for the wetlands around Mobile to play with other ragged, nearly orphaned children like himself. He had learned how to spot gators from the older kids, learned to tease them and throw rocks at them, but mostly how to avoid them, and was probably just lucky never to have been eaten by one since he was in swamp water more often than he was in bath water. He learned to identify cottonmouths and give them wide berth. All children know the urban legend about the boy who swung on the grapevine over deep water and came up covered in cottonmouths, screamed once, then disappeared forever. Leland could fish with a safety pin and some string, catch sunfish, clean and fry up the fish on campfires built by other kids or by some of the hobos who hung out near the shipping yards, hoping for enough work to buy another bottle. He ate better meals in the swamps than he did at home, that much was certain.

Life wasn't easy before his Ma died and was a whole lot harder after, when his Aunt Lily and her husband, Cletus, came to claim him at Children's Services. They lived in south Mobile in an apartment in an old shipyard building, just off Old Water Street. The neighborhood was a bad one but, by the time Leland was ten, he was one of the toughest boys in that area, the scourge of the schoolyard. His uncle was determined to tame the wild boy they inherited and used his studded leather belt to lay welts across the boy's back, legs, and behind. Toughened by his uncle's belt and his desire to survive against all odds, Leland learned to fight, to fight dirty, and to take control. He spent little time at the apartment on Water Street, using it only to sleep. He avoided Cletus as much as possible. Leland took to the streets. There were boys much larger than him who were sent home crying when Leland got this blank look on his face and just started swinging. He could take punches strong enough to knock a man down and seemed almost impervious to pain.

He didn't have time for much more than running the streets, stealing whatever he could lay his hands on and dodging the police. He ran the docks and learned how to steal enough food for meals when he wasn't fishing with friends. His aunt and uncle were usually too drunk to care whether he was home, safely tucked in at night, or whether he'd even eaten for days. When there was food in the house, which was rare, he learned to squirrel it away in hiding places. Neither of the adults was energetic enough to conduct a search, anyway.

Around the time he turned sixteen, he found a reason to attend high school regularly that had nothing whatsoever to do with scholastics. Her name was Katherine Anne Diebold, but her family called her "Kitten", and she was the most perfect creature that Leland had ever seen. Slim, so fair she was almost ghostly pale, as delicate as a flower, and wanted by every single boy in the Sophomore class. Because he had been held back twice in grade school for poor attendance and even poorer grades, Leland was older than many of his classmates.

The fact that he smoked and wore his t-shirt sleeves rolled and his jeans tight, more due to the lack of money to buy jeans as he grew than style but he let the girls choose to believe what they wanted, he was the "forbidden fruit", the dangerous "man" full of knowledge about how to flirt and please a woman. Not only had he caught Kitten's attention but, scrawny and wiry as he was, he was one of the most sought after boys in school. This newfound popularity surprised and astounded him but he certainly wasn't going to look that gift horse in the mouth. He thrived on the attention. Had his grades only taken a similar upturn, his life might have turned out so differently.

He gave Kitten her first kiss and managed to get to second base when he borrowed Cletus' car and took her on a date. She had told her parents that she was at a party with a friend. They parked on the delta and watched the sunset over the ocean, talked until there was not much more they could share, then they made-out for a while. He was the one who drew the line at petting. He didn't want her to come down off the pedestal he had her on, not until they were married. When he told her this, she just smiled her pretty smile and told him that he could go all the way, if he wanted, she had even brought along protection for him. He sighed and started the car. He took her home, still a virgin, still his reason to strive for a better life.

As it was, adults watched with horror as young girls sighed and giggled over his attention. Kitten had an older brother, Danny, who had become a new recruit in the local police department. He was horrified when he was told that his precious little sister was interested in and being courted by none other than white trash, Leland Casto. Danny had gone to grade school with Casto and had known that the boy was nothing but trouble from the day he was born. Other cops on the force verified his opinion, relating to him the many times Leland had run-ins with the law and how they longed to finally put the "pint-sized mad dog" away for good.

It became Danny's personal mission to make Leland's life miserable, determined to catch him in an act of larceny that would put him out of reach for a very long time. For two years, Leland was followed by a cruiser, watched before and after school and hounded by not only Kitten's brother, but also by many of the officers in his squad. Of course, eventually they did catch him and there wasn't much Leland could do about a charge of grand theft auto for a joyride that he and two friends had planned. Leland was sent away to Strickland Youth Center. When he came out, he found out that Kitten was engaged to be married to a young lawyer in town.

He got out of his uncle's car, walked to the Marine recruiting office and signed up. Within months he was in the Middle East, full of anger, full of hate, and ready to kill. He didn't just want to use weapons, he wanted to become one. He accomplished that.

*

Declan smiled at the sunlight on Melody's face, so glad that Gwen and Path were able to join them for a day of rest and relaxation in the sun. It was a wonderful way to spend the unseasonably warm spring day at the lake. They had found some bottles of good wine and chilled the bottles in the cold water. As they watched other teachers allowing the children to play in the shallows, they enjoyed their day off, just sitting by the lake and resting. Declan pulled the cork on the wine and poured glasses for Pathogent, Gwen, and himself. There was grape juice for Melody.

Gwen and Path were happy to have a chance to catch up with the young couple. It had been a long while since the four of them had found themselves with days off together on the revolving schedule that Dave had worked out. Dave had their days off planned months in advance so that some of them could actually plan trips elsewhere, siphoning gas, and using cars from Denver, should they wish to travel. Path and Gwen had seldom wanted to be anywhere but here in Golden with the children.

Melody was only a few months pregnant but had asked Declan to talk to Path and Gwen to see if they could just spend a few lazy, happy days together, appreciating all that had been accomplished here in Golden since those very hectic days two years ago. Now Golden was a village and some of the residents had even considered moving into more comfortable homes away from the camp, there were so many empty houses everywhere. However, so far it was just talk, no one really chose to leave the protection of being with the others just yet. Besides, there was a warm and loving sense of community that everyone seemed to share; even loners like Dave really enjoyed being with the children, teaching them, watching them grow.

Gwen was watching how skilled young Laurel was with the smaller children as she and her friends, Cassie and Christine, entertained the little ones. As one of the oldest girls, she was a natural at working as a teacher to the others. Gwen knew that Laurel had been several poetesses and brilliant women in her past lives, but she had told Gwen that she had also been a teacher many times, and a parent more times than she could remember. Laurel was strikingly pretty, a fair-haired girl with cornflower blue eyes. Gwen had worried about her crush on Conner, at one time, but Laurel had grown out of it and was happy to spend time with both Conner and Shawnee, the crush nothing more than a case of puppy love that Laurel seemed to realize before it became a problem.

Today she seemed a little distracted, watching the distance toward the southwest, as if there were something there bothering her. Gwen made a mental note to talk to her about it. Could this have something to do with the boy that Raven had told her about? El Paso would be in that direction, wouldn't it? Gwen found herself also worrying about that poor boy. What if he had been on his way to Golden and had been captured? Could that be why the children thought of him as someone who did not belong in the other village?

She turned her attention back to Declan who was talking to Pathogent about the cabin he and several of the adults were building. It would be a bit larger than the one he and Melody lived in now. "After all," Declan said, "I want several children, so does Melody, so our little one room unit just wouldn't be big enough, we still don't want to go back to twenty-first century ideas that a house has to be enormous and children have to have their own rooms and the family should lead separate lives. Most of our lives will be spent like they are now, out in the sunshine or in the open air."

"With everyone pitching in, that cabin should be ready in another week!" Path said, nodding, "it's been so wonderful watching what we can accomplish when we work together."

"We still haven't been able to talk you and Gwen into letting us build you a bigger cabin, where you can have a kitchen, a living room, privacy..."

"Why would we need that?" Gwen said, laughing, "I read outside, usually with four or five of the children, or in bed at night, and we take all our meals in the community kitchen and we like just walking into our cabin for the night, it's cozy, just perfect as it is. It's so similar to the cabin we had in the long ago, when I was Little Moon, or Matchsquathi Tebethto, and Path was Raven, or Siginak, it brings back wonderful memories. We do appreciate the fireplace, that was a wonderful addition. I loved that we were able to talk you into building a community library instead, so that the kids don't have to squirrel away books from Denver. They can have hundreds at their disposal at any given time!"

"I'm beginning to think that there's really nothing we can't do here. We've got some amazing technicians and incredible knowledge in this village, and I am learning so much from each of them, I never would have thought I'd be able to do some of the things I've learned to do," Declan told them, proudly.

Melody was watching the children at play and laughing to watch little Constance, who was now around three years old, as she was learning to swim, splashing and playing happily with a huge group of children taking care of her, not the least of which were her older brother and sister, Caleb and Crystal, and the first child to take a lot of responsibility for that entire family, Abi.

Thinking about Gayle's group, of which Abi was one of the oldest, Gwen turned to Declan and asked, "What about Toby, has his autism held him back? I haven't had a chance to talk to him one on one in ages, since I tutored him in English."

"Toby? Oh, no, Gwen, don't even worry about Toby, what he may lack in communication skills, he more than makes up in his understanding of how things work. He can take anything that's broken apart and put it back together completely repaired! He's been indispensable to many of the men, particularly on the construction crew. He only needs to be shown once how to do something and he finds a way to improve the plan. He measures so carefully and obviously understands complex geometry, he can look at a structure and figure exactly what materials we will need to duplicate it. Doing those things and knowing that he can do them so effortlessly makes him happy, he's such a happy boy. There's a lot of genius in Toby; it's hard to believe he's only nine."

She just could not help herself. Gwen was wondering who Toby might have been in another life.

Declan continued, bragging on his students with pride, "Emerald was another one we were worried about. Her trip across the country had been extremely traumatic before Lincoln found her hiding in that Louisiana sewer. The things that had been done to that child make me sick. She has put it behind her. She has blossomed. She's about the same age as Toby, seems to have an almost spooky ancient wisdom. When she says something, it's with such a frank honesty, she blows me away in class!"

Melody chimed in, "And some of the children are nearly musical geniuses. Emerald is one of them. She loves to sing, and when she sings, she has such a presence, I call her Billie Holiday reborn, and she just laughs. There are times when the whole class just stops singing to hear her. Those are what we refer to as 'magic moments' in my classes. Gwen, we have so many 'magic moments', I hope you will sit in on a couple of the voice classes again. I know you enjoyed those you did sit in on. I wish I could find some way for Emerald to hear Billie sing so she could know what a compliment that is. Maybe I'll talk to one of the engineers, see if we can rig up a record player to a generator... I'm determined that, whether musically inclined or not, every child will know how to read music and how to play at least one instrument. Music soothes..."

"Can you imagine having that kind of gift at the age of nine?" Declan laughed, "Melody has asked her to sing at campfire some night, to maybe boost her spirit. I don't think I want to know all that happened to that child but I hope someday she can just look back on it all and realize that she is strong, and that she survived."

Maybe it was a compliment for Melody to compare Emerald to Billie, and then, maybe it was a very good observation on Melody's part, Gwen thought, maybe

Emerald had been on stage while people listened to her velvet tones and melted. That incarnation, too, had known some pain.

*

Gavin had begun to realize that his dreams were more than just dreams and, through the encouragement of Travis, Laurel, and Yellow Feather, he learned that the dreams were real and that they really meant to help him. Though he was afraid to allow himself hope, he dared.

"All you have to do," Yellow Feather had told him, "is walk around the camp. I will be seeing through your eyes. You don't have to worry. I won't be able to affect your motor skills in any way, so I won't be doing anything to give you away but I might ask you to take me somewhere that looks interesting. Would you be willing to do that? We just need to see if they are a threat to us, if we need to worry about them."

It had sounded like a very good idea at the time but he found himself feeling very self-conscious, having someone inside of him. What if the boy called Yellow Feather could read his thoughts about Laurel, how embarrassing would that be? Also, he couldn't help but wonder if he was acting normal or if people around him would be suspicious.

With the new rules and the stricter enforcement of them, many of the men in the camp were actually working for the first time since they came here. The new rules didn't really affect Gavin. He had always been more than willing to work; he actually loved to work. It kept him in shape. He just went from job to job as cheerful as before. Sure, there were times when the people he was working with were doing less than he was, but he just worked harder to make up for it. It was like a challenge.

Right now he was assigned to work on helping to build what would soon be called the "mess hall." Casto had decided that everyone should eat their meals together and continue working until the camp was ship-shape. They had already constructed barracks and gotten rid of many of the shacks and haphazardly arranged tents. It was a new rule that only generals or higher had private quarters and those quarters had to be kept spit-shined and were inspected every morning by Casto himself. The officers inspected the barracks, with Casto only inspecting them every other week or so.

There was grumbling among the men that this was like being conscripted in an army but no one was brave enough to stand up to Casto or his generals. The punishment for refusing to work on assigned work details and live in the barracks was death. There had been a rash of deserters. Some had gotten away but most had been caught, and killed, slowly and painfully. Not only were they executed publically, but their bodies were meant to bear example to the others, left to rot where they lay, whatever the coyotes hadn't carried away.

He heard the boy's voice in his ear, "Is there any way you could go over near those trees and look toward the barracks and where those people are working?"

Gavin approached the general on duty and mimed that he needed to pee, holding his hands over his crotch and shaking, then pointing to the trees.

"Certainly, soldier, you've already done more than your share of the work, take your time," the "general", a man named Thrush, said nodding, showing a smile of snaggled and yellowed teeth. Gavin pretended to only recognize the nod instead of the words the man said. Though he was a tough bird and everyone on duty feared him, Thrush seemed to appreciate Gavin and was not so bad, not really. He always told Gavin what a good job he did and smiled at him, patting him on the back and rubbing his arm. No matter what the work detail was, Thrush always seemed to be in charge of Gavin's group.

Gavin wandered toward the trees and Yellow Feather directed him to stand behind the one that gave him the best view of the camp. Gavin looked where the boy directed him. He was glad for this chance to go into the forest because he really did have to urinate. He kept his eyes open and straight ahead but unzipped his pants and relieved himself. Both the concentration so that Yellow Feather could observe the camp, and the fact that he was busy relieving himself contributed to the fact that he didn't hear the noise behind him. He jumped as a hand landed on his shoulder and squeezed.

"I was hoping I could get you alone." It was Thrush's voice and he was standing close behind Gavin. He moved even closer and said, in Gavin's ear, "Now, son, drop those britches and we'll become even better friends and you'll never have to work this hard again." His hand moved slowly around Gavin's hips to touch his exposed penis.

Gavin pretended not to hear and turned swiftly to look, as if he were surprised to find that Thrush was the one pressing up against him. He pulled away and gave a questioning look, pushing the man's hands from him and trying to smile. The older man reached for the front of Gavin's jeans, then he rubbed the boy's crotch, and Gavin jumped back, shaking his head. This caused the general to turn red with anger and he reached to push Gavin roughly against the tree. Inside of Gavin, Yellow Feather was as enraged as the boy hosting him, "You're stronger than him, Gavin, don't let him do this to you."

Gavin struggled, knowing and fully understanding that the general could have him killed for insubordination, like so many had been killed when the work programs were first introduced. He shook his head again and tried to move out of the man's rough embrace as Thrush pressed his hips against Gavin's backside. He was both terrified and filled with rage, not knowing what he could do. This had never happened to him before, although he had witnessed it happening to others in the camp, sometimes by consent.

Thrush put his hands on Gavin's hips and tried to pull down his pants but Gavin was fighting and squirming. The man was warning him not to fight. He was threatening to kill him if he didn't comply, not seeming to remember that Gavin could not hear his threats. He reached a hand around to try to grab Gavin's crotch again. "Pretty boy, you make my pecker stiff as a board," he whispered, his mouth against Gavin's ear, his hand moving roughly to try to gain entrance.

Then, suddenly, another voice cut through the forest, "I do hope that you did not plan to rape that boy while on duty." The southern twang was unmistakable. It was Casto. "Because, if you planned to engage in a sexual act while you were assigned to be in charge of one of my work details, you are going to have to answer to me." He spoke with a clipped and direct manner, his accent thick, pronouncing each word slowly and distinctly, stressing every syllable with a lazy drawl. When Thrush pushed away from Gavin to turn, Gavin took advantage of being free and ran a few steps away, then turned, as if to defend himself. Then he pretended to notice Casto for the first time and reached down to cover himself, embarrassed to be exposed.

"You really don't want to be doing that to one of my best workers, now, do you? The boy is already deaf and dumb, you want to destroy his morale as well?" Casto was saying, like he was unable to believe the audacity of Thrush. "There are plenty of WILLING participants in this camp, he doesn't look all that willing to me, to tell the hard truth. What you do on YOUR time is your business, IF you do a good job when you're on duty; what you do on MY time is my business and right now, Thrush, I need to remind you, you are on MY time."

"Listen, Casto, I work hard for you, my friend. You need good men like me to keep these boys in line. I deserve a little break. If you look away, it won't take more than a few minutes and this pretty boy can go back to work. He does the work of four men anyway, so he'll make up for lost time when he gets back out there. Let's just pretend this is my 'lunch hour'," Thrush said, winking with a sly smile on his face, referring to the fact that many of the "sergeants" visited the whorehouse that Casto had established on their lunch hours, choosing sex over nourishment.

Casto listened, carefully, his mind boiling over with anger at the fact that he was getting backtalk from a subordinate. "Oh, I see, I should let you make your own rules now, is that how it is?" Casto purred, "Just because you prefer young male meat to the girls, you should get special privileges, is that how you see it?"

"No, I'm not saying that at all, I'm just asking for this once. Then, once he realizes that he's mine, I'll just pull him out of the barracks at night from here on out and screw him in my quarters." Thrush laughed, "You know how it is, you see something you want this bad and you feel like you're nearly going to die if you don't get it. I'm sure you felt the same way about Connie, right? I've been wanting this one for a long time now."

Casto smiled wickedly and said, "Okay, let me get this straight, you want to compare the way you feel to the way you THINK I feel about my whore, is that right? Well, you do have a point, you see something you want and you just get so hot thinking about it, keeps you up at night, then you start planning and plotting how you're going to make it happen, you're all distracted, feeling hot every time you see that person, looking for every opportunity..."

He clapped a brotherly hand on Thrush's shoulder, "I do understand, it gets to the point where it's all you can think about. You think you'll 'bout go crazy if you don't at least try at the first opportunity. Yeah, so distracted that you let your job go to hell...and, you know, like you said, he's worth four of you..." He held the gun to Thrush's forehead and pulled the trigger. The blood flew all over Casto and the tree where Gavin had just been standing was now drenched in blood. Thrush fell to the ground slowly, as if his body did not yet realize it was dead, falling in segments, knees buckling, then wobbling, then collapsing.

Gavin was careful not to flinch at the gunshot but he did allow himself to show shock and surprise at what Casto had just done. He fell backwards into the leaves and was kicking blindly, trying to back away from the entire scene.

Casto smiled at him through the blood, looking macabre and mad as a hatter with blood and gore dripping from his long, thin face, and said, "I know you don't hear me but I just never did cotton to no pedophiles. Do what you want with a grown up, whore or wife or whatever, but don't think about screwin' no kid around me. That's just evil." Then he laughed, "Any fool knows that kids are for eatin'!" He licked his lips, shook his head laughing at his own joke, and then pointed a bloody hand toward the work crew, "Now, go on back to work, I've got to find another man to be the work boss on your crew. Oh, hell, I know you don't hear me," he pointed again and mimed working. Gavin nodded his head slowly, and stumbled toward the work crew.

Inside his head, Gavin told Yellow Feather, "I gotta get out of here."

Yellow Feather answered, "Yes, you certainly do. We'll help you. I promise. Gavin, you have my word, I will help you, even if I have to do it alone."

Yellow Feather had seen their leader, and heard every word the man had said, seen everything that he had done, and it was far worse than he originally thought. The man was insane and exceedingly dangerous.

*

"This man has the most cold-blooded mind I've ever witnessed," Yellow Feather was telling some of the boys in their cabin. "Don't tell Laurel about this, but that Gavin boy is in grave danger in that camp. We have got to offer to help him escape."

"I was thinking about all that you and Laurel have told us and I sincerely think his greatest chance for escape is during those three hours of rest when he is on guard duty in the tower. You said that he is assigned the northernmost tower. I was able to visit him during last tower duty and he isn't far from trees. Since they don't have the area well-lit, he could just go directly north when he is relieved to sleep. I doubt very much that the other guards do much but envy the person relieved to sleep. I doubt they watch that tower any more carefully than their own perimeter. See what I mean?" Dakota answered his friend.

"I am trying to put myself into their places. We know that they have had no one even come close to their camp in a long time. They all feel this duty is fruitless and unnecessary," Dakota, who in another life was Chief Seattle, a capable and philosophical mind, said. "That would give him a three hours' start on any troops they might send, probably another hour before they could raise the alarm and prepare to follow his trail, if they could even find the trail. We could cover him until he comes to us, then lead him out of that area quickly."

"We'd have to do it on foot. Our best bet is the Franklin Mountains. We are all in far better shape than anyone you've seen there, right? We are accustomed to mountain terrain, we walk it daily, climbing all over the Rockies as we do. Those mountains are directly north of that camp and they actually meet the Rockies but it's a long trip; we'd be traveling through almost the entire length of New Mexico, as well as half of Colorado," Travis, who was Alan Turing in another life, said, running his finger along the map.

Coyote, the reincarnation of Crazy Horse, looked at the map as Travis traced his finger back down to the tip of the westernmost corner of Texas, west of the panhandle and nodded, "Long, long trip. How I wish we had horses. We'll have to find some dirt bikes, but how on earth can we ride them through all the mountains and carry gas? Who knows that terrain better than Little Crow? We need to seek his advice. He was Geronimo and he knew every inch of the ground around there."

"We can use the highway most of the way down, use a trailer to haul gas, too. We can approach on foot through the Franklins, hide our bikes just twenty miles or so from El Paso. If they do follow, and they might not even really care to, they won't know about us and they'll think he left on foot through the mountains. We'll leave the mountains for the highway and access our bikes and ride home," Yellow Feather, known to them as Tecumseh, said. "But, here's the thing, we HAVE to tell the adults, but we cannot allow any of them to go with us. If we are caught, we're just a crazy gang of kid survivors. They'll probably kill us, but we can't sacrifice any of the adults, the rest of the kids are going to need them all, if they are attacked."

"Fat chance the adults will allow this, knowing that we will have to take weapons and prepare for battle," Travis said, grimly.

"We can't let them think they have a choice," Yellow Feather said, without any sense of doubt in his voice. He had made up his mind to rescue Gavin. Nothing would change it, even if he had to go alone. "We are children on the outside but in here," he moved a hand over his chest, "we have the hearts and experience of warriors. I have no choice, in my heart, I know I must help him."

"I do have to remind you, my friend," Dakota said, slowly and making certain to meet Yellow Feather's eyes so he could read the sincerity there, "we have the 'experience' of warriors but not the bodies, not yet. Where once we were strong, muscular men who could travel hard for days with no worry, we have the limited stamina of growing bodies now."

Yellow Feather smiled and slapped his chest, "Speak for yourself, Dakota, I have been working out and climbing with Conner; this is as solid as I ever was."

They teased one another back and forth as young men will do but Yellow Feather knew what Dakota was saying. They would have to be prepared to battle men who may have trained for battle, men who probably served and trained for fighting. It would not be without danger.

*

"No," Pathogent declared, his face drawn and worried at the news the boys were sharing with him at their private meeting before the nightly campfire, even though Yellow Feather currently had the floor, "I can't begin to even think of letting you do this, it's too risky on so many levels."

"Pathogent, my friend, please forgive me, but we are not asking permission. There is no one in this camp that we respect more than you but you have to understand that we are already committed to this rescue. We have no choice and neither do you. We could have just left in the night, but we wanted to give you the dignity of a conference about this. We want you to know that we've been going over this for days and we are determined. Gavin's next tower duty is soon, and we have to be in place for his escape. I told him we would be there for him. I will not break my word. I truly believe that his life depends upon this," Yellow Feather sighed and continued, the gravity of the situation clear on his face.

"And now that he's met us and knows we are 'out there somewhere', his emotional and mental well-being as well," Yellow Feather told him. "After what I witnessed him going through, I set my mind and my heart to freeing him from that nightmare, and that is what I intend to do." He was unaware of the fact that, like the times when they were Shawnee brothers, he was talking with his hands as well as his mouth, "The men at this other camp are evil. He narrowly avoided being raped while I was inside his mind. He witnesses cold-blooded murders...cannibalism...acts so carnal that they appropriately named that place Hades. Demons truly live there."

Dave put a hand on Path's arm to stop him from saying more, and asked, "How many of you are going? We have a right to know who we are risking here. Am I not correct or have these rules changed, too?"

Yellow Feather sighed, feeling the sting of this accusation.

"We feel the need for no more than five strong warriors, those skilled with weapons enough to cover an escape, all experienced in battle," Coyote answered. "Certainly they won't come at us with full force and they don't have much imagination. They work in groups of ten, all of their duties, including those troops going after deserters are groups of ten. The most they would send for us is ten troops and we've seen their lack of discipline. They would go out with ten and come back with five. Their people are deserting at an alarming rate. We would not only be at an advantage because of our skill, but because they have no heart for what they are doing."

"I think I asked who..." Dave said, looking at Path and frowning, he met Yellow Feather's eyes and left no quarter for the boy to again ignore and skillfully bypass his question.

"Me, Coyote, Laurel, David," the boy, who was actually the youngest of the proposed rescue party, answered, then added, quickly, "and Haylie," he told them, his eyes holding theirs firmly and directly, "We have each decided to be included. We are not asking permission. We just want you to know. The others will keep you informed of our progress, and, if necessary, our losses."

"You keep saying that about not asking permission," Path said, smiling grimly, "but then you tell me that you are going, and you are younger than the others except for Haylie. Yellow Feather, she is a twelve-year-old girl who has lived through hell and then some."

"Who is ALSO our best shot with rifles, pistols, and bow and arrows..." Yellow Feather told him. "She is a better marksman than David, and he is the best of the boys. He is better than me, though I try my best every time. She is even better than LILY, and she was a marksman in her unit. Haylie has bested the entire field six times now, it made Lily proud to witness her skill...and, besides, she is determined to go. She will not allow us to leave without her."

"You are asking us to allow you to risk your lives based on dreams?" Layla said, incredulous over the entire proposition.

"Layla, we are not..."

"I know, we heard you, you are not asking permission," Gwen said, shaking her head, "and that really disturbs me. We are your teachers, your 'gatherers', so you call us. Yet, now you don't trust us to help make these decisions with you. I thought we did everything by vote here, vote around the campfire where everyone has a voice, young AND old. You knew that vote would not go your way, didn't you?"

Yellow Feather looked away from Gwen, unable to hold her eyes while disappointing her, to Pathogent, and then to Dave. "We could have left in the night..." he reminded them.

"I'm going with you," Dave, one of only four adult time-travelers, insisted.

"No...Dave..." Yellow Feather began, then stopped, he could not deny Dave's skill with weapons. There would be no argument that would make sense at this point. Dave was a marksman and had fought in battles overseas, so he nodded in agreement. How could he argue against the sensibility of Dave's assistance.

"And I know that Lily will want to go, too," Dave said, referring to the sharpshooting veteran who had saved Gayle's group as they traveled across the west many times over with her skill. He turned toward Pathogent to address him, "We will have to bring her into our confidences, I will talk to her tonight, let her know that the others still must NOT know about the children's skills. She is open and free-thinking. She will accept without question, a true soldier. She will keep this mission secret, as well."

Yellow Feather nodded, slowly, then turned to Path, "Does this change your thoughts?" he asked, seeming desperate not to anger or offend his friend, knowing that age and Gwen's fragile health were the only things keeping Pathogent from insisting on joining them.

"This is ridiculous, you cannot be serious!" Layla argued. The very thought of any of the children leaving the camp on such a fool's errand was more than she could stand. The thought of losing even one life from the camp was unconscionable to her. She looked to Pathogent and Gwen for support and her face dropped when she saw that they were faltering.

"I know what you're going to say, but," Gwen interjected, holding up a hand as Layla began to plead, "I honestly feel that they must be allowed to do this. It's about the life of a boy. They seem to find him very special and we don't know that he isn't. Even if he were not special, he is a child in grave danger."

"Gwen! They say they've DREAMED about this boy. That's ridiculous! Please say you know that it is too risky on such slim..." Layla argued.

Gwen turned to face the woman and smiled, fondly, at her friend, "Do I have to remind you how carefully we had prepared for your arrivals, always having just enough space prepared? Are you saying that my knowing that you were coming was 'ridiculous'? They have discovered other ways to time-travel, ways that we have never been able to develop. That doesn't mean those ways don't exist just because you and I can't do them."

Gwen smiled as she touched Yellow Feather's arm, "Please bring them all back safe, little brother." In the way she had referred to Tecumseh during their friendship, both in the past and currently, elders were "grandfather" or "grandmother", even if not related by blood; adults were always "uncle" or "aunt" and those younger than one, "little brother" or "sister" among the Shawnee. Her time with the Shawnee included her most treasured memories and Tecumseh had been an especially treasured friend, younger brother of her dear, close friend, Tecumapese. "Keep them safe. All of them."

It was decided there would be seven in the rescue party. Whether or not they agreed with the mission, the entire inner circle helped the children to prepare the group for their trip.

Quietly, when they were alone, Yellow Feather told Pathogent, "Travis can monitor us constantly. We are all in awe of his skill and power. He and Dakota will be able to tell you exactly where we are every moment. Travis was Turing, and he can travel at will. He was the one who learned to tap into that part of his mind many lives ago. He will be visiting us along the way, monitoring both the camp where Gavin is and our trip. He has been teaching many of us how to release ourselves into this, and four more of us are able to do it but none are as skilled as he. Travis will ease your mind, my friend. I cannot ask you not to worry, I know that you will, but Travis can visit us and tell you what we have found, what we are thinking. He can also share news with you about Gavin, the boy we must save. Both Travis and Dakota are extremely upset that they are not going with us, that they can better serve us here. You can help to comfort them by working with them to monitor us."

Path looked deeply into the eyes of his friend, hoping not to show the fear he was feeling for Yellow Feather, or Tecumseh. When he had known Tecumseh before, he as Siginak, lost him so much earlier in life than was right, than was fair. It worried him that this history that they shared might be repeating itself. "I second what Gwen said, keep them safe...keep YOU safe." They touched foreheads and then parted.

When they were gone, Pathogent went to find Travis. Travis, as usual, was working over charts and mathematical equations only a genius like himself could begin to understand. Path sat down beside him, smiling, and said, "Now, this mind travel thing. We have another hour before campfire. Teach me."

Travis smiled, "It will take far more than just an hour, my friend, but we will begin tonight and I am certain that you are a quick study." He was secretly happy that Pathogent had finally come to him. Admiration for the older gentleman was ingrained among the children, but none more than Travis. Travis considered Pathogent one of the calmest, most considerate human beings he had ever met, calmer than Gwen, calmer than anyone in camp, and full of ancient wisdom that he wanted to learn from. This would be a mutual session: Path would have to give as well as take. Travis could not wait to enter that mind. Pathogent was one of the few people that Travis felt comfortable around since he was a loner and trusted so few people in any of his lives. And now, strangely enough, there was Gavin...

*

The next morning, the camp was in an uproar over the absence of seven of their number, everyone demanding to know when the decision was made and why it was not made by consensus at the nightly campfire, why it had been kept from them. There had never been a greater sense of indignation over the fact that a decision was made without bringing it to the populace. It seemed that everyone held Pathogent personally responsible and Gwen was getting frustrated at the obvious anger the group displayed.

"To allow Dave and Lily to disappear on some secret mission with five of the children is something unheard of," Gayle protested. "Vacations are one thing, but we have never taken so many children far from the camp. You say that your magic protects them, but certainly there is a limit to the range of ANY magic. Have you tested your theory? Is there anything you've done in the past to test this theory?"

Declan agreed with her, "I want to take a group and follow where they have gone. We really don't know what might be out there waiting for them. We've been so fortunate for the two years we've been here, why are we taking such a big risk right now, who decided this?"

Pathogent was disturbed that the word had gotten out so quickly about the travelers who had left camp in the evening the night before, first to travel down to Denver to get motorbikes and trailers, then to pack for the trip south. Why had it not appeared to everyone as if they were simply going down for supplies or to check on the meeting place at New Hope? How did anyone come to assume it was more than that before he had a chance to prepare for tonight's campfire council? One look at Layla was enough to tell him who had leaked the news of the mission. He glared at her, feeling betrayed, and she looked away quickly, though still indignant, her chin set and raised with defiance. To her this was less a matter of betrayal and more simply caring for the safety of those on this mission. While he understood her position, it made him angry that they had not been able to discuss this before she involved all the others.

"No, Declan, please don't do that, please listen to me, we will know if they need us. Only then will we consider going outside of Golden's shield to either defend or bring them back," Path said, firmly.

Gwen looked at Melody and knew that she shared Declan's and Gayle's concerns. Of the twenty to thirty adults surrounding them, only Conner and Shawnee seemed calm, withholding judgment however much the group had been stirred into revolt, waiting to hear what was going on from Gwen and Path before voicing a decision. She added, "We can only tell you this. Every single one of them volunteered for this mission, every single one. It has never been our intent to keep anyone here against their will and you know that quite well. Path had nothing to do with these plans. He simply learned about the plans when I did, there was little we could do to stop..."

"They are CHILDREN, Gwen! This is insane, what could Dave and Lily have been thinking taking children, and why the children they selected?" Janice asked.

"Dave and Lily only volunteered to go with the children. They are not responsible for this decision. They simply could not let the children go off without their protection..." Gwen defended.

Conner spoke up, "It's enough for me to know that Gwen and Path approved this and it should be enough for all of you."

"That's not how things are decided here, is it?" Zeke spoke up, gently but firmly disagreeing with Conner. "I mean, it hasn't been to date. Are things changing? I didn't know that we were having secret missions now, since work crews and the like had always been decided at campfire in the past, like all things. I kinda like being allowed some input; this just feels a little, for lack of a better word, disrespectful."

At the grumbling around the crowd, Declan quickly changed sides, no one was going to speak ill of Gwen and Path. Neither of them had ever done anything but good for the people of Golden.

"We did not 'decide this' nor 'approve it' but I trust them," Path told Zeke, holding up a hand to Declan and smiling at him, before he was able to express his defense of them, "we simply did not stop them when they came to us to tell us that they were leaving, whether we approved or not. That said, we trust each and every adult and child in that group and know that each of them gave this serious consideration before coming to tell us. As they said to us, they could have just snuck away in the middle of the night, leaving us all wondering. They didn't want to cause us that kind of concern so they came to us and told us of their plan, I was going to tell everyone at tonight's campfire, please believe me, that really was my intent. I was preparing my news in these notes." He held up the paper in his hand.

Shawnee spoke strongly and calmly, as she did with her exuberant classrooms, "Enough of this. Whatever the driving factor that took them from this camp, I am certain that it was important enough for it to remain secret, and our causing a fuss may actually be counterproductive, may even put them in danger. I don't want any of us going off half-cocked and taking a chance to ruin, or even endanger, whatever this mission might be. I know Yellow Feather and Coyote are two of the wisest boys, very mature for their age. They would never endanger Laurel, David, and Haylie without good reason...they would never needlessly risk any of the children's lives."

"So, is that why they've been running around these mountains where there are wolves and bears and other dangers, unsupervised?" Lisa spoke up. She had traveled with Declan's group across country and had always been one of the most outspoken regarding the risks posed by wild animals. She had always been opposed to some of the freedom the children had when it came to running wild through the forest on their days off school and other duties.

"They are wise children, and almost always armed and capable," Shawnee said. "They are probably safer than any of us. The forest animals are respected by them and return that respect."

Lisa rolled her eyes and turned away, saying, "As if a hungry mountain lion is going to refrain from eating a child out of RESPECT, please! Honey, I respect your beliefs, but they are just 'beliefs', after all, not far from superstitions if you will forgive me for saying it."

"Wait just a minute, Dave and Lily are with them," Gayle said, reversing herself and leaning more toward Path's and Gwen's calm front, "nothing will happen to any of those children as long as those two draw breath. I traveled cross country with them and the safety of the children was always paramount to them, in any situation. They both risked their own lives many times to rescue children. We brought in a lot of kids on our journey and they survived because of the courage of those two wonderful veterans. I would trust them with the life of my own child. They are two of the best, most self-sacrificing people on the planet and two of the most skilled fighters, not only with weaponry, but in hand to hand combat. I trust you, Path. If you say this was okay, then I am pulling back my concerns."

"So it's just anarchy then, is that what this community is devolving into? I was hoping for far better than that," Brian countered. "It's not that I don't hold Path and Gwen in the highest regard, because, believe me, I do, but I thought we had a sense of 'community' here and I was hoping for far better than people just up and deciding that 'this is how it's gonna be' and just doing it. I thought we were organized in work groups and in classes to keep that kind of thing from happening. I thought we decided things by consensus, not by young 'warriors' going off on the offensive." He noticed how Shawnee's nostrils flared at this statement and seemed embarrassed by his own words, "I'm sorry, that was uncalled for. I know better than to say something like that, it was ugly and I'm ashamed. But what I'm trying to say is, what if they are followed back to us? What if they draw something bigger and stronger down on us? Are you all facing that possibility?"

"Aren't you getting a little carried away before you even know what you're talking about?" Conner said, calmly, ignoring the slight and the emphasis on the word "warriors." "Who said that there was anything out there to 'draw down on us'?"

Brian looked toward Layla for support and she finally admitted, "I told them that the rescue group that went out last night was going to rescue a boy from another camp, a camp full of evil and ugly people. The people in that camp have already killed off other groups. They probably think they're the only camp on the continent. I would prefer that they not know that we exist. According to the kids, they are the worst sort, cannibals and murderers."

"So you assumed the worst?" Shawnee said, rocking Little Moon back and forth in her arms as she started to fuss, as if the baby could feel the tension in the group. She comforted her infant. "You assumed that they would become aware of us, just because our group goes to scout them out?"

"They aren't just going to 'scout them out'; they are going on a rescue mission. There is a child, well, a young man, being held at the camp and they are going to save him. It will be a very dangerous mission. There could be many of that other camp chasing them when and if that boy gets away," Layla told them, defensively.

"What are you talking about? How could they possibly know such a thing?" Brian yelled.

Path closed his eyes. It was going to be impossible to keep the secrets now. This opened the window too wide. Suddenly everyone was arguing, the tension was almost impossible to get under control. This group had never raised voices with one another but this confrontation quickly dissolved into angry words being thrown.

"PLEASE stop arguing!" a young voice said above the din, commanding attention in a way that was obviously uncomfortable to the teenager, one of the oldest of the children in Golden. Travis winced as all heads turned toward him. He was tall and slender, very non-imposing, but very shy and withdrawn. Few of the adults had ever heard him speak above his soft and calm modulation. He hated attention; he hated to have every eye and ear on him but he was informed by the other children what Path and Gwen were going through and he came forward bravely, if not boldly, and he was not alone. Dakota walked on one side of him and Abigail on the other as they approached the adults. Perhaps twenty of the other children fanned out behind them.

"Perhaps we should introduce ourselves to give you a hint at why we know what's going on elsewhere, and why we are asking for you to trust us to handle this. You have all accepted what Path and Gwen have told you about their 'travels' through time. What you don't know is that we all, every one of the children that all of you protected and brought to this place, are also 'travelers', we have lived and remember many lives." Travis smiled, shyly, "In perhaps one of my more famous lives, I was called Alan Turing. I helped to build a machine that would decode the Nazi Enigma code, that wretched difficult project," he admitted, shaking his head, "but I was also once called Benjamin Franklin. I have full memory of all of my lives and the things I learned while alive in those times." He looked to Abigail for support.

"I was Elizabeth the First, daughter of Henry VIII in one of my most memorable 'visits'," Abi told them. She actually transformed with her body language to take command, like royalty, like a queen, "It was a hard life, a dangerous one but I proved myself strong and resilient, despite my father's 'indiscretions'. I was brave, even when faced with threats of beheading and imprisonment. I've had many colorful lives, which is one of the reasons I have always had trouble taking orders," she looked apologetically at Gayle, who smiled back at her in awe having known a strong and courageous Abi, a little skinny girl wise beyond her age, because she traveled from California with her. "You may also be familiar with Alice Paul. I was a rabble-rouser then, too, which is why it irks me that you don't consider the girls on this mission as capable as any of the boys. That's particularly insulting to me." She stood defiant and proud, her hands clenched into fists at her sides.

"And I have had many admirable former lives that I am proud to have been able to witness. One of them," Dakota told them, softly, "was my time as Chief Seattle. I think you knew me for some wise comments I've seen in books from time to time, but I prefer to think I was much more than those few borrowed words in time. I was also once, strangely enough, since I was more often Native American, a man called Winston Churchill; that life was more recent, and yet, still known for quotes more than for the accomplishments..."

Conner allowed a little chuckle, "Hardly, oh, my friend, your accomplishments were hardly insignificant." His grin was so wide it almost hurt. He was thoroughly enjoying meeting the "former lives" of these wonderful children he had been "teaching." Now it struck him… amazingly, that the children could have been teaching HIM.

Travis continued, having put together in his mind what he wanted to say before giving the adults a chance to question them. "And I am capable of being in constant contact with the group. My mind can connect to any one of them, but let us first tell you who those 'children' are who chose to go on this mission with Dave and Lily. Yellow Feather was many great beings in his lifetimes; one of them was Hiawatha, another was Corn Planter, and some of his more known ventures in recent history were as a man called Tecumseh, and in THAT life he was a leader even as a boy. Believe me, he is quite capable of seeing many perspectives of strategy, and he will have those of us here in camp to guide and advise him and he absorbs that advice. He is not someone who goes off, how was it that you put it, half-cocked? Coyote was once, in very recent history, called Crazy Horse. I think many of you have heard of his courage and wisdom. He was also once a man called Thomas Jefferson; you may have heard of him, too. There were only twenty or so years separating those two lives of his, which might explain why Crazy Horse seemed 'born wise' by his people," Travis smiled, smugly, "and maybe it was cosmic irony, a way of showing Jefferson how wrong he had been about the 'red man'."

"No less important are the other three. David is good with marksmanship because he was once a man called Daniel Boone. And he lived as Mark Twain, or Samuel Clemens, actually. And in another life, he was known as Teddy Roosevelt. Rather impressive credentials, agreed? Still worried about these 'children'? Let's not leave out our 'fragile' young girls. Laurel was a strong pioneer woman named Mary Draper Ingles; no fearful, fainting, fragile thing, she escaped being captured by Shawnee warriors, who had taken her from her home in Virginia to what is now Ohio, near its border with what is now Indiana. She escaped and found her way back home, through the wilderness, following the rivers to find her way, nearly dead but strong enough to survive. Yet, in a more recent life, you might have admired her as Eleanor Roosevelt. She has been a poetess more times than she can remember, hence her romantic flair." At this, Conner looked at Shawnee and smiled. Laurel had been his star pupil and Shawnee had pointed out a crush that Laurel had once had for her handsome English "professor."

"Oh, and then there's poor little, tiny, helpless Haylie," Travis continued, "I am not surprised that you are so worried about her. Yes, she is small for a twelve-year-old, but she is small in body ONLY and she is stronger than any of you could imagine. Many of you know how she's shaming us all in her skills with weapons. It came easy to little Boudicca, the woman who made even the Romans shudder; she was also known as Annie Oakley in one incarnation. There's nothing that girl can't master. She's fearless and cautious. That other camp wouldn't know what hit them with her, David, Dave, and Lily firing at them."

The word "dumbfounded" did not describe the reception to his words. Everyone was silent as they took this in. These were the children that they had spent the last two years with and none of them suspected that the children were capable of having lived as such historic figures.

Travis smiled, grateful to be nearing the end of his speech. "I don't want to mislead you. Of course we are 'dropping names' to get your attention. Many of us, like Gwen and Pathogent, have lived hundreds, perhaps thousands of very ordinary lives as very ordinary people happy just to be alive. We have just chosen some of the names you would know, some of our more colorful and memorable lives. You would hardly pay attention if I told you I was an accountant named Thomas White, in Hoboken, New Jersey, which, by the way, was a very interesting existence..."

He shrugged and went on, "I have been ordinary and normal in most of those lives, but the ordinary names wouldn't be impressive enough to get you to listen. Isn't it more impressive to let you know that you have an incarnation of Galileo in your midst, right there in your science classes? Or that DaVinci now takes painting and drawing lessons from several of you? I love to be the one to inform you that some of you have been hiking with

John Muir. Imagine that, or that a few of you are trying to teach animal psychology to Jane Goodall or Dian Fossey. I will admit, it is equally impressive and awesome to me that Marie Curie and Sojourner Truth are among us...but, you see, we wanted to enjoy a real childhood in this incarnation."

"And that is why we kept our secret from you," he sighed. "I am sorry if you feel that we should have been more honest and open with you but we had a good reason: living the life of a child is very freeing, very refreshing, and carefree. We actually needed that, to recharge ourselves, to get back into touch with the things children notice and enjoy. I treasured the joy of watching ants at work or counting stars or wondering if I were going to get more freckles. I guess we should just celebrate the fact that we were given two years of joy before being forced to reveal ourselves." Travis looked drained after this speech. It was more than he had wanted to do; he was such a private and shy person, this had taken too much out of him and he looked pale and tired.

He and several of the other children looked so sad it nearly broke Gwen's heart. Pathogent noticed how stricken Layla looked, realizing that she was the one who was instrumental in bringing this to a head. During the silence, everyone struggled with the fact that, for whatever reason, this knowledge had been kept from them... and then most of them realized that the last few hours were part of exactly why that was necessary.

Conner was the first to speak, "Thank you for telling us, for trusting us to process the truth, Travis...Alan..." he smiled, embarrassed, "however you wish to identify yourself. I still see children with my eyes, even with my heart. I still want you to enjoy the childhood you deserve. When we get through this, you must all go back to being the same children we know and love. Right now I just want to know what I can do to help."

Travis smiled, with gratitude showing in his eyes as he looked at Conner, "I will monitor this closely. You will all know if we need help. If you think that we are not worried about our friends, please believe me, we are worried, very worried, I am upset not to be concentrating on them at this moment. I wanted to go along but they knew that I would be more help here, monitoring both their location and the other boy's. His name is Gavin, by the way. I want you to know that he is good at heart, and strong, and very brave. He needs our help and, whether or not you agree, we have decided to help him. We don't want to appear ungrateful or disobedient. However, we cannot allow ourselves not to help this boy. Something tells too many of us that he will be very important to us. Even IF he was a nobody, famous, or noteworthy in all his past lives, he deserves our help. He is terrified. He is unhappy AND, most important, he was on his way here when he was intercepted."

This was news to even Gwen and Path, though she had wondered about it many times, and they looked at one another, wondering how many other incredibly important children were waylaid.

*

Shawnee tucked Little Moon into her cradle and smiled, gently touching the downy hair on the infant's head. She ran a finger down over the tiny nose to the little perfect angel-wing lips. She could feel Conner come up behind her and leaned back into his warmth as he wrapped his arms around her waist. He whispered into her ear, "I can finally put my arms all the way around you again," he teased, "welcome back my slender beauty."

She smiled and looked down again at their child, "Did tonight make you wonder if she might have lived other lives, if she might be like the other children, a reincarnation of greatness? Is there a possibility that there is a reason for all of these time-travelers to have come to this place and time, bringing skills and wisdom and power from the past to help rebuild the future?"

"I like the way you put that. It makes it all more sensible to think that might be the reason. I was tending more toward thinking that everyone is a time-traveler but we were the defective ones who had no memories of our former lives." He smiled over her shoulder and joined her in staring at their beautiful sleeping daughter. "It makes it even more of a privilege to be their caretakers, their teachers, to having been chosen to guide them here. Yes, I have to wonder who she was, what we may learn from her. Could she just be our normal baby, or is she going to be revealed to have been reincarnated for a purpose. Oh, Shawnee, I hate to admit that I hope not, I hope there isn't a burden of fate put upon her shoulders. I understand what was stolen from the children tonight, they just wanted to enjoy, for a little longer, the gift of being only children, having no responsibilities but growing and learning and having fun." He choked up on those last words.

"They still are," Shawnee whispered through her own emotion, putting her hands over his, embracing the feeling of his arms around her, "they still are children, whatever their minds have seen or done, they are still children and I will continue to treat them as such. And, when they bring that boy back to us, we will allow him to be a child again, too."

"I know that Gwen is trying to pretend that she is not worried sick about them, but I would wager that she won't be getting much sleep while they are gone," he said, bringing his hands up to massage her neck.

"How long will this venture take?" she wondered, hoping that the group would not be gone from camp more than a couple days, a week at the most.

"I was talking to Travis about that, it's only about a ten-hour trip on the highway from Denver, but they plan to take it slowly, five hours today and five tomorrow. They will be making camp tonight, but he is routing them differently on the way back, so it should only take about ten hours of travel time on the way down, another three to four hours to walk in over the mountains to where they hope to meet up with the boy from El Paso, then perhaps much longer on the way back, in case they are followed. They don't want to lead anyone back to the Denver area. If worse were to come to worse, since they are on dirt bikes, they can take to the mountains again to elude anyone who might try to tail them."

"But, if they are followed, how can they avoid that?" she asked. He was still standing behind her beside their daughter's cradle but now he was massaging his hands through her hair and rubbing her shoulders, trying to get her to relax.

"By killing any and all who follow, I guess," Conner said, matter-of-factly, as if it happened every day, as if they would be capable of such a thing. "If need be, some of us can meet them part way and add our fire power."

"Conner, whatever they were in former lives, those children are not killers. They won't know what to do. There is a big difference between shooting targets on a range and taking a life," she worried.

"Dave and Lily know what to do. You know from your own history that Tecumseh and Crazy Horse would know what to do. That was why I was so relieved to find that Dave and Lily had gone with the children. They killed in the war, and they killed many on the way to Golden to protect the children. According to Gayle, they will not hesitate to make certain that no one follows them to Golden, no one. If they have to drop behind and pick off anyone or take a different route to make certain the children aren't in danger, that is what they will do. I think Travis told us enough to help us to stop worrying so much and yet, you are thinking of reasons to worry. Let's not court dismay, my love." He kissed the back of her neck and she closed her eyes, warming to his ministrations.

"Come to bed, my gorgeous woman, let's help one another distract from these futile worries," he said, smiling, successfully hiding his own nagging fears. Fortunately, she had not even thought of the fact that the other group might have "travelers" as skilled as Travis and the others. He would not allow himself to voice that concern to her. Though he so rarely hid any of his thoughts from her, this would not be something he would allow her to consider.

*

Gavin felt himself breaking out into a cold sweat. This could not be happening, he could not become sick now, he could not miss his tower duty right now, when there was hope of escape and rescue on the horizon. He had awakened this morning knowing that, sometime in the night, a fever had broken. His clothing was damp from sweat, his head felt heavy and his whole body ached. He pushed himself to finish his work on the trash collection crew. Tomorrow was his tower duty and he had to be present in that tower! The others had come so far to help him, he could not allow this opportunity to slip through his fingers.

He dragged his trash collection bag toward the assignment board and checked again; there, as always, was his name under the assignment for the north tower. Everything was going as planned, everything but this darned flu, or whatever it was. He wiped the sweat from his brow and continued on toward the fire, where he would dump the papers he had gathered. As usual, even sick, he had gathered more trash than anyone else in his work crew. He dug a gloved hand down into the bag to bring out some trash to throw on the flames. He looked down to see a list on one of the papers, written in a childish scrawl with words badly misspelled.

Maik 'em cleen camp.

Apoint genrals.

Werk at orgenizing horhouse.

Charge werk vowchers for hors.

Kill desserders.

Bild bareks.

Invaid dreems.

The last entry froze his blood. He had already guessed by the list who might have written this. Casto was making every effort to bring this camp into order. He had appointed leaders to ensure that every effort was made to make Hades into a camp to be proud of. It seemed that Casto was behind every effort thus far. That was bad enough, but he never dreamed that Casto might possibly be able to see into the heads of others the way his friends, Laurel and Yellow Feather could. "Invaid dreems." How could Casto be capable of doing what he had just discovered about himself? He wanted nothing to harm Laurel or Yellow Feather. Tthey had been very kind to him. What if Casto knew about their plans, what if it was a trap?

He wondered if he could steel his mind against unwelcome invasion? It seemed there should be a way. He felt certain that he would have been aware of Casto's presence in his dreams. Wouldn't he? There was always a subtle warning, a difference he could feel. He was always aware when Laurel was going to appear: he began to feel warm inside; it was almost like he could hear her breathe. Her breath was more welcome to him than a summer breeze on a hot, dusty day. With Yellow Feather, it was a sense of strength and power coming at him. The other boy, the one named Travis, he thought he could actually feel Travis' kindness, as if Travis didn't feel comfortable approaching him without warning him first, kind, considerate, hesitant, a true gentleman. He would clear his throat, as if entering a room and wanting to announce himself.

No, he was certain that he would be aware of Casto, the way the man made his skin crawl whenever he pulled a work crew inspection or paid a surprise visit at the barracks to make sure everyone was keeping his bunk and locker clean. Gavin's was always not only clean, it was military clean, just like his new work boss had taught him. You could bounce a coin on his bed, he made it up so tight and his clothing and boots were folded and stacked just like Sergeant Casey had taught the entire barracks. Nothing was ever out of place in Gavin's locker because he did not squirrel away candy or tins of food, as some of the others did. He didn't post naked pictures from magazines, either, but those were allowed, even if he had.

Casto would always smile and tilt his head in Gavin's direction when he inspected the boy's locker. Sometimes he would use him as an example, insulting Gavin because he didn't think the boy was capable of either hearing or understanding. "You boys with brains need to learn from Simpleton here, he's the only one of you who does it right. Now, I'm going to have to ask you, why is that? Why is it that a boy with half his wits can do a better job than all of you? I'm not going to tell you again, you don't bring your lockers and bunks up to my high standard, you're going to be working latrine duty for a month. No, make that two months. Is that understood?" It sure didn't help to make Gavin popular with his barrack mates, but he didn't care, he would soon be gone.

These thoughts didn't help Gavin feel better, that much was certain. He slid the paper into his pocket and hurried to dump the rest of the trash onto the fire and stepped away quickly. He was already sweating. The fire made him feel miserable. He went to the water bucket and drank several ladles of cool water. He thought about the fact that he maybe shouldn't be drinking from the ladle that others would be using. They, too, might end up with this flu. Then he realized that a good dose of the flu might be just the thing for this camp. But, then again, maybe that's where he got it. Suddenly the "community water bucket" lost its appeal.

He walked swiftly to disappear behind a building and puked his guts out.

*

They had made good time following along Highway 25, even when there were cars log-jammed in the highway. Their trail bikes easily detoured out through the woods to rejoin when the highway was maneuverable. They left route 25 for 84, then hooked up with 54 which took them close to El Paso. They were overjoyed to witness the resurgence of wildlife, both on the ground and in the air.

They stopped just about three hours from where they wanted to enter the mountains above El Paso and camped, building a fire and enjoying the beauty of the night sky above them. The mountains would hide their campfire from the group at El Paso, even those in the towers. They had carefully planned and gone over the maps, communicated with Travis extensively, and had eaten a hearty dinner of canned beans and rice. Then Dave suggested that they all try to sleep so that they would be fresh and in good shape to greet the mission awaiting them.

Laurel lay on her back, staring up at the stars, trying to resist visiting Gavin's dreams, knowing that he, too, needed a good night's sleep. His tower duty would begin early in the morning. She sighed aloud. Haylie raised up on one elbow and looked at her, smiling, "Are you worrying about tomorrow?" she asked.

"Shouldn't I be?" Laurel answered, turning on her side toward Haylie, "Are you?"

"I guess I don't have the common sense to be scared!" Haylie said, with a smile, "I'm excited, you know, like before Christmas or when you are going to start school. That kind of excitement, the kind where you don't know if tomorrow's going to be the best day you ever had or the worst, but you're excited just to be doing something so new to you that it gives you butterflies."

"Excitement of the unknown," Laurel said, smiling back. "Listen, Haylie, I really want you to be extra careful. These are extremely dangerous men. Think of them as mad dogs, because that's basically how they act. Gavin is a brave, strong man and he's terrified of them, especially their leader who is ruthless and cruel."

Something strange came over Haylie and she said, almost as if in a trance, "The night before a battle is when you must clear your mind of fear and not build the enemy into a giant to fear, and know that, if someone must die, it must be the enemy, not you. You must face them with no hesitation to kill or you will be killed. My living will celebrate my enemy's death every day that I breathe."

Laurel had a feeling that she might just have met the ancient Celt, Boudicca. She stared at Haylie and felt a strange feeling of historic privilege come over her. It was amazing to be able to say that she had met and talked to someone so brave and strong that she had held the Roman Empire at bay.

Haylie returned, in a flash, her crooked smile on her face once more, "Coyote was so excited to see that herd of wild horses yesterday. I will wager you that, as soon as we get back to Golden, he will take another trip down to where we saw them and try to come home with a few."

"It was a beautiful sight," Laurel had to add, "I have to admit, I was excited seeing them, too. I only wish we'd had time to stop and watch them. It was so wonderful that they survived. It was a huge herd! I think that David was watching them with yearning, too, I don't think Coyote will be alone on his excursion. Now, Haylie, we'd better try to sleep, we do have to have clear heads in the morning."

*

Dave relieved Lily who had taken first watch. She was sitting up on a rise where she could see far into the distance.

"Ready for tomorrow?" he asked her.

"Ready as I'm ever going to be," she assured him, smiling. Lily knew that Dave cared a great deal for her and she found herself wishing that she had told him a long time ago that she returned those feelings. The fact that he loved her was enough for her right now. It gave her warmth and courage, just as it had as they were crossing Nevada, escaping terror along the way. Telling him now seemed somehow fatalistic, as though she were doing it in fear that they both might die tomorrow. She didn't want to allow Dave or herself to think that way, although she had extracted a promise from Haylie that no one else knew about. She and "Annie Oakley" had talked privately for some time, the child not even pretending to have the voice of a child as she allowed her past persona to discuss something extremely serious with Lily, her mentor and friend.

She looked at Dave, realizing that she returned the love that he felt for her and wishing they had the time to explore those feelings. But now was not the time. That man had always been too busy to breathe, helping to maintain order in Golden, acting as right-hand man to Pathogent, keeping them all safe from harm by patrolling the perimeter, something only she and Dave actually knew. For the two years that Golden existed as the gathering place, Dave had kept them safer by patrolling and keeping watch over the village every single night as others slept. She had awakened in the night, knowing that she was safer simply because he was out there, keeping them safe.

She thought about the burden she had put on the young girl child. Annie/Haylie completely understood her request since it was exactly what she would want given the same situation, and she gave Lily her solemn vow, staring directly into her eyes as she asked for the same promise from Lily.

And now here was Dave, ready to relieve her watch early, knowing that she was tired and needed sleep. Dave, always looking out for everyone else. How she embraced the love she knew that he felt for her and wished she could tell him so.

Dave sat down beside Lily and they both looked up at the stars. It was always easy talking to him when they shared a moment like this. Lily had always had a problem talking to other people, growing from a lifetime of foster parents who shattered trust. That lack of trust and comfort in one-on-one situations with other people was one of the reasons she joined the service. She thought that perhaps depending on others for your very life might teach her more trust. It didn't. However, meeting Dave, who had been through many of the same nightmarish scenarios as she had seen in the Middle East, allowed her to finally feel close to another human being. That, and the love they shared for the children they protected, gave them a strong common bond. Sometimes she wished that she had the courage to tell him how much he really meant to her. She had to hope that he just knew.

They talked for a long while before she went to her bedroll. The night was moonlit and visibility was good. She nodded when he sent her for her sleep and he settled into his turn. She reluctantly said good night to him, kicking herself mentally for not being able to tell him how much she loved him.

*

Lily had been only seven when a multi-car accident took both of her parents and left her an orphan. Until that fateful day, she had been a happy, healthy child of two loving and devoted parents. There were no grandparents or siblings so Lily was left an orphan, ward of the state. Her first set of foster parents were a little strange, but good people, not energetic and athletic as her parents had been, nor intelligent and curious as they had been. They were just stable, sane, hard-working salt-of-the-earth people. They had given up fostering when they had a child of their own, so Lily was once again without parents at the age of ten.

The next set of fosters were nice and lots of fun, at first. The woman, Jill, was beautiful and fun-loving, took incredibly good care of herself and taught Lily how to use her charm and good looks. The man, Carson, was handsome, intelligent, and adventurous, seldom home because his job as an attorney occupied much of his time. And when he wasn't at the office or in court, he was at the gym playing basketball, handball, or any array of sporting activities.

Lily spent the first three years with them in a state of joy. She was able to join so many clubs at school. Jill enrolled her in other activities, music, art, dancing. It was easily one of the best years of her life. She became popular at school, had friends to sleep-overs, and her grades were better than they had ever been. Life seemed almost too good to be true. Lily enjoyed a dream life of privilege and security.

Then the bottom dropped out of her life when one night Carson visited her room while Jill was away on a cruise with friends.

Lily didn't know if the molestation would ever end. It seemed that Carson was an expert at planning for them to be alone. She lived a tortured life for the next year, wondering how to tell Jill, not knowing where to turn. Eventually, Carson had convinced her that Jill knew, and that felt like the worst betrayal of all. When her grades dropped and she stopped going to activities, Jill began to worry and signed her up to speak to a psychologist.

What she revealed to the psychologist ended her life with Jill and Carson. She had heard that they divorced and that Jill had taken Carson for everything that she could. Jill never talked to Lily again, so Lily could not help but assume that Jill blamed her every bit as much as Carson, however much the psychologist assured her it was untrue.

Lily withdrew from life going on around after that and just kept her head down and her mind on studies, waiting to be old enough to be on her own. She kept her body in shape, knowing that she would need to be strong for what she had planned. She enlisted as soon as she graduated, hoping to get a college education on the GI bill, which is exactly what she did. She was a loner, never really getting close to anyone, moving from relationship to relationship emotionlessly. She had only been discharged from the service for a short time before the wars and troubles began.

*

Dave was not surprised when he was soon joined by Yellow Feather.

"Can't sleep?" Dave asked.

"No, and neither can Travis. We've been in my head, writing so many different scenarios. The thing we have going in our favor is the trail bikes. He said that Gavin told him that there are nothing but big trucks in that camp. Those would be great chasing us over terrain like Franklin, but we get into the Rockies and we could easily lose them in forests. Our bikes can go where their trucks cannot. We also have the element of surprise. He said that most deserters are tracked on foot. They will not expect that Gavin will have access to a bike."

"Yellow...um, Tecumseh, I have something I want you to promise me," Dave said, considering this the perfect time to broach the subject that he and Lily had discussed at great length. "If Lily and I feel it necessary to drop back, even drop out, to cover the escape, promise me that you will keep everyone going forward. We know our way back home and we are both used to hard travel, your young bodies are not. If we tell you to go on without us, trust us. We'll make it home our own way. We just want to make sure that you don't stop and come back for us."

"But Dave," Yellow Feather started to say.

"No, no 'buts'. Lily and I know what we're doing. I know you've been in battle, my friend, but that was with a seasoned warrior's body. It's not the same thing as the body you now possess. Lily and I are the seasoned warriors here. Promise me that you will trust us and listen to us when we tell you to go on."

Yellow Feather sat in silence. It had just now occurred to him that such a thing might happen. This crazed leader might bring a large force to the chase. There was no way that they could allow that force to go anywhere near Golden. Dave was right. He and Travis had been guilty of being too optimistic, of not anticipating the very worst. His past should have taught him differently: Tippecanoe and later the Battle of the Thames should have taught him that it was a grave mistake to underestimate the enemy.

If Dave and Lily weren't enough, they would have to call Golden out in force, to build a wall of defense somewhere halfway between El Paso and Golden. The enemy could not be allowed to discover their sanctuary. His eyes met Dave's in the moonlight and he gave a slight nod of his head. Dave appeared to visually relax, now that he had gotten the word that he knew that Tecumseh held sacred.

*

"You're thinking of them again, aren't you?" Gwen whispered, her mouth close to Pathogent's ear in the darkness of their cabin.

"It's all I can do to stay here and not go awaken Travis, if he IS asleep, which I doubt. I've been bothering him constantly for reports. I know that he's getting frustrated trying to keep me happy. This is their last sleep before the rescue and he wants to allow them that." Path turned onto his side to face her, rubbing his hand over her hip, just to touch her and to soothe her. "That poor kid has the world on his shoulders right now. I know that he would rather be with the group than monitoring them."

"I liked Declan's suggestion to prepare vehicles for movement, in case we are needed. Every minute might just count and now we are ready in a 'stand by' situation.

The armory packed into those jeeps and RVs should be able to stop a large enemy force," Gwen said, running her hand through Path's still thick, black hair, only streaked with gray at the temples.

"We have to hope we haven't underestimated the size of that army." Path pondered, "We can't allow them to breach the defenses, should we be called south. We cannot allow those monsters to come within reach of Golden."

"There's still the shield," Gwen reminded him.

"Yes, there is still the shield, so long as they don't have their own magician," Path offered, arching a brow. "We know so little about this group, which is what makes me nervous. I've always heard that you should never underestimate the enemy."

"But Travis said that there is great unrest in that camp, that there are more and more deserting every day and only fear holds them together, fear of that leader of theirs, who sounds like a devil to me."

Path winced, "I don't think he's more than just a crazy, uneducated man, but then again, I don't want to underestimate him. We will be ready, as Tecumseh says, because we must. I love the quote attributed to him, even if I didn't get to hear him say it: "So live your life that the fear of death can never enter your heart." We've talked about this before, we've been given a gift, these beautiful years together. I'm willing to give my life to insure that Golden stay free and the children stay safe."

"Let's hope that it will not come to that," Gwen said in a whisper, "let us hope that it is simply a rescue, nothing more. However, don't even think that I won't be there by your side."

Path smiled. He knew better than to think he would be able to talk Gwen into staying in camp while he went off to "war." Not his warrior queen.

*

Travis felt it and it sent a shock wave through him. It was like something was trying to drill into his mind, like some foreign insect was trying to find entry. He sat up straight in alarm and pushed hard to reinforce his own thoughts, closing off even Tecumseh, closing his mind to Gavin. Right now he had to prevent entry and he needed all his efforts to concentrate on this wall he had to build to keep the invader out.

It was repulsive to him and he wondered if it felt like this when he entered the mind of others, like he was some kind of parasite, trying to worm into the thoughts and dreams of others. He felt his stomach flip and he felt like he might vomit. It had been so sudden and so repulsive to him that it made him dizzy. This wasn't like a *blink* or even a lateral travel; this was like an eel or a tentacle was working up his back, trying to enter through the brain stem or any point of entry it could find. He shivered, then sent out a thought to Tecumseh, "Guard your mind, someone is trying to enter."

"I know, I felt it," was the instant answer.

"I won't sleep NOW!" Travis assured him. "I can't afford to let that 'thing' into my dreams."

"Nor I," Tecumseh agreed. He sat up and was alarmed to see a coyote not ten feet away from their camp. When it saw him, it moved just a few paces away, then stopped and stared at him. It shook its head and reached a foreleg up over its ear as if trying to jar something from its head. He watched it carefully. Had something entered the mind of the coyote to use its vision? Was he being paranoid? Was it possible to use random animals in such a way? He tried to shake that thought from his mind, it was too much like the horror stories he had read back on the reservation, where a satanic being would use ravens or other animals to spy on the "good guys." But there was something about the way that coyote seemed bothered by something in his ear. Could it simply be ticks or fleas and was his imagination running wild?

He normally would do nothing at all to a wild animal, preferring to live in concert with their right to exist but he threw a rock to see if he could scare the coyote away. It moved only inches, as if not the least afraid of the rock, but then sauntered off to find some prey. Tecumseh sat shivering, unnerved. What had just happened with Travis and with the coyote did not bode well to him. He wanted this mission to be over. He promised Gavin that he would help him and he would, but it needed to be a successful mission. He felt responsible for the others. He could not allow even a single life to be lost.

*

Dave stared up at the clear sky and counted the stars. It was amazing to him to be under this beautiful star-filled canopy and yet expecting enemy action. This was so different than going to a foreign land, living in an unfamiliar climate and facing enemies so very different from the people he had grown up with. This was a day before, but he could not really get it through his mind what they might actually face.

He and Lily had private conferences that the others were unaware of and their prime directive had always been to protect the children at all costs.

Dave smiled. He had already had a longer life than he had ever expected to live but now there was Lily. When he thought about her, his ears would grow warm, something that was a throwback to a shy, awkward little hillbilly boy from Arkansas who never really thought that a girl could possibly be interested in him. And yet, there seemed to be some kind of response from Lily, more than simply friendship, or was this just him being hopeful?

If it was his imagination, he wanted that imagination to continue giving him this absurd scenario where he stood a chance with that amazing and beautiful woman. He looked toward the sleeping camp, realizing that there had been so many times when, as he guarded Golden, he realized that he was essentially guarding Lily, hoping that someday she would return the feelings he felt toward her.

Guarding Lily and, because they were with her, guarding all the others, he kept a watchful eye on their surroundings, his ears attuned to any sound.

*

Dave had such a normal life growing up that he could hardly relate to anyone with problem parents or siblings. It wasn't that he didn't know how fortunate he was. Several of the kids in his class were living with foster parents or had a single parent household while his Momma and Pop were loving, tender, and kind. He was an only child who grew up defending the weak and always trying to make peace between kids who were, for one reason or another, at odds with each other. They were simple folk, his family, hard-working and strong in their faith. They attended church every Sunday of their lives, with their son happily in tow. He worked hard to win favor with the church elders, a trusted young man, growing up with strong family memories and strong faith in God.

Both of his parents were so proud of him when he joined the service. The entire community was proud of their hometown boy. He loved the way his parents glowed as the entire church held a potluck dinner to say good-bye to their "soldier." He was able to say farewell to people who had known his kin for generations. It made him feel warm inside to think that he was going to war to insure their safety and well-being.

He had kept the letters to his parents light-hearted; even during the very worst of the fighting and stress, he made his deployment sound like an adventure. His father wrote that he read the letters in church and that everyone was so proud of the good that he was doing overseas. There were a few moments when he sincerely doubted his mission when he heard stories of atrocities committed against civilians by fellow soldiers but he kept his own cause noble and did nothing to be ashamed of in the defense of his country.

He never wanted his parents to know the truth about the atrocities that he witnessed and the nightmare he found himself entrenched in. There were times that he thought he would lose his mind if he witnessed another senseless killing. He was sickened by the enthusiasm some of the soldiers brought to their duty of killing, even innocent civilians. He waited out his tour of duty like it was a prison sentence, hoping and dreaming of the day he would be home and breathe free. The innocent civilians in this foreign land were living in his concept of hell.

If only his folks could have lived to see his homecoming reception. If only his dad had not had the major, fatal heart attack and his mother had not fallen in the shower of their home. If only they had not owed so much on the house to have had it repossessed by the bank. If only.

The world was so full of "if only" for him for too long. He could have had a job with so many businesses in his hometown. There were many friends and former neighbors who approached him with offers. But, Dave had not seen much of the country and he decided to simply wander, nothing to hold him, no reason to stay. He was basically a well-educated, soft-spoken, kind-hearted homeless veteran with no real goal in life but to be wherever he needed to be if he could help someone. He would often work for his keep on farms and homesteads as he traveled around the country, especially for people who were in need of someone giving them an honest day's work for an honest day's pay.

He could not remember why he had ended up in Provo, Utah, but he was living homeless in the park when a very pretty young girl still in uniform, fresh from her service overseas, saw him and offered to buy him coffee. After just a few hours of talking to Lily, Dave had decided that Provo might just be as good a place as any...at least for a while. The bombing did not surprise him, nor did the many deaths. He hunkered down in the park and waited some of the worst of it out, trying to decide what to do. It had been a good place to stay but now there were so few survivors and they all seemed to be gathering belongings and heading for the coast. So he decided to wait to see which way the wind blew, the park his new home.

At least until that pretty young thing named Lily came to him with her new friend, Gayle, and asked him to join them in their caravan across country, heading into the mountains for who knew what beyond. He helped to make certain they were armed and prepared, although he was surprised to find that both of the women were quite capable and had already loaded a camper with necessities. Then his life as a protector once again made sense as they rescued child after child in their journey, risking life and limb, every risk well worth it.

Those memories were held precious in Dave's heart.

*

Casto hit his fist down on the table beside his bed. He had never encountered anything like it, he had sent his mind out, just like always, just the way he did when he knew that someone was approaching Hades. His anticipation of visitors had earned him respect and no little bit of fear.

His skill had others thinking he was magic. The fact that he always knew who was coming and why they were coming had built a legend around him. This time was so different. Though he could feel that someone somewhere was approaching the camp, he could get no clear message as to why and how. He was straining his brain until it nearly hurt, growing angrier by the moment.

That damned coyote could have been anywhere west of the freaking Mississippi for all the good it did entering into that stupid canine brain. All that coyote could think about was catching moles and getting away from that kid throwing rocks. He needed it to stop and check out how many of them were there but he'd only seen two kids. Damn it, where the hell were they? He had felt two minds pondering Hades and he rode that link back to the minds that sent out the thoughts but those damned minds were strong enough to evict him. He had never encountered resistance before. What the hell was going on? It was like their brains were made of concrete, they shut him out so effectively. What kind of people could do that?

No matter, he would have the camp ready for visitors. They would have another feast coming to them and his legend would grow. It would be better if he knew where and when they would hit camp but he'd start tomorrow, mustering the troops, making sure the chase vehicles were ready, if they were needed. He'd be ready to deploy a hundred men, easily. Damned if he'd let them send out those feelers and reject him like that. He'd find some way to break into their thoughts, some way, damn it!

He lay down beside Connie and found that he felt annoyed at her presence. Her snoring was irritating and disgusting; and he didn't want to sleep on a small portion of his bed. He wanted his whole bed. His mood was going from bad to worse quickly. He shook her to wake her up, "Get dressed, I need my sleep," he told her. She grumbled, a little too much, so he slapped her ample behind and teased her, "Go'wawn, sleepyhead, I'm too tired to listen to your bitchin'. Don't go away mad, just go away." He chuckled at his own cleverness.

As if he were offering a consolation prize, he told her, "You can take that wine with you, I need to keep my head clear." She rose, groggily and muttered under her breath, pushing the hair she did not even have back from her face, as if the memory of hair controlled her motions, so she ran her hands over her smooth scalp. She tried to orient herself and stomped a few steps from the bed. She was angry at having been roused so abruptly from her deep REM sleep. She had been dreaming about horses running across the prairie and wanted to crawl right back into that beautiful dream. She grabbed the bottle and, still half naked, wearing only an oversized t-shirt, stumbled drunkenly from his quarters. He watched her go with relief. The girl was nothing but a distraction: a beautiful, smooth, sleek, slender distraction, and he didn't need a distraction right now, even though his body was already responding to the sight of her long legs and shapely ass.

He was still angry that he couldn't successfully enter the minds out there in the darkness. The boy had looked to be Native American. Maybe he was like some kind of Shaman or something, maybe that was the answer. "Well, little boy, I'll be wearing your scalp on my belt come a day or two, let me tell you," he thought. "Don't think you didn't piss me off, little Cochise, but vengeance will be mine, you little red devil." His mind searched for every epithet he could hurl against the boy, comforted by his own sense of superiority. How he would love to say every single word of that to the boy's face. How he'd love to watch that face become aware that he was going to lose, and lose big.

He lay back on his pillow and stared at the ceiling. Nothing about the terrain gave it away. Texas was a big damned state, for all he knew they were coming up from Mexico, and didn't that make sense? Of course, the kid was probably from one of those damned southern tribes. It would be just like them to have survived the bombings and all. Damned immigrants! He'd have watch from the southern towers doubled for a couple days. Like hell he'd let anyone in this camp think he wasn't ready and waiting. They'd be wanting to steal food and vehicles. He'd have surprises waiting for them, just you wait.

"I'll send your asses back across the Rio Grande so damned fast, you'll wish you never even LOOKED North. Damned immigrants, god damned freeloaders."

*

Gavin entered her mind gently and carefully, not wanting to awaken her. It was soft and comforting, just being with her when she was sleeping. It felt wrong to do this, but he just really couldn't help himself. She was dreaming about horses, watching them running across a plain, kicking their heels and tossing their manes. She smiled in her dream and that smile lit up her face. He gently left her mind so not to awaken her and tried to sleep. Tonight he would see her in person. Tonight he would actually be able to touch her.

Suddenly he felt as shy as he had always been with a girl. What if she didn't like the real him? What if this whole rescue was just out of pity for him because she was so kind and sweet? He frowned, worrying. The most frightening of all was thinking that he knew that he was already head over heels for her. What if he was assuming that she felt the same way but she was just being nice? How would that make him feel? What would it be like living in that other place, lovesick and rejected?

"Stupid, stupid, stupid, stupid," he thought. Why was he doing this? Why was he keeping himself awake like this? Was it the fever? Was he still sicker than he had been when he lay down? Earlier tonight, he had fallen into bed and passed out cold, no memory of even pulling the covers up over himself. Now he was drenched in sweat again, feeling one moment cold and clammy and the next suffocating and hot. Damn, this was going to be hard, he was just so sick! What timing!

He reached to his bedstand in the dark and took another five aspirin from the packet he'd been given in the medic shack, and drained the water from his glass. He had to be better, he just had to.

The next thing he knew, the big bell was being rung six times and it was time to go to mess for breakfast, then change to report to his tower duty at nine bells. He forced himself to drink some coffee and eat some canned peaches. It was all he could do to keep it down. When he reported for duty, the line boss, Pit Bull, looked at him and said, "Boy, you look like hell, sure you can serve?" Then realizing that the boy was looking at him dumbfounded, shook his head and said, "Oh, hell with it, there's nobody else anyway, might was well be sick up there as anywhere." And he sent Gavin to his tower.

He normally climbed the ladder fast, not daring to look down but today he had to stop five times on the way up, clinging to the ladder, feeling sick and dismal and dizzy. When he got to the tower, the dizziness sent him spinning and he went to the railing and vomited over it. The taste of sour peaches in his mouth was hard to handle but he tried to shake it off and simply leaned on the stool, hoping the world would stop spinning so fast. "Oh, God," he thought, "why is this happening now, was I not meant to live free? Is this working against me so that I stay here forever or get killed for trying to leave?"

He felt Travis enter his mind. "Are you okay?" was the first thing Travis said as he felt swept away by the vertigo and nausea. Travis grabbed the sides of his desk to anchor himself against the nausea and worried about Gavin. He could actually feel the fever and the nausea in the pit of his own stomach, as if he and Gavin shared a body.

"No," he spoke inside of himself, "I am sick as a dog but, even if I have to crawl, today is the day." He tried to put up a brave front, standing taller and taking a deep breath.

"We can have them hold up, wait until you feel a little better," Travis said, full of concern and empathy. Gavin knew that he was especially going to like Travis who, like him, was shy and reserved and quiet. Travis was as kind as a boy could get. "You don't want to take a chance of falling off the bike, Gavin. If you're this sick, maybe we should wait," he counseled.

"We only pull tower duty once every month!" Gavin told him, mentally. "I don't think I have that long. This camp is getting worse, the workers hate the line bosses, or sergeants, as Casto calls them. Everyone is grumbling and unhappy and full of hate, there are fights in the barracks every single night, rapes, screaming, knifes drawn and used. I watched a guy in my work group get killed for taking too long a break the other day, man! His line boss just shot him dead, right there in front of the rest of us. We are virtually slaves, we are expendable. Although, I don't know how much longer that will last, at the rate of murders and desertions, this camp is getting smaller and smaller, and there's no way to increase the population. All the whores are aborting any pregnancies and no one here seems to realize what that actually means about their future." He talked rapidly, excited and alarmed at how bad he felt but also how precarious his position.

"Slow down, Gavin, we're going to get you out, we promised. We do have to warn you, we think someone in your camp is capable of entering minds. Guard yours carefully. It feels dirty when he tries, like some kind of worm wants to enter at the base of your neck. I don't know if it is from your camp, but we think it probably is," Travis told him. "Be careful, guard your thoughts if you feel this happening, I'm worried that you might be too sick to fight it." Travis kept his voice calm and soothing, hoping that Gavin was not already too stressed and ill to think straight when he needed to be careful.

"Gavin?" Travis finally thought to ask, "What IS the population?"

Gavin did some math in his head, forty men per barracks, six barracks, fourteen sergeants, or generals as they referred to themselves, giving themselves promotions, and twenty-two escape chasers. He ticked it off and told Travis, "Not counting the whores, about 267, including Casto, give or take a few of yesterday's murders."

Travis seemed happy with that number. His group must outnumber Hades. But weren't most of them children? Gavin took a deep breath and tried hard to relax as a cool breeze moved across his brow like a caress. Travis seemed to have read his thoughts, "Yes, she sent that. She cares about you more than you know," he told him.

Gavin closed his eyes and for the first time in days, smiled.

*

"These mountains are too easy," Haylie said, laughing, "this isn't even work! But I do wish it weren't so hot. Am I talking too much? You are all so quiet. Should I stop talking?"

"We will need you to stop talking when we get closer; we don't know how much the wind can carry sound around here," Yellow Feather told her, watching the sky and the ground around them for any animals or anything that might host the enemy's mind like the coyote last night. "But right now, I am actually enjoying the fact that you are talking so fearlessly. It is good to be so confident. I share your confidence."

Dave held up a hand to stop them, as dusk was settling in. "Now that we can actually see the camp, Lily and I are going to look for good places to shoot from, should we have to cover Gavin's escape. There isn't any vegetation. We'll have to use the lay of the land to our advantage, it's all we've got. Haylie should probably seek an aerie, too. Her keen eye is better than anyone's. Haylie, what do you think of that little outcropping up there, do you see it?"

She leaned back and looked up and grinned, "Perfect." Confident in her skill, Dave knew that she could shoot the eye out of a pigeon at a tremendous distance. This also put her further from harm, which was something else he desired.

After she left them, Dave turned to Yellow Feather and said, "Lily and I discussed this, and you gave me your word, if a force comes after you and we get separated, keep going toward home, do not stop for anything. She and I are trained reconnaissance and will eventually find our way home safely, but we want to cover your tails and make sure no one follows you back home." None of them allowed themselves to think or say the words Golden or Colorado since they found out about the mind invasions. "We will find our way home, believe me, trust me," Lily nodded and smiled, reinforcing what Dave was telling them, adding, "trust us, like we trust you."

David, Laurel, Yellow Feather, and Coyote all winced at what he was suggesting. They had all wanted to stay together in a tight group but they understood what Dave was planning and they could not argue with the fact that this was "warrior wisdom." They rested as they waited for the time to move forward closer to the camp.

Yellow Feather told Laurel, "Gavin told Travis that his turn to sleep was at ten bells and he would be able to sleep until one bell, so that gives him three hours of time that they won't expect him to be accounted for. They probably won't be able to realize he's gone for another half hour, at least. That gets us back to our bikes, then we hit the trail hard for home."

Laurel nodded. She knew that he was making it sound so easy because he wanted to keep her calm but her insides were rebelling against that. She resisted the urge to try to reach out to Gavin. After what Yellow Feather told her about last night, she wanted to keep her mind from opening up and being receptive. They had all been warned to keep their guard up, allowing Travis to communicate since he could block any invasiveness better than they, and Travis had told Yellow Feather that he and Gavin had already discussed that possibility, so Gavin probably had his mind locked down anyway. She sighed, it would be so comforting to know that he was okay. She had caught a little of a conversation between Travis and Gavin and knew that Gavin was sick, not too sick, she hoped.

She, David, Yellow Feather, and Coyote moved forward closer to the camp. At full dark, they would move to the little copse of trees to wait for Gavin. Gavin was close. Tonight she would finally see him for real, be able to actually touch him. She was almost embarrassed at how excited that made her, even thinking of him made her blush.

*

He could not see them and he was trying as hard as he might, watching the horizon, wanting to make certain that, if they could be seen, that he saw them and warned them off before one of the other guards caught sight of them. They were close, he knew that much, but they were good and they were careful. He saw nothing but the usual rolling brown hills leading toward the Franklin Mountain Range. Not a glimmer of the sun reflecting off a rifle, nothing. He rested his fevered head against the barrel of his rifle as waves of nausea continued to threaten to knock him down.

The seven bells had sent the guard to the west of him down to sleep. He would be next. He was nervous, but not afraid. There were worse things than dying, and living here in Hades was getting to be a whole lot worse than anything that could happen tonight unless they were captured and he had to watch his rescuers endure torture. That alone would be far worse than anything imaginable. He had to stop thinking such things. He thought about what Travis told him about someone in the camp trying to read their minds and he wondered who that person could be. He had to hope beyond hope that it wasn't someone close to Casto because word would go out faster if Casto got wind of it.

He decided to think about something else entirely and took his mind back to his childhood. His brother, Dale had been four years older than him but always seemed far more grown up and capable than Gavin. He, of course, was the first to do everything. By the time Gavin did those things, walk, run, ride bikes, all the normal boy things, no one took much notice, except Dale. Dale was the one to urge, teach, and congratulate him all through his life, through school and everything. The folks were too busy with Nascar and going places with their friends, and drinking, there was always alcohol in their home. When Gavin was selected to go to the state finals spelling bee, it was Dale who strutted proudly through town telling everyone who would listen what a smart boy his brother was. Dale was the one who begged, cajoled, and shamed his parents into finally attending and being in the audience with him when Gavin placed third among thousands of kids statewide. When Gavin got all A's his final year in junior high and was placed in Advanced Placement classes in the college preparatory group, Dale took him out to dinner to celebrate, just the two of them ordering from a menu like grown-ups. His big brother had been proud of him and told him so nearly every day. Dale had been the only real father that Gavin had known and it was Dale who had fostered Gavin's desire to know everything that he could possibly know about the world.

Gavin smiled to himself, thinking that all of the men in this camp thought him incapable of thought beyond rudimentary levels. While most of them had pretty much rejected education, he had absorbed it like a sponge. Had the world not ended when it did, he might have gone on to one of the finest colleges, if he'd been able to win enough scholarships. Dale had been working towards that goal, saving money every week out of his pay to help Gavin pay for living expenses if his grants and scholarships hadn't been enough. When Gavin began mowing lawns and got an after-school job washing cars, he contributed to the fund. Dale was his entire support system and, with his brother gone, Gavin had just pretty much lost hope and decided to struggle just enough to survive. Losing his voice to trauma was almost a blessing. When everyone thought you were not only deaf and mute but mentally deprived, they tended to let you just pass under their personal notice and, other than noticing his brute strength, no one really noticed Gavin much here in camp. That alone had served him well and kept him relatively safe, until the pedophile, that is.

He grimaced at that memory. Although he and his girlfriend had made out, kissing one another and mutually enjoying some light petting, he was still a virgin. He honestly had just never really pushed the opportunities with Sandy, even though he knew that, at times, she would have let him have sex with her. He had visions of going to college and becoming successful, then coming back and taking Sandy away from the trailer park life they had both grown up sharing. Her folks had been as tuned out as his. It had also been all about Nascar, smoking dope, and drinking beer with them. As a matter of fact, they had been friends of his folks, which was how he and Sandy met.

All these memories, he made himself relive them slowly to pass the time and, when he ran out of memories, he began to think his way through books, beginning with one of his favorites, "A Tale of Two Cities," moving through "The Three Musketeers" and "The Count of Monte Cristo." He had moved through more modern novels like "Animal Farm" and "1984" when nine bells sounded and he realized that in only one hour, he would be free. He shook his head and went into "Don Quixote," one of the few books he'd ever really struggled through. Though he loved the story, Cervantes' style had been a little harder for him to read than others, not as challenging as James Joyce, but challenging enough.

*

Casto lay in his bed trying hard to get some responses other than those in camp. He searched through every mind that he could enter, even those relatively blank. Then he decided to make certain that the guards on duty were being diligent. He had never done this before but it would be a good way to see if they were sleeping on the job. Nine bells had just rung so the most northwest and southeast towers were in their sleeping mode, so he began with the northernmost tower. Looking at the roster he saw that "Simple Kid" was how they described the person in that tower. He smiled, it was as good a name as any for that strong little deaf mute ox. He wormed into that mind, picturing his thoughts going in at the base of the neck and moving upward.

It wasn't totally empty as he had expected but the kid was picturing a crazy man on a horse jousting with windmills. He laughed to himself. He remembered watching that cartoon when he had been a kid. So, the boy had childhood memories similar to his. Shaking his head, leaving the boy with the image of an aged knight on a swaybacked steed, with his jousting pole nearly dragging the ground, and a short little humble man on a burro by his side, he moved on to the mind of the guard in the northeast tower. Nothing more to learn from "Simple Kid" but the fact that he was both alert and awake.

Here was more fertile ground as he found the guard thinking about Connie and the man actually had thoughts about trying to save enough to buy a night with her. Casto noted the name, writing it slowly on his pad, while allowing the man to continue thoughts that would lead to his own death....

*

Gavin shivered as he felt the invader leave his mind. It had been exactly as Travis had described, like a worm. Because he had expected it, he kept his mind on Don Quixote, going over a scene that he was very familiar with. He did not push the invader out of his mind but tried to think about hooking onto that "worm" to follow if it left. He wanted to know where it came from. He didn't allow his mind to feel what his stomach felt, that it was a sickening feeling as it entered, searching his thoughts. He pictured the confused and noble chivalrous knight of La Mancha defending the honor of the breathtaking Dulcinea.

As it left his mind, he allowed his thoughts, blank now, to follow. When it returned to its source, he felt the source evaluating, laughing at Gavin's assumed interest in "cartoons." Gavin's stomach rolled: it was Casto!

He pulled back before he could be identified and gasped. Casto was suspicious! Could this endanger his friends? Suddenly he felt a friendly presence in his brain and

Travis' voice said, softly, "Don't worry, Gavin, your Sancho Panza is relaying this intelligence to his friends. I'm here for you."

It gave him comfort in two different ways, the fact that Travis had actually witnessed what had just happened without his knowledge, so Travis was pretty darned capable and talented. But he drew some kind of comfort from the fact that he had read "Don Quixote", as well. So, Travis had found a way to enter another's thoughts undetected. This was something Gavin definitely wanted to learn. Little did he realize that he already had done so when he entered into Laurel's mind while she slept and Casto's just now, as well.

*

Yellow Feather had been listening intently as the hours passed. When he heard the bells, the thought of the absurdity of it all went through his head. Measuring time in increments had not even been re-established back in their camp. It seemed relatively unimportant. Everything was less rigid, more relaxed, you slept when it was dark, if you wanted to; many of them found darkness a signal to enjoy the observatory they had set up for star-watching. There were never strict rules about napping during the day. All chores were so easy and shared by so many that they didn't take so long and left a lot of leisure time to explore, sleep, read, or simply play. Everyone shared every duty willingly. There was no "military" sense to it and he hoped that it would never become necessary to track time. The sun and moon signaled time for campfire discussions and work details. Early morning was a good time to work in the summertime, before the heat became a deterrent. How much more sensible and relaxed it was there than here.

They all heard the bells, which was the signal for Gavin to climb carefully from his tower to escape. They watched through their binoculars. The guard in the northwest tower would be sleepy, having just awakened from his own sleeping period, but the other one, the northeast tower, that was the one they were most concerned with. So far, that guard was just sitting on his stool and looking back over the camp. So long as he stayed in that position, Gavin was safe. They could see a distant figure climbing down a ladder, stopping more often than they would like. When he finally hit the ground, he stayed low to the ground and ran into the hills, toward them.

"We see you," Laurel sent a message to his mind. "Just keep coming straight..."

As they watched, the guard in the northeast tower stood up and moved, facing away from them, then turned to walk back to look northward.

"Drop to the ground!" Laurel told Gavin's mind.

He didn't hesitate. He hit the ground in a long dive. He had purposefully worn dark clothing so that he would tend to blend in, but they were all afraid that the guard might be able to detect motion, however camouflaged Gavin might be. They watched as the guard went back to his seat.

"Okay, come straight ahead," Yellow Feather urged.

It all happened exactly as planned and they waited for Gavin to reach them. When he did, he stood still for a moment, trying to chase away the dizzy feeling but giving them a grin. "I guess that you are Yellow Feather, Coyote, David, and Laurel," he said, turning from one to the other and guessing correctly on each one. He tried not to look too long at Laurel but he was so happy to see her and she was even prettier than he had pictured in his head, even prettier than she had looked in the minds of the others. He smiled shyly at her and she boldly stepped forward and took his hand. "Oh, Gavin, I'm so glad you are safe." She hugged him. He had never felt anything so good and welcome as her hug.

"We're not safe yet. We've got to hurry to get back to our bikes before you are missed!" Yellow Feather reminded them.

"Where are Haylie, Dave, and Lily?" Gavin asked, looking around.

"They are in hiding; they will be covering us and will follow close behind," Yellow Feather told him. "Come on, everyone, we've got to hurry to put some distance between ourselves and this camp and it looks like Gavin is going to need our help. Man, you ARE sick, you're burning up!" He and Coyote stood on either side of Gavin and he put his arms up over their shoulders. They helped him to hurry at a good pace but he was having trouble even with their help.

"I'm so sorry!" he told them, feeling terrible that they had to struggle so hard to help him.

"We can carry you, if need be," Coyote told him, "stop apologizing."

"All I could think about was how many people died of the flu and other viruses and now here I am sick and you guys are still risking your own health to help me. How am I ever going to be able to repay you?" Gavin asked, nearing delirium, his fever was getting so bad.

David was complaining, "I still know I could have taken that other guard out, if you guys would have just let me try. Arrows are silent. I know I could have hit him and we wouldn't have to worry for six hours instead of just three..."

"Shhhh," Laurel said, "remember what we decided a long time ago about unnecessary deaths? We don't want to be as bad as them, we only kill in self-defense, David! Yellow Feather, I think Gavin's going to faint. What can we do?"

"No, no," Gavin insisted, "I have to hold on. I'll be okay, just keep me moving forward."

With the burden of Gavin's illness, they were making half the time they had planned. At this rate, they would still be at least an hour, perhaps as much as nearly two hours, from their bikes when his "sleep time" ended. They had to hope that an alarm took a while to raise in Hades, because at this rate, there could be a pretty dangerous chase many, many miles from Colorado.

Travis told only Yellow Feather's mind, "I am thinking of telling Pathogent, Conner, Declan, and the others that we need to send reinforcements down to intercept you. This isn't looking good."

"I'm agreeing, my friend. I don't see how Gavin will even sit a bike. We will be traveling so much slower than planned. We planned on putting Haylie in one of the trailers but we may have to ride him double with one of us; it's going to be risky."

They continued to struggle through the long hike through the Franklin range.

Dave, Lily, and Haylie melted in out of the darkness to fall in behind them but occasionally moved forward to allow another to drop back to take turns carrying Gavin's weight to help him flee. There were times when they were able to pick up the pace to make up for the times when he had to stop and vomit from the exertion.

*

Casto had drifted off to sleep after visiting each guard and writing down intelligence he had learned from his time in their minds. Too many of them would regret their treasonous thoughts about this guard duty being a waste of time and their leader being a madman. He would show them what a "madman" could do when faced with insubordination. One thing he realized for certain, they had some useless, stupid people up in those towers, seldom were any of them doing their jobs, too busy daydreaming or even doing things like playing solitaire or masturbating. He felt the heat of anger rise up and knew that, if he continued to search minds throughout his camp, he would end up putting his own concentration off.

He would deal with them all in due time.

Let them wonder how he found out. Let them blame one another for the intelligence he had gathered.

Visions of dominance and bringing people to their knees danced in his head.

*

At one bell the light was flashed into the north tower, waiting for Gavin's signal that he was awake. There was no response; they flashed him again. The guard in the northeast tower grumbled, wanting his turn to sleep so he flashed his light toward the north tower, too.

"Come on, kid, wake up!" He turned to the center of the circle and flashed the central guard office, letting them know that something was wrong.

"Awwww, HELL," one of the guards, a man named Grayson, at the central tower grumbled, "damn kid in the north tower is still asleep."

"He was looking pretty peaked earlier, I'll bet he's up there puking," the line boss, known to everyone as Pit Bull, said.

They signaled the northeast tower to begin his sleep time and went walking toward the north tower to wake up "Simple Kid." Pit Bull stood back to let Grayson climb the ladder and waited. The shout from above turned his stomach. The kid wasn't in the tower.

"Please let him be in the privies or in his bunk sick," Pit Bull said aloud, "I don't want to be the one to report another desertion to Casto! That's five in the last two days!" When Grayson came down from the tower, Pit Bull ordered him to go search the privies while he went to the kid's barracks to see if he was down from the tower sleeping it off.

It was well after two in the morning when they went, reluctantly, to wake Casto. Pit Bull knocked at the door and was hesitant to enter, even when a voice from inside told them to do so. He went into the dark and waited while Casto lit a lamp, dressed only in his jockey shorts; then, looking around at the spotless sleeping quarters that he had never seen before, meekly gave him the news. Casto looked weak and fragile with so little clothing on but Pit Bull knew better and was shaking with fear. He told Casto about how sick the kid had been earlier in the evening and suggested that the boy might have gone somewhere off in the brush to sleep his sickness off or to vomit. He told him that there was already evidence of that having happened on the ground outside the tower. He continued to talk, trying hard to fill the long space as Casto just stared at him.

"Shut up!" Casto growled, "Dammit, I'm going to make an example out of this one, I'm so sick of this! Get out of here and sound the alarm! I want at least three retrieval units out there right away."

"But, boss, what if the kid is just out there somewhere sick? What if he's not a deserter, what if he's just out there puking his guts out?" Pit Bull objected.

"Don't nobody know that, do they? For all anyone knows, we got us a deserter on our hands and when we find him, I'm going to have him skinned alive to show everyone how we're going to handle deserters from here on out!" Casto was furious, his mind should have showed him the kid's intentions. What was that crap about an old man jousting windmills?

"Tracks pointed north," Grayson said, spitting into a cup. Grayson dipped his snuff and carried a cup with him everywhere he went to spit the disgusting fluid into, what wasn't in his beard and on his lips, that is.

Casto stared at him, long and hard, his lip curled back in disgust, "You get one drop of that stuff on my floor and I'll be skinning two today!" Casto yelled. Grayson backed toward the open doorway, ready to make his own escape.

Casto stepped into his jeans, pushed past Pit Bull, and went out to help raise the alarm. He wanted men on the trail right away. It was already almost three bells and these idiots had taken much too long to find out that the kid was gone. He was cursing under his breath and knew that he needed to get himself under control so that he could send his mind out to try to capture clues. If he left it up to this motley crew, that idiot kid would be gone forever; unless the hungry coyotes already got him. He chuckled to himself: the kid was pretty big and strong; he could probably take on a coyote or two. But he'd bring that monster down a peg or two today, he sure would. They'd be eating him in a stew, come evening, best worker or not.

He raised enough cane to bring all the barracks to attention and ordered three groups to follow tracks, another two groups to work around the perimeter to see if there was sign of any other desertions. He fully intended to find anyone they could for this lesson that his camp needed to learn. Then he stood in the center of the confusion and closed his eyes, trying to calm himself enough to concentrate, knowing that it would not be easy with all the shouting and running around him. He spread his arms and tried to put himself into a calming trance but it wasn't working. He wasn't getting anything over the screaming and shouting and calamity of his own camp's call to action.

Then, suddenly, a voice came into his head, loud and clear, "You're going to lose, Casto, just keep your men in camp or risk losing everything. You follow, you die." The voice left his mind before he could even think to send anything to follow. It snapped off like someone turned off a radio dial, just died out instantly. Casto stood in a rage, "Who was that?" he said aloud, causing those walking past him to hesitate and look at him, curiously. "Who was that, damn it? It sure as hell weren't the kid, he don't know nuttin'. Who is helping him?" He shivered at the thought of someone more powerful than he. That just wasn't going to be allowed, he would have to take this challenger down.

His face was flushed with anger. He looked over and saw one of his men standing there, watching all the running about, confused and uncertain what to do. Casto looked at this blatant inactivity in the face of his frustration and it enraged him even further. He stopped one of his soldiers from running past and took a knife from his belt, then moved straight for the hapless, bewildered man. The first strike cut the victim across the gut, a deep and vicious wound. As he bent over, Casto raised the knife and buried it between his shoulder blades, then raised it again and again and again. When the dead man fell to the ground, Casto leaped down on him and continued to stab the body until he, himself, was covered in blood. A rabid-looking, heathen fiend arose from the carnage, ready to lead his camp into battle. Covered in blood and wild-eyed, Casto ran to rally his entire camp into preparation to follow the lead of the groups he had already sent out. His own men looked at him in fear. It was obvious to them that the man had completely lost his mind but, with his murderous rage, none of them was brave enough to disarm him or disobey.

Now there was a cacophony of sound in his head, so many voices, most of them young, the voices of children, all talking at once. And they were all laughing and taunting him. Oh, would he show them. Yes, he would have the last laugh on those laughing children. He'd sink his teeth into their tender, little throats, he would. He sent that message roaring through his brain.

*

Pathogent turned from the group who had entered the mind of the stranger so very far away and paled as he realized that he would be leading even some of the children in this rescue mission against several hundred armed and dangerous men. Even among those in Golden, there were people who were against this entire mission, wondering if they were not now taking the role of aggressors by taunting this enemy camp. He didn't know when it happened, but the children had risen up in a group with more bravado than he expected. He and Gwen were the only ones capable of joining their mind meld with the man known to Travis as Casto and, although they had been shocked and dismayed at his capacity for violence, the children ended up sending out the laughter, showing him that they were not afraid of him.

Travis agreed with this tactic, arguing that they needed to keep this villain disoriented so that he could not zero in on the rescue group. If the men in Hades were following, let them have to work hard to find the trail, let them have long periods of searching to slow them down.

Pathogent stood, facing the adults, and informed them that he wanted volunteers and was amazed that nearly every single person stepped forward. He looked at Gwen when Shawnee stepped forward with Conner, Little Moon wrapped in a long cloth and tied to her chest, sleeping peacefully.

"No, some of you must stay here with the younger children, some of you need to help Gwen..." he began.

"Not on your life," Gwen insisted, "others will stay with the children, but I am going with you. Our strength, combined, will be enough..." she said, hinting at the magic they had been capable of in the past. Pathogent knew better than to argue but looked pleadingly at Shawnee, "Sweet granddaughter, please stay here with our Little Moon. Help Layla and Janice and the others keep the smallest children safe."

Shawnee started to protest but Conner turned to her and his look told her that, he, too, could not bear the thought of risking his wife and child. "I would be too worried about your safety. I wouldn't even be able to think clearly."

She wanted to shout a protest, but her hand went to the curve of the tiny back on her breast and her features softened. She nodded, her eyes locked on Conner's.

"Conner," Pathogent continued, "I want to ask you to stay here, too. They need your calm mind here with them. They need to feel safe and protected. They will need someone that they all look up to...please...you and Shawnee are trusted, loved..."

What he didn't need to say but what everyone knew to be true, was that Conner and Shawnee had become the younger Pathogent and Gwen to many in Golden and were trusted and loved every bit as much as the older couple.

Conner's eyes narrowed, resenting the fact that he was not going to be given the chance to prove his courage in the face of this threat. It was strange for him to feel emasculated when he considered himself a feminist in every way but this. Then he regained control of his ego and nodded, understanding that leaving the camp defenseless was equally intolerable. He had to make certain that no invading force would find Golden defenseless, should the shield falter, or, heaven forbid, fall. He winced at allowing that thought because it would mean that Path and Gwen would have fallen. He nodded acquiescence to Pathogent who gave him a quick smile of admiration and an almost fatherly love.

Path's heart swelled with pride at all that his "descendants" were doing to protect the children and to keep their village safe from harm. He watched as they worked, running and shouting instructions to one another, working as a great and organized team to arm those leaving and those staying.

More than half the camp was loading into cars and trucks to go to shield and retrieve their brave group of rescuers. Adults were shocked at how thoroughly armed with weapons the older children were. Bows, arrows, knives, and guns that were never even seen in camp appeared from nowhere as the men added these to the weapons from the arsenal, including any that hadn't already been loaded in their earlier preparation..

Pathogent, working hard with the rest to load the deadly weapons he detested, took a deep breath, his eyes seeking Gwen, who was busy talking and working with those who were staying behind against their own urges to join the defenders. She looked up to meet his eyes and sent him a weak smile. She knew what he was hoping, that, if they played it right, none of these weapons would be necessary at all. But at what cost? The last time they tried something of this scope, they had both nearly flamed out of existence.

*

During the Spanish Inquisition, Gwen was accused of witchcraft and was found guilty. Her punishment was going to be a public burning at the stake. When they tied her to the pole, surrounding it with kindling, Pathogent, in his struggle to save her, had let loose with all of his magic to stop them; she joined, linking into his power. They were actually able to kill a panel of Inquisitors in the hot wave of anger and rage coming off of them. Their actions freed other prisoners of this heinous and unjust tribunal. Yet, when they struggled to rein in their combined blast of power, the *blink* took them in a whirlwind of light and heat and power.

In the abyss of the *blink*, she could hear him but could not see him: "I think I may be mortally wounded, Gwen," he had told her, whispering through his pain. "I didn't know this was possible, but I feel like I'm in a strong fade."

"Don't say that, it's not possible, we are energy, energy cannot die."

"I think we transformed all of our energy into a blaze and may have destroyed whatever we are made of, or whatever I am made of. Are you not wounded? Oh, tell me you're not wounded..." he asked, hopeful that it was only he sapped of all strength and feeling his life force slipping away.

She put a hand to her stomach, where her own wound had burned completely through her very core of being and sighed, "I am wounded, my love..." her voice faded to nothing.

It was an eternity before they *blinked* into another life again, both of them shocked and surprised to find that their energy had survived, that some thread of life force had sustained them. They were both unsure why or how but knew from that point on that they would have to pay dearly for any energy they borrowed and gathered. Magic came at a high cost, the bounty of which they were both ready to pay again, should the need arise.

Today they understood that they might be facing that choice again. To save the lives of the children, they both knew that it was a choice that they would make, if necessary. This wasn't about them, this was about the future of the planet they had both come to love. Neither of them would hesitate.

*

Five full hours after Gavin climbed down the ladder, two hours behind their plan, they made it to the bikes. They had to stop to rest several times and give him water. He was feverish and severely dehydrated and had vomited or dry heaved many times along the way. They were all fearful for him. He was gray with sickness, dark circles under his eyes from the fatigue of pushing himself so hard. As they passed the new outcroppings where Dave and Lily and Haylie had rushed to hide again to monitor the escape, Yellow Feather sent a message to Travis, asking that he give the three sharpshooters a complete report on the fact that even Yellow Feather was simply too weary and would be in need of rest before mounting the bike. He and Coyote had practically had to carry Gavin, alternating occasionally with David who insisted on taking his turn to help.

Gavin had, about an hour and a half ago, asked them to leave him behind. He realized the danger he was putting them in as his sickness grew worse and regretted that he had ever sought their help. Now there would be seven brave people who would die with him, rather than just his dying. He grew even more delirious realizing the danger he had put them in and how he was going to be unable to protect himself, let alone Laurel and her friends.

Dave reported, through Travis, "There are huge dust clouds in the distance, possibly no more than two hours behind you. Get on those bikes and ride."

"Not without Dave," Yellow Feather objected, "Tell him to come down, we ride together."

Travis reminded him, "He said, 'You gave me your word, boy. Lily and I have already discussed this, we are going to give you some lead time by staying behind. We'll catch up, remember you promised to keep going, no matter what.' Get Haylie down, let her and David ride in the trailers so they can shoot behind them and you'll have the extra bike for Gavin."

"Gavin is in no condition to ride," Yellow Feather argued in his mind but there was an immediate reply from Gavin that all of them could clearly hear. They were surprised that he was capable of monitoring all their communications.

"I will ride, I have to, there is no other choice," Gavin said.

"No," Laurel said, "ride with me. I am great on these things, we can ride double, I'll be able to stop if I feel you slipping."

Gavin shook his head. "Too dangerous, I could pull you off the bike or make you wreck. No, I'm going to have to ride. Besides," he added with a weak grin, "the wind will feel good. I am looking forward to it."

They unloaded some of the gear from the trailers on some of the bikes to make room for David and Haylie, unhitched the unnecessary ones, and called for her to come down to them. She reluctantly obeyed, although she wanted to do the same thing as Dave and Lily, shoot from hiding to give them more of a chance of escape. However, she could see that the plan to have her shooting followers was also brilliant. She had shot from a moving horse before. A steady motorbike would be almost too easy.

At their insistence, Gavin rested as the others prepared the bikes, then mounted one, struggling to clear his head.

"Travis said that he can tell when you are going to need him. He's going to stay in your head and talk you through this," Yellow Feather told Gavin, aloud, blocking his mind from anyone's intrusion, fearful that the mind-intrusion from Hades could happen again and hear their plans. "Prepare for him to yell at you when he feels you slipping out of consciousness. Our 'family' left about three hours ago to come help us. We should rendezvous with them somewhere around Duran, New Mexico, if I'm doing my math correctly. That's figuring in the delay and all, since they are making such good time and we...well, we aren't. It will take us at least two-and-a-half, maybe three hours to get there, if not more. We'll stop whenever you need to, Gavin."

Gavin smiled at this, "I hope he does keep me awake. I don't want any of you stopping because of me. We've got to get out of here."

Only Coyote dared to look behind them. From his lower vantage point, he could not see the dust cloud that Dave had described but he could see a haze that indicated that something was there, in the distance.

They began to pull away on their bikes, gaining speed now that they were on the open highway. One thing they had going for them: those following them would have to stop and check a trail that went up and over rocks and rugged terrain, leaving little trace in spots. It wouldn't be an easy trail to follow, especially at three o'clock in the morning. And now that they were on tarmac, they would not be raising dusty evidence in their wake. Even if the enemy got really lucky, they should be at least a couple hours behind, as Dave estimated.

*

Time ticked away as Dave and Lily, too far apart to communicate and with none of the communication skills of that the young ones shared, listened intently. They both occasionally allowed themselves to doze in that half-alert way they learned when serving on duty. Neither of them had ever lost that skill. It was something no combat veteran would ever forget, how to grab a few winks of sleep but still be able to come fully awake, aware, and in fighting mode.

They both heard vehicles in the distance, not too much more than an hour-and-a-half after the kids had left on their dirt bikes. Dave shook himself awake and tensed up, ready to lay down some fire and delay the enemy. He could only hope that Lily was doing the same and would be able to escape if they faced overwhelming odds. There were only two trucks coming, but they were coming at breakneck speed over the hills and rocks of the northern foothills of the Franklin range. As Gavin had informed them, they might be one group of ten or twenty, at most, if there were two groups, one in each truck. These were military vehicles, with benches in the back. It was possible to have as many as eight troops in back with a driver and passenger in the front of each. Dave grinned to himself, lining up his rifles on the ground beside him, liking the odds. That meant that he and Lily would only have to take out ten each to be safe enough to escape. He looked down the scope of his rifle and drew a bead on the driver of the lead vehicle. If he timed this right, the truck in the back would hit the one in front and they might even have fewer combatants to take out.

To his amazement, he heard another shot besides his own! Lily had the exact same idea. Sometimes he felt that he could easily want to marry that girl, he thought, smiling. Who was he kidding, he could have easily married that girl months and months ago! The driver slumped over the wheel, taking both slugs in the chest and dying instantly, causing his truck to veer and weave and the truck behind tried to brake too late, crashing into the lead truck, just as planned. There was a moment of screeching metal and the loud percussion of impact, dust flying in a thick cloud around both trucks, then the firing started as the survivors of the crash began firing wildly, trying to determine where the shots had come from. Dave grinned and said to himself, "This is a damned turkey shoot. Have at 'em, Lily, you damned fine filly!"

*

Casto heard the words in his head, "This is a damned turkey shoot..." and the rest. He cursed as he saw the cloud of smoke in the distance. From the mind he had entered, he could see the wreck and his doomed soldiers. At the head of a fleet of twelve other trucks, being led by the third truck of the original reconnaissance group, he hoped to get there in time to point out the position of the sniper. He wanted that head on a pole. "Damn it! Damn it!" he yelled, feeling impotent as he realized that the trucks were further in the distance than it originally looked. He lost connection with the sniper and cursed again.

He urged the driver to go faster even when he realized that the gas pedal was already on the floor of the truck. They were flying over rocks and rough terrain, and, though very dangerous, his group was doing an incredible job of making good time, but it wouldn't be fast enough. He was already counting twenty men lost of the hundred and fifty he set out with. More than half the entire population of Hades, aside from the women, was on this mission. He would show this deserter AND his accomplices that he meant business! No one made a fool of Leland Casto, no one!

*

Lily and Dave met at the dirt bikes and he already knew that she would be excited and in a fevered pitch about having to have left so many good weapons behind. When they started to mount the bikes, he told her, "No, the kids took the highway, we're going overland, due north, maybe some of the trucks will follow us instead. Even so, our only chance of survival at this point is to hit some big trees that those trucks can't follow through. They are too close behind. You got this, Lily?"

She smiled and nodded, revving the engine of her bike. Then, impulsively, she leaned toward him and kissed him on the lips, "Stay alive, handsome, you and I have got some serious talking to do when we get home."

His expression of surprise made her laugh, but then he gave her a huge smile, "Baby girl, I think we're speaking the same language. Let's give these hostiles a run for their money!"

The kids had already carefully made certain that all of the bikes had full tanks and had unhooked the trailers to make maneuvering easier. Now the two of them drove back and forth, obliterating tracks leading onto the highway, and left the highway, making it appear as though many bikes had gone that way, due north, and headed for more mountains to the north. They would lead the enemy into the Rockies, hoping to lose them there.

*

Gavin had to stop to vomit and wipe the sweat from his face but Travis was true to his word, currently reading "Moby Dick" in his ear, booming the voices of Ahab and almost making him seasick with the descriptions of the tossing of the Pequod. That aside, it really was helping, listening to Travis read as he rode the bike in the darkness. What also helped was all the sleep he had gotten the day before. He was not tired, just nauseated and feverish and exhausted from the exertion of the hike. He took the canteen Laurel offered, gasping a little at the touch of her fingers against his skin, then splashed water into his hand and rubbed the coolness onto his face. "It's okay, I'm ready again." He looked at her and smiled, embarrassed, speaking from his mind to hers, "So romantic, all this vomiting and stuff, huh?"

"Oh, Gavin, I just wish there were something I could do to help you," she told him. He could tell it was sincere, but that might be how kind she was to everyone. She was obviously an empath. He couldn't allow himself to think that he might be as important to her as she was to him, and, just as he was thinking it, she answered in his mind, "Oh, but you are." He smiled and met her eyes, wishing they were safe and alone.

They both ran back to their bikes and started them again. Coyote was staring off to the south, hoping that the lights he was seeing were streaks of morning, not headlights; it was a strange, eerie glow and, while it was still some distance away, it was too close for his comfort. He thought that it must be a large convoy of trucks to make that much light on the horizon. Gavin saw him staring and looked back, then they joined the others back on the highway. Riding full out on the road, with the throttle wide open, was actually a good feeling and helped to keep Gavin going, but Travis was his lifeline. When and if he ever met Travis, he knew that he would love him like a brother, like he had loved Dale. He rode close to the back of the pack, making certain to keep Laurel in front of him, wanting to protect her if need arose.

Yellow Feather was watching the road signs and the mileage carefully. They were only about an hour from Duran now, only another hour which put them only about two hours from the others, Pathogent, Travis, and the rest. He knew that he was pushing Gavin harder than was wise, but he also had felt a strong presence behind them, perhaps as many as a hundred coming from El Paso, in the place even the residents had aptly named Hades. Those residents were being led by a madman who would stop at nothing to taste the blood of what he considered to be upstart, taunting children. He had to hope that Gavin had it in him to keep up with this breakneck pace.

*

Declan gave a wry smile as Travis read "Moby Dick", sometimes aloud. He knew that Travis was doing this for the benefit of the kid they were saving. Declan grimaced when he had heard that Gavin was sick but, since he and almost everyone in their camp had been exposed to many viruses as they had crossed America on the way to their mecca, it was unlikely that Gavin would be a risk to the entire village. At least that was what they all hoped. More than anything else, he worried about Shawnee's baby and Melody's pregnancy, wanting nothing to risk their health. Sure, he had always heard that the mother's immunity protected a baby for a long time after birth, but how could they be sure? Perhaps they should almost quarantine the rescue group for a while. Then he shook his head for worrying about such things when this rescue and the battle that may ensue were imminent. It was almost crazy where the mind would go when worrying began.

His SUV was loaded with weapons, while others held children and adults who would be, perhaps, using those weapons against other human beings. This wasn't something Declan had allowed himself to completely wrap his head around yet; he had always argued that, should they find other living beings, didn't they owe it to them to try everything possible to live in accord? Wasn't the fact that there were so few survivors on this earth at this point something that needed serious reflection? The pacifist in him rebelled against the thought of what the next hour or so might demand of him. He had resisted the resistance back home in Ireland, rebelling against the violence and senseless deaths; avoided confrontation when possible on the trip across this continent; now he resented the fact that this other group of survivors might draw them into a fight. Knowing that he would do anything to keep his wife, future child, and the others safe, he set his jaw and wondered what lifelong philosophies he would have to overrule in the next few hours.

He was a lot more than just a little upset over this entire turn of events, and then there was something about the children being able to communicate with their minds, like Travis was doing right now. This was almost as hard to accept as what they had learned from Pathogent and Gwen shortly after their arrival at the camp; now the kids were time-travelers with extra talents that even Path and Gwen had not mastered? This all seemed like the plot of a fantasy fiction, something other-earthly. Declan had always considered himself a romantic, but also pretty grounded. He loved flights of fancy about the fairy and the other unseen worlds, but he never entertained the fact that he might be asked to believe them someday. Now the veils were thinning between fantasy and reality and he was unnerved by the possibilities. Would his own child be normal? What WAS normal? Was there a new normal?

He looked over at Travis, who could not be drawn into conversation while he had pledged to keep talking to keep Gavin alert. The kid had amazing dedication. Travis was the kid who had refused to leave Nashville if his then pregnant female dog were not able to go with him, forcing Brian and Dani to find trailers for their motorbikes so that he could haul Bella across country with him. The two pups she whelped, born in St. Louis, were grown dogs now. Archie and Lulu had brought a lot of joy to the children and many of the adults, who found that Archie was a natural hunter and Lulu was a fearless protector. The children took her everywhere. Pompeii, the other dog in the camp, was pretty much devoted to the children, as well, but more as a playmate and goofy entertainment. Bella was the lady dog, the *grande dame*, preferring to sit with her head in Travis' lap and have someone stroke her velvety ears.

So, now he was thinking about dogs. It was funny where the mind went as you were driving any distance. It had been a while since he had traveled so far, preferring to stay pretty close to camp or occasional trips close-by or up into the mountains. He remembered to prompt himself that no one could even think of the location of their camp, just in case the other side had a mind reader or two. He scoffed, "And what are the chances of THAT, boyo?" Travis looked at him and arched a brow, to which Declan laughed and said, "No, just talking to myself, sorry."

He looked as they approached a mileage sign and remember that Travis had said that they expected to rendezvous in Duran. The sign said that Duran was thirty miles ahead. He nudged Travis and pointed. Both of them could feel their tension mount, knowing what might lie ahead, neither having ever experienced battle.

*

The lights had indeed been headlights and they were gaining ground behind them. The four bikes had just had the gas tanks filled with the last of the gasoline and they were going as fast as they could, just slightly lighter now, without the gas cans. David and Haylie signaled one another, preparing their rifles for firing. Should any of the trucks get close, they hoped to put a hole into a radiator, or maybe take out a driver; one lead truck could be caused to swerve in front of the others and might slow them down a bit. Now if they just would get in range. Things were ticking in Haylie's mind like added wind velocity and the forward momentum of the trucks. She knew her range when she was still and the target was moving. She even knew her range when she was on a horse and the target was moving. But these bikes were flying now.

Then she decided just to be still, to embrace the state of quiet and calm she entered when shooting, and assume that her accuracy would be the same, given that she would be holding the gun solidly when she shot. She grinned over at David, licked her finger and put a bead of spit where the tip of her sight would be, had she not had a scope. David laughed in appreciation of her antics. They had to push the thought of the danger away and stay calm so that their shots were true. Better to amuse one another than to show fear and terror. Neither wanted to even think about the fact that they might have to take a human life to save their friends.

Coyote was checking his rearview mirror, constantly watching as the distance between those headlights back in the distance and their group narrowed incrementally with every mile. There were so many of those damned trucks it lit the morning sky and they were tearing up the highway at breakneck speed.

"Gavin, are you okay?" Travis asked, taking a short break to drink some water, closing the book on his finger to mark the page.

"You can stop reading, my friend. There's no way I'm going to do any passing out or stopping now. They are narrowing the gap. My adrenalin is pumping like crazy," Gavin told him. He could hear Travis and Yellow Feather discussing the distance between the group of bikers and the trucks coming south, holding their friends.

"If Haylie and David can do a little damage to them when they get closer, we might be able to buy enough time to rendezvous in just ten minutes!" Yellow Feather and Travis figured the miles between them. "Stop and prepare in five and cover us as we approach. It looks like there's a rise ahead that might be perfect for our group to fire from." It was like working out one of those impossible math problems in high school: If a car, if traveling south at 70 miles per hour, and a train is traveling north at the same speed, and the distance separating them is 520 miles, how many minutes will it take until they pass? Declan could hear just Travis' end of the conversation and shook his head at how incredibly smart these kids actually were. He chuckled, reminding himself that many of them had been the geniuses of the past.

Travis sent a message to one of the kids riding with Pathogent about stopping and arming in five minutes. Pathogent did not even question the intelligence. He simply nodded and agreed that it was what they would do. The children passed the word from truck to truck.

They set up quickly and waited, seeing lights in the distance and knowing that the gap between the two sets of lights was narrowing dangerously fast. The archers were ready to send arrows raining down on the trucks and the guns were all loaded and ready. However, Pathogent and Gwen were determined that neither would be used any more than absolutely necessary.

Haylie brought her scope to her eye and aimed, taking her deep breath and finding that inner place that kept her steady as a rock. She found the spot where the radiator would be but then raised the sight and saw the grinning, brutal face of the driver who intended to not only catch the kids but ram them into oblivion. Her finger squeezed the trigger at the same time that her shoulder anticipated the recoil. The bullet shattered the windshield cleanly, not deflecting the momentum at all, and hit the driver right between his eyes, exactly where Haylie had aimed. She cursed herself for letting anger guide her bullet…she should have shot the radiator.

The driver was killed instantly. The truck swerved wildly, causing the one behind it to hit a rear fender, then the lead truck was leaning over on two wheels, skirting the guardrail dangerously before swerving back into the path of the other trucks. It narrowly missed them but caused them to slow down as it then ran up the embankment on the other side of the highway and flipped into the air as if performing an acrobatic feat, tumbling back on itself a little off center and rolling into a sideways skid. If anyone was alive in that truck, their "friends" didn't even pause to determine that or help, as they cleared the danger and continued the chase.

David aimed as Haylie gathered herself for another shot. He was more determined to hit either the radiator or a tire, at the very least. The trucks behind them had lost a moment slowing down because of the lead truck, and had given them more space than they needed but David still had a clear shot to disable the truck or throw steam up and block visibility. His bullet hit the truck with a twump.

Return fire whizzed around them as the passenger in the truck leaned out the window and fired. They knew to weave their bikes in an unpredictable pattern but some of the bullets were coming close.

Suddenly steam started pouring out from under the hood of the truck as hot water escaped the radiator. Visibility was limited and the driver cursed as he was urged to continue on the highway toward the speeding bikes.

Dawn was breaking over the eastern horizon to their right.

Yellow Feather's voice broke through the din, "Up ahead, they are up ahead!" And they could see lights in the distance. The drivers of the trucks behind them could also see the line of trucks facing them, blocking the highway, their bright lights blinding, not more than a mile in the distance, and started slowing down, not knowing what they were facing, surprised to see any organized opposition to their tyranny. They continued forward slowly, rolling to a stop within shouting distance from the other trucks, some of the "soldiers" jumping from the trucks and running forward to aim their weapons. Suddenly a shower of arrows rained down on them and many of the enemy soldiers were hit.

The bikes continued, speeding up, heading for the safety of the wall of trucks and their friends. Cheers went up behind the lines as the four bikes sped toward them even though some of the group from Golden realized that two of the rescuers were missing. As soon as the bikes came to a stop, the boys and Laurel dismounted, smiling and happy to be alive. Haylie was gathered up by several of the other children and hugged, as was David. Yellow Feather looked at Pathogent and smiled his thanks. "Perfect timing, my Siginak," he said, softly, and took Path's hand in his.

Gavin looked around at all the strangers, wondering if he would be able to tell which one was Travis. A shy, thin, sixteen-year-old approached him from the crowd gathered around them and said, in his familiar voice, "So, Gavin, at last we meet." Gavin started to shake the extended hand, then took hold of it and pulled Travis into a hug. "Damn, man, you're my hero, a handshake just isn't going to get it!" he told Travis with his mind.

The celebration was short-lived as they watched nearly a hundred armed men line up to aim guns at their group. However, bullets that they fired at the rescuers seemed to deflect off an invisible wall, frustrating the enemy. Another volley of arrows scattered many of them but they simply came back to line up again, even though the shots they fired met resistance. Then a very thin, blood-covered man with a bull horn moved to the front of the motley crew of misfits and announced, "It seems y'all think you have some kind of advantage over us," he said, drawling his words out slowly. "While I gotta admit, I'm surprised to find such a big group this time, I have to warn you, we have defeated every enemy we've come into contact with and we don't aim to lose this time, neither. Losing is just not in my vocabulary. Now, I might consider letting some of you live if you hand over my deserter, or is it deserters, plural, that you have among you? You give us that big, dumb kid and we consider letting you live, now you're not going to get a better offer than that, I can assure you."

Gavin seethed, silently telling Travis, "That's Casto."

"I know," Travis said, aloud. "We've had the pleasure of meeting minds." He arched a brow and looked at Gavin, amused. "It was a very short meeting."

Laurel walked to where the two boys stood and slid her hand into Gavin's. He looked at her in surprise but squeezed her hand warmly, thinking how small it was compared to his, how he wanted to shelter her completely in the palms of his hands. Then he put an arm protectively around her shoulders and pulled her close, kissing her forehead and smiling his thanks to her.

Both groups were sizing up the other and they allowed a great deal of time to pass while the tension grew. Arrows were nocked and waiting, guns were at ready. Some of the men from Hades felt their hands and arms shaking from holding their guns at ready too long. They knew that Casto was desperately trying to get some idea of how big the enemy force actually was. But weren't most of them children? Who needed to fear children? Then the men reminded themselves that it had been mostly children holding the bows and loosing the rainstorm of arrows down on them.

Casto paced in front of his men, showing no fear to the enemy. Casto actually did not know the word fear, it simply was another obstacle to him, this confrontation. He knew that, given enough time, he would figure out a way to make this all work out to his benefit. He looked almost comical, a bantam rooster strutting and posturing. Pathogent looked at Declan and shook his head. While he knew that the man was dangerous, having been told of his ruthlessness and bloodthirst, the man was ridiculously strange-looking and cocky, like a hairless Barney Fife. Even from this distance, his hairless head and the lack of eyebrows made him look like a walking egghead. Even the blood covering his body made him look comical, like he was wearing it as some kind of tattooing or fake bravado. He kept a non-stop narration of his intent, trying to use psychological intimidation, pouring threats through his megaphone.

Casto only stopped speaking as one of his men came running up to him and whispered something in his ear. Casto put the mic to his mouth and said, slowly, "I just got news that we were joined by one of our other groups who chased after another couple members of your little biker crew. They went northwest and tried to disappear among the trees. It appears one of them didn't make it and the other one...well, see for yourself." He motioned a truck to pull forward from the back of the pack, other drivers moving their trucks out of the way to let this one through. Tied to the front bumper of the truck, her feet on the bumper and her waist tied to a framework meant to transport equipment was Lily. She was in terrible shape, nearly unconscious from what had probably been a hard chase, a rough capture, and then being tied to the front of a speeding vehicle going over rough terrain.

The Golden group took a collective deep breath.

"I can't let this happen. Trade me for her," Gavin thought to Travis. He took several steps toward the front of their line. He was visibly distraught to have caused such a horrible thing to happen to one of his rescuers. She was obviously barely clinging to life. He moved his mind from Travis to Yellow Feather, who stood staring at the scene in front of them, his jaw clenched and anger written on his face.

"Don't be crazy," Travis told him, "after all she did to insure that you were safe, she would never forgive us for doing such a thing. Besides, you don't think he'd actually HONOR that trade, do you? He'd only have both of you instead of only Lily. Don't do anything foolish, she's tougher than she looks."

"No, she's half dead, don't you see her wound?" Gavin said, feeling the pain in empathy. The rest of them saw it when he thought it. She was bleeding from a wound low in her side. Laurel reached a hand forward, as if her empathy were causing her to try to stop the flow of blood, tears flowing freely down her cheeks.

Every single person from the Colorado group watching this tableau could feel their heart beating faster and felt great sorrow, knowing that they were helpless to help Lily, as heroic as she had been to so many.

Haylie moved forward and tugged on Pathogent's arm. He leaned down and she was whispering in his ear, "She made me promise her something, Pathogent, I promised both of them, her and Dave, both!" He listened closely to what she had to say and knelt down beside her to take her into his arms. She cried as he held her, then he looked deeply into her eyes and nodded. He whispered into her ear and hugged her again. She moved back, out of sight.

Casto raised the bullhorn to his lips as he walked toward Lily, "Now, I don't want you to think that I wanted to harm this pretty lady. I'm actually mad that my men damaged her so badly. After all, she would have made a good addition to our whorehouse, a fresh, clean, well-fed woman like this, it kinda turns me on even thinking about it. I'm sure there's more than a few of you who've thought about the things this little bitch could do for you, huh? But, I do have this ace in the hole now and I'm thinking, you wash my hand, I wash yours, you know?"

Declan moved up beside Pathogent. "Can't we just shoot this monster?"

Path smiled and looked at the pacifist standing beside him, the irony was not lost on either of them, then said. "The only reason that man is alive right now is the fact that Lily is still alive. He harms her further and he's a dead man."

He said it with such a cold conviction that it sent a shiver down Declan's spine.

Casto, liking the sound of his own voice, kept going, "Now, we are all down here salivating over the idea of having a few of those plump children you've got up there for dinner, and I don't mean as guests, sitting around our table." At this, his men laughed and raised their weapons over their heads in agreement. "But, and I do mean BUT, we might consider letting you take them home with you, if you just hand over the deserter, you see, he pissed me off. He's a disobedient soldier and he was given a job that he deserted. And I just don't like disobedient cowards who desert their posts." He took a knife from his belt. Pathogent tensed.

"I'm waiting! You have two minutes to turn the dumb kid over to me. What good is he to you, anyway?" He located Gavin and looked straight at him, pointing with the weapon and taunting, "You dumb shit, what good are you to anybody?" He stood, letting time pass, swinging the knife back and forth. Then he shrugged. He watched as Travis and Laurel held Gavin back, struggling to keep him from coming forward. Holding the bullhorn in one hand and walking nonchalantly with the knife, Casto crossed in front of Lily and shouted into the microphone, "I'm not going to ask too many times! I will cut her into pieces if you test my patience. You see, me and my boys have developed a taste for raw meat, and this well-fed filly will be eaten right in front of you, right in front of all those little children, one slice at a time if you don't give me what I want."

They could hear Lily's cry of pain and, as he passed so that she was no longer blocked from view, they could see that he had cut her deeply across her stomach, just below the ropes. Blood oozed out around the long wound.

"Strike one," he yelled into the megaphone, "you don't even WANT to see Strike TWO or THREE!" Casto yelled.

Lily was looking up at them, struggling against pain to retain consciousness, she seemed to be seeking someone. Any lip reader would have been able to see the two words she was repeating over and over, the words coming forth in choking sobs of pain, "Please...Haylie" Her eyes scanned her friends, holding no judgment, only love, and they all tried to send her love in return. The cut was deep, between that and her wound, she was already dying. Gayle was brought to her knees in sorrow, Lily had been her own personal hero many times as they traveled across Nevada and Colorado, Lily had saved the entire group of weary travelers time and again with her eagle eye and deadly shooting skills. Brittin, Gayle's lover and companion, was on her knees beside Gayle trying to help her get through this, crying with her. Lily's eyes found who she was looking for and locked on, saying one more time, "Please..." she sent a silent message to little Haylie.

Casto made another pass in front of Lily and this time a scream came ululating over the distance, when he cleared his pass, his arm moving violently upward with a flair, they could see that he had cut her across the face, her cheek laid open, one eye blinded with blood coming from the socket.

Two shots rang out from behind them and everyone of the Golden group turned to look in shock. One shot missed its target, the other did not. Lily went limp but Casto realized that a bullet whizzed by his face so close that it was a near miss. It even grazed his forehead, but hit the man behind him and that man fell to his death. Casto turned in panic and looked up toward the group, then yelled at his own men, "Kill them!"

The Golden camp stood looking at two children, both down on one knee with rifles still smoking from the shots they had fired. David had missed his shot at Casto, but Haylie had kept her promise to Lily. Pathogent felt the rage building in him from what these children had been forced to do and to witness. The fact that the men meant to kill them all was enough, but the torture of Lily would seal their fate. Gwen stepped to his side and they clasped hands and then lifted their hands toward the sky. A strong wind began to blow, as if they had called it up. Even their own camp was shocked to witness this harmless and wonderful elder couple appearing to join forces with nature to bring some kind of mystic power to play. They both seemed to take on an odd blue glow, first it seemed cold, like ice, then everyone could feel their heat building.

As Casto's men started to move their trucks forward, Pathogent yelled, "Stop!" and the trucks hit what could only be described as an invisible wall. Then, to everyone's amazement, Path and Gwen began to glow like they were both on fire. With no need to amplify his voice with a bullhorn, Pathogent told the enemy, in a voice so unlike his own soft and quiet one, this new voice ringing loud and clear off the surrounding mountains to echo for miles, "This is your only chance, men from Hades. Any of you who wish to flee, may now do so. If you stay with your leader, you will die. He does not have that choice, however. He cannot leave here today. He alone has already sealed his fate. If you leave now, know that if you ever come at us again, we will kill each and every one of you and burn your camp to the ground."

Nearly a hundred voices screamed into Casto's head, "NOOOOOOOOO!" was their message. He dropped to his knees only two yards in front of Lily, his hands over his ears, screaming at the cacophony in his head. His screams were confusing his men who gathered around him, trying to understand what was happening.

Suddenly, one of the trucks lifted into the air and flew horizontally into the cliff on the other side of the road, smashing the truck as if it were made of balsa wood. Travis looked at Gavin in shock, then understood what Gavin had just done. "Let me try it with you!" They both closed their eyes and concentrated on another truck, lifting it into the air with only their minds and throwing it into the cliff where the first truck had splintered into tiny, smoking bits of twisted metal. It was easier when two minds combined. The other children looked at Gavin and Travis in awe.

Most of Casto's men had already begun to scramble toward the trucks at the back of the convoy, hoping to be able to escape the carnage, praying that their truck would not be smashed against the hillside.

Path signaled to Gavin to stop to give the enemy a chance to retreat.

Path turned to look at Gwen and they smiled at one another but it was a horrific smile they shared, it was a smile filled with knowledge of such power that it could destroy everything and everyone in their path. It was also a sad smile of finality, of a choice that they had not really wanted to make but had known was inevitable as soon as they saw Casto's version of justice. They both looked toward Casto and moved forward together, walking directly toward him.

The man looked at the two people who were obviously some kind of magicians approaching, capable of making themselves look fearsome and even glowing with some kind of inner light. He wanted to laugh, he wanted to tell them that he had some magic of his own he could show them but he stood in fascination as they tried to frighten him with their parlor tricks, their sideshow antics. The noise in his ears had suddenly stopped. Thinking he had effectively blocked it, he smiled and he rose to his feet, full of confidence again.

"Kill THEM!" he screamed at his men.

Only two were brave enough to move forward. Gwen raised a hand and they flew through the air like puppets, thrown up against the trucks with such a crushing impact that they were instantly dead.

The confusion in the enemy camp was horrible to witness. Some of the soldiers rushed at Gwen and Path and suffered an even worse fate than the first two. One merely exploded. A group threw up a shield around Casto, still fearing him enough to want to protect him. No one had ever witnessed seeing a person melt until the moment Path pointed at one of those guards and caused that to happen to him, his companions screaming in terror and scrambling away from Casto's perimeter. Pathogent and Gwen walked fearlessly to the truck that held the body of Lily and stood in front of her, spending a quiet moment with her and the flames went blue and soft and, in some strange way, sorrowful; they were touching her gently and insuring that she was truly gone and was no longer suffering. Together they unbound her and gently laid her on the ground at their feet. Then they turned their entire wrath on the few men surrounding Casto, approaching close and increasing the blaze that was quickly consuming them all.

The screams were deafening. The older children hid the smaller children against their chests so they couldn't see the conflagration. Yellow Feather went to Haylie and knelt down beside her, crying with her over the task she'd been burdened with and the promise she had been forced to keep. He held her as she wept bitterly in his arms, a child no more. He sat cross-legged on the ground and gathered her into his lap, whispering comfort into her ear. Several children were also hugging David, comforting him. They gathered strength from one another, knowing now that they could work as a unit, that the future was more secure than ever with their combined strengths and talents.

Laurel looked at Gavin and wondered what he was doing. His eyes were closed and his head was tilted back, then she saw that Travis was doing the same. She tried to enter their minds but found herself blocked. She looked helplessly at Coyote who smiled at her and said, "It's okay, I think they're with Path and Gwen. They now know how to do that. They know all that Gwen and Path know about calling up the magic. They alone have tapped into it, into the force that the four of them now share." He nodded toward the utter destruction of the enemies below.

Most of the men from Hades had backed trucks up and were fleeing, heading back toward Texas. Trucks were hitting other trucks in their panic to get away. The children watched as several trucks not already disabled were disappearing over the horizon.

Casto stood, defiantly laughing, actually expecting some kind of magic to come to his aid. When he realized that nothing was happening as he tried to duplicate what Path and Gwen had done, his eyes widened and he grimaced in frustration.

Gwen and Path appeared to be embracing Casto as they surrounded him and took him with them as they blazed in a tower of flame. The three of them were visible in the white hot light in which they were the center. Suddenly the tower of light grew brighter and more intense and blinding, then they simply went invisible in the white heat of it all. In a matter of only moments, there was nothing left but ash and a charred and partially melted, smoking tarmac where they had stood. When the noise stopped suddenly, everyone realized that it had been a deafening roar, like the roar of a furnace, even from this great distance, that they had not really noticed until it had stopped and they witnessed the abrupt silence.

Declan's face was wet with tears as he had watched his ancestors to the bitter end, expecting them to come back to him after destroying the enemy. He stood rooted to the spot, unable to move, unable to believe that they were truly gone. Gayle moved to comfort him. Over their time in Golden, he had quickly become like a brother to her and she knew that they all, those of the group who were descendants of Pathogent and Gwen, felt like family. He held her as they mourned their losses, joined by Brittin, whose love for Gayle made her part of that family core.

"They aren't coming back, are they?" Laurel said, through her own tears, choking on sobs. She felt an arm go around her and she looked up to see that Gavin was back to normal. She turned and cried against his chest and he held her, stroking her hair and trying to soothe her. He held her like a fragile and precious artifact, wrapping his arms around her and making a vow that nothing would ever hurt her while he lived. She snuggled into his warmth like a kitten, realizing that this was the man of her dreams yet he was real; he breathed, he was no longer just someone living inside of her head. He comforted her the only way he knew how. He was amazed at how good he felt right now, fever and nausea completely gone, a new strength surging through his body, as if the sickness had burned from him when he was with Travis, Path, and Gwen.

He smiled over her head at Travis. The secret they shared would have to be discussed in great depth. He now knew how powerful Travis truly was, how much power had been transferred from Gwen and Path to them both. Gavin was still unable to believe what he had learned when he had allowed his mind to go into the conflagration with Travis. He now believed that the universe was filled with energy that was available to him for the asking and he knew how to harness that power with his friend.

Young twelve year old David was in a state of deep grief over losing his hero, Pathogent, blaming himself, "Why did I miss? How could I miss? If only I had hit him..." He was wandering in a circle, saying this aloud to himself.

Lincoln went to his knees in front of David, tears staining his own face, yet looking deeply into the boy's eyes, "Do not think that Pathogent didn't plan this, he knew this would happen, he told me this would happen. He did not expect or want you to kill Casto, David. He loved you and did not want that burden on your young shoulders. He might have even deflected the bullet himself. He did not know that you were going to try to kill Casto or any of the enemy. He didn't want or expect it of you. Now, I know that you two were very close and he wanted me to assure you that you were always very, very special to him, you were his 'right hand man' from the very start, and one of the bravest boys he had ever known. While you were gone down there to El Paso, he was worried sick. Yes, David, he loved you like a son, he wanted me to tell you that." He held the young boy and let him mourn, whoever this child had been in other lives, right now he was just a child, a very hurt and bewildered child.

Everyone looked around for Yellow Feather and Coyote but could not find them among their group. Then they looked to where the conflagration was still smoking and found them there, performing an ancient rite of mourning, giving Path and Gwen's spirits back to the ancestors where they would walk in peace and glory. They had already been joined by Cody and Haylie. Soon the others drifted toward the spot as well, to honor the rites being performed and to say goodbye in a better way, for mutual closure. Hearts were breaking and throats closed with grief, but they had one another and Golden was safe, however great the sacrifice. However greatly they had been outnumbered. As Lincoln said at the end of the ceremony, "Until their energy *blinks* again, and may they get to spend many lifetimes together."

It was the good part of an hour before they even thought about going back to Golden. There was the numbing effect of the grief and the fact that some of them still held out hope of seeing Path and Gwen again and were afraid to leave them behind. The men and women had taken Lily's body from where Pathogent and Gwen had gently put her and, wrapping it in blankets, placed her, lovingly, on the bed of one of their own trucks to take her "home" for burial. Gayle had taken Haylie aside and held her, assuring her that she had been far more than just heroic, giving Lily a far more honorable death and stealing the joy of torture from Casto. "After all," Gayle told her, "she was a warrior, like you. And you gave her the warrior's death that she wanted. I know she would thank you, if she could, Haylie." They talked together, away from the others for a long while.

Yellow Feather stood, looking south and waiting, even as everyone was loading up the weaponry and supplies that had been so hastily unloaded when they had arrived at the rendezvous point. Coyote and Travis went to where he stood, and stood on either side of him, looking into the distance with him.

"Are we going for Dave, my brother?" Coyote simply asked, stopping elbow to elbow with Yellow Feather, knowing where Yellow Feather's thoughts were traveling. "If so, Cody said that he will go with us, he is already talking to Little Crow, who knew this land so well. He will be the tracker we need if we want to stand a chance of finding him out there."

Travis said, "I can't get a fix on his energy, there is a chance that he is dead. I would say it's more than a chance. I can't imagine him allowing them to take Lily, were he not dead..."

"Unless he was wounded," Yellow Feather said, turning to meet Travis' eye, "I can't get him in my mind either, but then, Dave was always a tough one; he could block us like nobody's business. Remember when he was thinking about how much he loved Lily and he blocked us to keep his thoughts private? Grinning at us like a cat who ate a canary? If he is out there, he might be blocking us so that we don't worry, so that we don't risk capture to rescue him. He has no way of knowing what happened here. He might be wounded, and Dave is a survivor, he might be holed up somewhere, healing, until he is strong enough to come home. I cannot go home thinking that I could have helped him."

Travis nodded, he knew that it wasn't just the "boys" going to find Dave, but four of the greatest spirits of all time. This rescue mission would be conducted by Tecumseh, Crazy Horse, Chief Joseph, with Geronimo as their tracker on this dry, arid land, his own home turf.

Travis clasped Yellow Feather's hand in his, then said his goodbyes to Coyote, Cody, and Little Crow. As they prepared the bikes to leave, Declan approached the group. He already seemed to know what they were planning and showed no sign of disagreement. Although it was still hard for him to wrap his head around the reincarnation thing and the fact that Little Crow was only nine years old, he knew and approved of their plan. These "boys" had already proven themselves to him time and again. "Why don't you take one of the trucks?" he suggested. "That way, if you find Dave, you've got a way to bring him back if he can't ride a trail bike."

"We will be going over rough terrain. I think I know where Dave and Lily left the road and we'll be able to find where the Hades men followed them cross country," Coyote said, "our trucks probably won't be able to climb where we're climbing."

"Well, they found Lily, so they must have been able to climb. Besides I didn't mean one of our trucks," Declan said, nodding at one of the deserted army trucks that the group from Hades had left behind in their hurry to leave the fight. "They probably even have spare gas in those babies. They were prepared to travel, after all."

Yellow Feather smiled and nodded. They found one of the trucks, undamaged, with the keys still dangling from the ignition.

"Can any of you drive this thing?" Declan asked, smiling. "Do you need me to come with you?"

"They can't drive it, but I sure as hell can," said Randy, one of their heavy machine operators, who worked closely with Dave and Clint, and helped to bury the residents of Denver with excavators and bulldozers. "Declan, I don't even WANT to be the one to face Melody if you don't come home with the others. This would be far less dangerous to me, I assure you. I'll take this adventure. If this baby can't follow you into the wilderness, Yellow Feather, you can leave me parked and I'll wait until you bring Dave to me. Then he'll ride out of there in style."

Brian insisted that he was going with Randy, too, if for no other reason than safety in numbers. He climbed up into the truck with no hesitation.

So it was settled and, after loading food and other supplies, including medical supplies, into the truck, the search party left to go south again. At the same time, the others headed home to Golden.

*

It had been a strange feeling, coming back to Golden without the original founders. There had been both cause for joyous celebration and mind-bending grief. They had laid Lily to rest and built a cairn over her grave, she was surrounded by the entire village, each person grateful for her courage and sacrifice. There was no shortage of words being said over her. She had been loved and respected by all. They held a memorial for Gwen and Pathogent and held one another together, knowing that they had no choice but to move forward, one day at a time. Their mutual grief stunned the entire village but they had to move forward to honor their ancestors' sacrifices.

Torn by guilt that his rescue had cost them so dearly, Gavin expected a cold reception but was surprised by how quickly he was accepted and surrounded by love. Gavin, who had lived in Hades, literally, found that Golden was the closest thing to Heaven that he could imagine. There was so much joy and laughter here, even with the sorrow of losing three, and maybe four of their beloved citizens. Golden was still like a village of lights. He found that he especially looked forward to the nightly campfires, where gifted musicians performed, people told fascinating stories, both true and fiction, and everyone experienced such a sense of camaraderie and love that he felt warm inside just being allowed to be a part of it.

The work here was so easy! Everyone pitched in. No one was a boss; they simply planned a project and carried it out together. He had never had it so easy. He could not even begin to feel tired, there were just so many helping hands that every task was accomplished easily and quickly. He was learning to help build cabins and houses, garden, clean, help with laundry, and cook. There were no gender specific jobs, there were simply tasks to be done and never a shortage of people to help. There was so much leisure time that he almost felt lazy!

During some of his down time, he had come to enjoy climbing with Conner and several of the others. Laurel was beside him in every other activity he enjoyed and he found himself falling even more in love with her, were that even possible. There was only one adventure that she waived interest in, actually abhorred, and that was his new passion, climbing. It was exhilarating to him, climbing a cliff, conquering fears and insecurities, putting faith in your belay. He was slowly and surely, with Conner's guidance, overcoming his lifelong fear of heights and he learned that it was more about learning how to be safe, secure, and skilled. She understood this when he explained it to her but she used the time he was away climbing to catch up on other interests.

Travis had, of course, become like a brother to him. They seemed to be learning from one another. Travis was teaching him how to *blink* sideways, to visit other minds even on other continents and he and Travis were both becoming more certain of the magic they had learned while in Path's and Gwen's minds. They were able to keep the shield from dissolving and possibly expanded it to include much of Denver, although they wondered if perhaps Gwen and Path hadn't already begun that feat. Travis was determined to help Gavin discover who he had been in other lives. But one name came shining through and, though he knew that the name was supposed to have been nothing but legend, he was forced to wonder...could Gavin truly be Merlin?

Gavin loved Golden like no other place he had ever been. And then, of course, there was Laurel. She really did feel the same about him as he felt about her, much to his amazement. The first time they kissed was burned in his memory. They had been at the campfire and she asked him to walk her to the girls' cabin that she shared with several of the others. They walked in silence. She had always communicated with him inside of his head. Everyone was surprised that he hadn't found his voice yet after Travis had told them all that his muteness was trauma-induced from the shock of losing his entire family and how he found them. He had been examined by Lincoln and Gayle who found him healthy and could not find any physical reason for his handicap.

He and Laurel talked with one another in their minds and he was telling her how happy this entire camp made him feel, how wonderful it was to be sharing space with adults as kind and loving as Declan, Conner, Shawnee, Melody...how the joy of the children filled him with a happiness impossible to express. How quickly these good memories were replacing his nightmare memories of Hades.

"Aren't you ever going to kiss me, Gavin?" her voice whispered, softly.

He stopped and turned toward her, slowly. Oh, how he had waited for this signal from her. He drew her close and she stood on her toes and wrapped her arms around his neck. He bent his face to hers and let his lips ever so slowly meet hers, wanting every second of this to count and become a memory, loving the velvety feel of her lips, loving the softness he found there. He carefully tightened his arms and lifted her toward him and the kiss deepened and lengthened. It was a long time before he let her move back to earth. He loved the feel of her in his arms, her curves, her slender, sweet-smelling body, the way she sighed deep in her throat drove him mad with desire. He could smell the clean scent of herbs on her neck, where she sometimes rubbed lavender or rosemary.

She sighed again and closed her eyes for a moment, then told him, aloud, "That was my first kiss. I am so glad it was you."

His mind struggled, oh, how he wished he could tell her the same, that he had never kissed another girl, that, although he was a virgin, that he had never made out with a woman, but it would not be the truth. But it was the truth that this was his very first kiss of love. "It won't be your last," he assured her.

"Silly man, I know what you were thinking and you need to stop regretting your life's experience," she told him. "I'm glad you practiced before. That was why your kiss was so amazing, so good. I need you to teach me, show me how to make things better. My heart is beating so fast it feels like it's going to jump out of my chest! Is this normal?"

"It better be!" his thoughts told her. "I feel the same and I want to think I'm pretty normal."

"Oh, Gavin, you are never going to be seen as 'normal', you are far too amazing," she told him, her words stumbling and naive and clumsy. She chided herself, tripping over the poetic and powerful brain that she possessed, tripping over the way she longed to express herself. She had been so capable of expression in all of her other lives, what was happening to her?

He could feel and sense her frustration at herself. He knew that she was trying to compose something profound for the moment. So he did it for her. Quoting Byron, he soothed her mind with words similar to those he knew she sought, "When age chills the blood, when our pleasures are past, for years fleet away with the wings of a dove. The dearest remembrance will still be the last, our sweetest memorial, the first kiss of love."

She took a deep breath and met his eyes, unable to believe how quickly he was able to reach into his trove of knowledge and come up with that beautiful verse. He would never forget the beauty of her lip quivering to fight back tears and her deep sigh. It was a sigh of coming home to something you never knew was "home" until you found it, of knowing that you had found the person you could trust with your heart, a sigh of resignation and bonding and love. He felt that sigh deep in his heart because it was how he felt, too. And then, suddenly, he found his voice, it came back to him as suddenly as it had left him and he used it to say the thing he most wanted to tell her, "Laurel, I love you."

She looked at him in shock and they laughed together as she realized that the sound of his voice was no different than the sound of it in her head so, at first, she hadn't even realized that his lips had moved. When it dawned on her that he had actually said those four words aloud, she was laughing, then she was crying, and he was holding her, both of them overwhelmed with emotion. He put his head back and laughed aloud, for the first time in years. She thought that the sound of his laughter was the most beautiful thing she had ever heard, aside from, that is, his declaration of love.

*

Conner sat and talked with Declan, Melody, Travis, and Gavin, having invited them to join him and Shawnee for dinner. Everyone in Golden was getting used to the fact that Gavin's voice had returned to him and appreciated the fact that they could now converse freely and hear his words like any of the other boys. Since the two "boys" were looked upon as two of the new leaders of the children, he wanted to learn as much from them as he could and sought their counsel regarding where Golden might go from here, hoping that they could give him insight. As they relaxed after the meal, Shawnee poured coffee all around and she and Melody sat at the table with them as they talked, Little Moon having been fed and snuggled down for the night.

"I had no idea how much time Pathogent and Gwen gave to everyone but, now that everyone is coming to me, I'm feeling a little overwhelmed and not really sure I am up to the expectations of everyone here," Conner admitted to them, with a sigh. He reached over and put his hand over Shawnee's, "After all, we're NOT Path and Gwen, we don't have their magic, nor their connection to everyone; we're just normal people, no former lives to guide us, no eternal wisdom to share."

"No, you are not Path and Gwen," Travis began, stirring several spoons of sugar into his coffee, mellowed with chicory, Shawnee's specialty. He smiled slowly to reassure them, "But you are Conner and Shawnee, and believe me, that's enough. You are well-respected and loved and wise and Path knew that you were capable of taking over in advisory capacity when they were gone. Everyone could see that he was grooming you four for this from the start. He knew that you and Shawnee would be the strong voices of reason and Declan would be the soft and tender spiritual guide." He grinned and directed the next comment to Declan, "I'm sorry, you know it's true, everyone is always expecting you to make their worries go away and make them feel better and you always rise to the occasion, don't you? And Melody is like a warm momma figure to just about everyone she meets. She was taking that position long before Gwen ever started to slow down."

"But now, knowing that you all bring so much to the table, so to speak, that so many of you have so much accumulated knowledge, I feel foolish even thinking about making decisions without consulting you two and Yellow Feather and many of the others," Conner admitted.

"But we don't want you to feel either foolish or that you need to consult. This beautiful village is running itself quite nicely. You had to have been able to see that a long time ago," Gavin offered, feeling a little shy about jumping in, considering that he had been here such a short while. "You see, we WANT to be allowed to grow into ourselves, as you well know. We want to be treated like we still need guidance, advice, corrective action and, despite whoever we may have been in former lives, we DO need that. If you keep feeling that you need to ask permission or please everyone, this will become too much like a government. We, none of us, want that. We want someone stable to hold the horse at a steady canter and, if you become an overbearing dictator, we'll knock you off the horse and put someone else there," Gavin teased. "We will still have the same voices as everyone else at the council fire and that's enough for me."

"It feels very comforting to do everything as we've always done, by consensus around the nightly fire," Travis said, smiling and nodding in agreement with Gavin. "I still get a lot of comfort, looking forward to the council meetings and voting by consensus. It has always been a time of comfort and joy to me to be able to sit amongst my friends and hear them discuss everything essential to the running of this village; it's just such a sense of community and cooperation. I wish I could put it into words how it makes me feel. It's like going 'home' to your grandmother's house and having her make your favorite meal without having to ask what your favorite meal is. It's like the comfort of really belonging to something bigger than yourself. Most times the things you bring up don't even make it to 'vote'. They are passed by a simple agreement after hearing others out. It is working for us. We're not yet so big that you have to worry about 'elections', boards, committees, don't you agree?"

Declan nodded and smiled, his arm protectively draped over the back of Melody's chair, his hand idly rubbing her swollen pregnant belly. "I agree, wholeheartedly, I'm willing to put a lot of this back onto the nightly council now that the shock of losing our founders is beginning to wear off just a little. I'm sure Conner feels the same. We simply want to enjoy our growing families and watch our beautiful children being raised with some of the brightest and best children ever to have existed."

"I think that things are falling back into place faster than I actually expected," Shawnee admitted. "I have to say that when you all returned without Path and Gwen, I thought we would suffer chaos for a very long time, but everyone here is so capable and strong. Look what we endured to come here, look at our mutual struggles and how far we've come with the efforts of everyone. I've never lived in a community where everyone knows what to do and just pitches in, listening to the voices of experience, eager to learn. I love Golden, what we've accomplished here. I hope we never really change the basic tenets of what we started here."

Melody smiled at her friend, Shawnee, and lifted her cup in agreement.

"But you will have to accept it," Travis warned, "people have come to think of you as the leaders. I don't want to bring up something incredibly sad but there were only four ADULT time-travelers that you were all aware of, and if Dave...well, it doesn't even really bear thinking of right now."

"There are quite a few in this room capable of the title of leader, and several others who are currently out there looking for our Dave," Conner reminded them. "Now we have had a taste of discord, like we had just before our rescue group went south to rescue you, Gavin. I think it gave us a chance to examine what we have accomplished and how well it works. Even when Pathogent was unjustly being challenged for what people felt was a decision he had no right to make, he allowed the power of the conversation to go back to the 'council of many' rather than make excuses for himself. Your intercession happened at the perfect time, Travis, it helped us all to realize that there are going to be times when we may have to face discord and realize that it can't always bring about a perfect decision that will please everyone."

"I will always be happy to give you insight into whatever you need from me," Travis told them, sincerely, "but know that I am also time-traveling and experimenting and continuing to learn and explore the universe. This is very important to me and I see it taking up a lot of my time in the future and I am growing more and more jealous of my free time. Does that sound selfish? Let me assure you, I am here, but sometimes in physical essence only, but I'm always just a tap on the shoulder away."

Gavin explained to them, "Travis has long been capable of time-travel in his current state, and is just as capable of pulling himself back to this time and place when necessary and he is teaching me. We learned so very much when we were conjoined with Path's and Gwen's minds, as well. We don't want to freak you out, but there are a lot of things that the children have been doing and are capable of that you are totally unaware of..."

"So, while you are sitting in my classroom, you might be in the past?" Shawnee asked, full of wonder.

"Or the future!" Gavin laughed. "Where do you think we get some of the answers?"

"So, you could go into the future and tell us if we find Dave, if he lives?" Shawnee asked.

"No, it doesn't really work that way. We cannot 'affect' the past or the future. Much like Gwen and Path, we aren't even aware of what happens or happened in many of our lives. Like they did not realize that they had conceived children, thinking it was something they were always denied. We might go into the future and see a Dave who isn't really there. Wait, this is hard to explain. Just put it this way, we may see a future that could be altered by something we do here tomorrow, does that make sense?"

"Then what's the point of visiting the future?" Conner mused, thinking this through, logically. "I have to say, I don't envy you boys, this seems so complicated, I think I'm happy just living the life I'm living, particularly now," he said, his eyes sending a message of love to Shawnee.

"Who knows what we might learn? Something I learned from time-traveling helped me, as Alan Turing, tweak my machine just when I was about to give up on that wretched project. And, like human nature, I've actually forgotten what that was; for the life of me, I did not retain that 'spark' of essential information once my goal was met. The project just fell into place and worked and that, essentially, was the only important thing that mattered."

Melody smiled, but there was a little crease of concern on her forehead, just halfway between the eyes, "Is any of this dangerous for the children? I mean, is there a chance that someone could suddenly just disappear and we never see them again?"

Gavin and Travis looked at one another and smiled, "If anyone did, we'd go get them!" When Travis saw the stricken look on Melody's face, he backpedaled, apologetically, "No, Melody, none of us bodily disappears; it's not necessary, it is only our minds and awareness, you could say it's our 'energy' that is doing the traveling. We care deeply about one another and we are all truly and completely learning so much about what we can and cannot do, we're developing skills that will make the future unique and wonderful. If Gavin is in another century, traveling in another host, I could bring him back to himself in a flash. We all are learning how to do that. Please rest assured, this experimentation is no doubt why we were born the way we were born, why we've lived so many lives. We cannot stop our destinies. You would not want to stop our destinies, we are all just riding on this big blue ball, shaping the future the best we can. I find myself so excited by the possibilities I sometimes have a hard time explaining it all."

No one could see inside her cradle but, as she slept, an angelic smile of agreement rested on Little Moon's precious tiny face.

*

Two weeks had gone by with no sign of the rescue crew who had gone out searching for Dave but Travis assured them that he was in contact with the boys and that everyone was okay, though very hungry and frustrated. They had found the place where Lily had been captured and a trail of blood indicated that Dave, too, had indeed been injured, severely.

Now they expected the rescue group to find the worst. They had found his bike abandoned in a dust-filled arroyo. There was no more blood but they still found little sign to go by. Had they not taken Little Crow with them, they would never have found the tracks from that point on, but he circled the arroyo, carefully, not giving up and eventually found a shoe-print nearly erased by the blowing wind and, after moving on in that direction, finally found traces of a trail again. They followed for several miles, going up into the hills near Santa Fe, New Mexico.

Randy and Brian were still able to follow them, sometimes detouring around trees, but soon catching up with them again, the truck able to climb and maneuver, up and over rocky places. They wondered if Dave might not have stopped in Santa Fe. They had nearly run out of food and needed to see if they could find something in the town. The boys did find a supermarket and were happy to find enough canned goods to renew their energy, eating canned fruits and braving some of the other choices, as well. Brian, too, was happy to find fruit. He felt drained and he had not been in the elements like the boys were; he marveled at their stamina. He had to give them credit, they were tough young men.

They had just walked out of the grocery store when they heard loud and discordant singing coming from somewhere down the block. Looking at one another, wary of an encounter with possible deserters from Hades, they followed the sound.

Sitting on the sidewalk, outside of the liquor store was where they found him. He was singing, delirious with fever and trying to drown his pain with Vodka. As they approached, he looked up at them and smiled, "Are you ghosts visiting me again? What? Yellow Feather, Cody, Coyote, is that you? You came to bother me again, to try to urge me on? Aww, boys, did those bastards kill you, too? I just can't find it in me to move. I couldn't save her, I couldn't even save myself. Just go away and leave me alone, I don't need you to tell me I failed her. Why didn't they take me instead of her, why am I alive?"

He was filthy and ragged, his clothing barely hung together by threads and his leg around the wound was nearly black with infection and possible gangrene. He had, indeed, been shot in the thigh, lucky that the artery had not been hit or he would have bled to death. As it was, the wound was infected and, worse yet, crawling with maggots. The heat and the terrain had taken a heavy toll on Dave, but his emotional pain of losing Lily to the enemy had brought him to his knees.

Dave had given up. Dave had prepared to drink himself to death. It surprised them all to see him this way. He was delirious and incapable of realizing that they were real. He passed out at their feet.

Brian pushed through the boys and looked down on Dave and grew very serious, seeing how bad the leg looked. "This is a big town, there have to be doctor's offices and hospitals, we need penicillin and electrolytes. I want to flush that wound with clean soapy water, see if you can find some, let's get him to a doctor's office so I can get him up on a table and see if I can clean that out enough."

Dave regained consciousness for a moment and looked up at them and grinned, "My wound? Here's how you clean out the wound. Look at those drunk little worms!" He poured Vodka onto it and seethed pain through his teeth. Then he started singing just a few notes, stopped and looked at them and said, looking at Little Crow and

Coyote, "Well, hi there, boys, are you in my dream, too? Go inside, there's plenty for everyone, first round's on me!" He laughed hysterically and almost fell to the side. He was having trouble just staying conscious. "Oops, I plumb forgot, you kids aren't old enough to drink, whoever you were in another life!"

"Good lord," Brian said. "Come on, boys, we're going to have to carry him." He helped Randy hoist Dave up into his arms, carrying him like a child. Randy was big, and very strong, and Dave, who had always been lean, was a shadow of his former self.

They sent Little Crow ahead and he found a dentist office only a half block away, so they carried him there. Fortunately, it had been a place set up for dental surgery so there were a table and a room full of medications and instruments.

"I don't want to mess with the wound more than to clean it and take the dead tissue from the edges, but we've got to get him to Gayle and Lincoln after we clean and dress it. See if you can find some antibacterial ointment, Neosporin would be great. Those maggots might have been helpful, actually, but I want to get them out of there," Brian said, relieved to have found Dave before the wound would have killed him. He tried to control his gag reflex at the sight of the squirming larvae in Dave's wound.

Randy held Dave down while Brian washed and cleaned the wound, the best he knew how. They winced at how much pain Dave was suffering. They washed him, carefully and gently, and then Coyote came in carrying a change of clothing. They had already cut the dirty, filthy rags off of him and they were able to clean him gently and dress him in clean and soft, non-binding clothing. They cut the leg off the soft cotton pajama bottoms Coyote had found and dressed him carefully. They had earlier forced ipecac into him so that he would vomit and clear his system of alcohol so that the antibiotics and pain medication would have a chance to help. The room was stinking with the smell of infection and disinfectant and was filthy with gore and vomit so they rolled him into another chamber to keep him clean.

"I'm no doctor, it's the best I can do," Brian told them. He turned to Yellow Feather, "I don't know if he's going to make it. Maybe tell Travis to keep it quiet about us having found him until we are sure that we are bringing a live Dave back to Golden. Tell him to just prepare Gayle and Lincoln for what we're bringing in."

"Which is?" Yellow Feather dared to ask.

"A probable amputation, possible gangrene," Brian told him, grimly. "Now, let's get him in the truck while he's knocked out. We're going to have to desert the bikes because you will all need to ride in back and keep him quiet and make sure he doesn't go delirious on us again."

"I want Little Crow to ride in front with you guys," Yellow Feather told him, softly. "I don't want him witnessing any more of this than he has to." He grinned, embarrassed, "After all, he still is a child."

Brian nodded and agreed. They made a bed on the floor of the truck and wrapped Dave warmly and carefully, hoping he would sleep all the way to Golden. Brian stopped twice to check on Dave and administer antibiotics. Randy rode in back with the boys to make room for Little Crow in the cab.

*

They arrived in Golden in the middle of the night. Gayle and Lincoln and Travis were waiting with a make-shift surgery set up for an examination. When Lincoln saw the leg, he looked at Gayle. They both looked grim. "We're going to need more than we have here, wake Clint and Randy and tell them that we're going to need the surgery room we used for Gwen and they need to get the generators working again."

Gayle turned to Brittin, "Please find Stephanie, Maria, and Courteney. tell them we're going to go down there again, and we'll need them to sterilize the room as best they can. We're all going to have to transport Dave down to Denver to see if we can save his leg."

"Save his leg, hell, the question is, can we save his LIFE?" Lincoln said, truthfully.

It was a very long night for them all but they decided to let the children sleep. Conner and Shawnee stayed behind, so did Declan and Melody, but nearly all the other adults went to Denver to see if there was anything they could do to help. Dave had been there for each and every one of them, sleeping outside the perimeter many nights, just to insure their safety. Dave's presence had made nearly everyone in Golden feel safer. This was a time when they all wanted to give something back to him.

Several of them already knew that they could give blood from the tests run before Gwen's surgery, and Gayle was arranging that step before surgery, working carefully with Stephanie and Maria. She alternated between taking blood from donors and checking the pre-surgical tests that Lincoln and she had decided they wanted.

"Was it wrong of us to give him the ipecac?" Brian wanted to know.

"It might have saved his life," Lincoln told him, "or maybe his liver, at least. It was essential to begin a course of antibiotics. No, Brian, you did a really good job for someone who isn't a trained physician, you actually did better than a good job. Now, leave it in our hands and see what we can do."

"Are you at least optimistic?" Randy asked, upset that they could not get him here any faster than they had.

"Optimistic about saving his life?" Lincoln asked. "Working with Gayle, I am very optimistic. Saving his leg? Not so much. However, we know Dave and we're going to do everything we can to save it. We know he would not do well being 'dependent' and losing Lily is enough loss for him to bear."

Hours later, Stephanie came out to tell those waiting in the hallway, "He did great through the surgery, neither of them...Lincoln, nor Gayle, would give it up, they skin grafted the wound and think that he might not need amputation. Most of the infection came from the bullet still being in there and bone fragmenting from his femur. But his femur didn't break. The bullet came so darned close to the artery, you were right, Brian, too darned close. Only time will tell...and now they want you all to go home and go to bed so that some of you can give us breaks later today."

*

In time, Dave healed well enough to walk again, although his limp was extremely pronounced and he needed to use a cane. Brian crafted him the most beautiful cane made of oak with carved animals all the way down, twining through bushes and leaves, animals they were finding living in the forests around them. Dave was speechless at the beauty of this gift and was proud to use that cane. He talked a lot about Lily to everyone who wanted to talk about her memory. He told them all the details of the wild chase he and Lily had led through the rough terrain, the shooting and Lily's capture. He described how hard he had tried to keep that capture from happening before he lost consciousness. He told them that he figured that the guys from Hades thought they had killed him and left him for dead.

He was pleased when he saw the beautiful grave that they had placed her in, happy to hear that they had been able to bring her body home and he spent a lot of time there, keeping it beautiful. Some of the village suspected that he often slept nearby, continuing to protect his Lily. He made it clear to Haylie that he felt that what she did for Lily was heroic. They had a very long conversation about it, both of them crying and comforting one another and he told her that it was unfair for both him and Lily to have extracted that promise from her but that he was glad that they had. He said it all in one final sentence, "Better at your skilled hand than the torture of that despicable monster."

When they told him about Gwen and Pathogent, his jaw would twitch and they knew that it hurt him more than he would let on. He had lived many parallel lives with both of them and had come to love them like family. Although they knew that he thought of them ALL as family, his history with Path and Gwen could not be denied and he felt a great loss not being able to see them again. There was so much sadness he was forced to face as he healed but heal he did, and, in the process, helped others heal from their guilt and pain, especially Haylie and Gavin.

But the thing that brought Dave joy was that the rescue was successful and he and Lily did not sacrifice in vain. He was genuinely happy that all of the kids, including Gavin, were safe and together again in Golden. He made certain that Gavin knew that and that he was happy that they had him join their group. Gavin was always so willing to help and take on more than his share. He was a great addition to every work crew and the entire village was happy to have him. Besides, he made little Laurel glow with happiness and Dave was certain to tease them both about that mutual feeling they shared with one another.

He especially showed excitement when Coyote and David came back from a short excursion with two of the wild horses that they had seen on their way down to Texas. Coyote had already nearly tamed the mare and they were certain that when the colt was old enough, he, too, would make a good mount. The village quickly built a stable and corral for the horses. Coyote beamed over his acquisition and every single one of the rescue crew had known that this would happen. He couldn't get that herd of horses out of his mind. Laurel offered to help Coyote and David care for the beautiful animals, hoping that there would eventually be more horses in Golden.

Dave leaned on the top rail of the corral to balance himself and asked Coyote, "What's her name?" as he watched the beautiful golden mare toss her mane and prance around the enclosure with her solid black colt by her side.

"Lily, of course," Coyote answered, softly.

Dave could not answer, but he put a hand on Coyote's shoulder and squeezed.

*

Months later, the village was given another reason to celebrate as Melody and Declan had their son. They had struggled with the name, since they wanted to name him after Pathogent, the man Declan considered almost like a father but that name would be a strange burden for a baby, however much the humor of it impressed the man who chose that name for himself. Finally, they named him after one of Declan's ancestors and Melody's great-grandfather, who had both been Pathogent's hosts in other lives. The whole village welcomed Brendan Jacob Donnelly as the newest citizen of Golden. Little Brendan was a robust, long, round thing and everyone teased Melody that she might have actually eaten TOO healthily while pregnant. He had his mother's dark hair and grey eyes, but with an impish look like his father, so he was a delightful mix of all the ancestry brought to his genetic make-up. Declan called him his little *sidhe*. Only hours old the child was so full of joy and pleasant to be around.

Melody had the same group around her that Shawnee had for the delivery of Little Moon and they all felt the absence of Gwen and Path quite strongly when remembering that night, none more than Melody and Declan who had wanted more than anything to share this special night of their life with them. Brendan was born in the morning, greeting the dawn with a robust first cry and then seldom crying from that point on. He was a treasure and the visitors filed past early, then resumed again after lunch, giving Brendan and Melody hours alone for bonding. Conner called Brendan "the entertainer" since, were he to follow in his parents' footsteps, he would take the stage in one form or another, an actor and storyteller like his father or musician like his mother. It would be his nickname for the lad for life and the boy would come to embrace that title in honor of his father's and mother's talents and enthusiasm for life. "Uncle" Conner would always be an integral part of the child's life, as well.

Celebrating that night around the fire, there was another well-received announcement, that Brian and Dani were also expecting. He had come home from the rescue to the news that Dani was waiting to tell him. They had waited until they were certain to announce it at the campfire. Dani admitted that she had hidden it for quite a while and that she was due in only a few months.

Everyone was happy that Melody not only felt well enough to attend campfire so soon after giving birth but that she also wanted to play them a few tunes of good cheer on her violin.

"You know I love my violin, but it's a fiddle when it plays music like this," she said, tapping her toe and grinning, playing a few tunes for the children to dance to. Declan held Brendan while she played and he watched her with glowing pride. They danced happily among the younger children, and then she encouraged Emerald to sing "Summertime", to her accompaniment and everyone was thrilled to get to hear the girl's obvious talent. And, although she struggled to overcome her shyness, Melody was encouraged by her friends standing beside her and holding her hands, Haylie on one side and Raven on the other.

When she finished, Conner stood up and smiled at the faces around the campfire, faces he had come to recognize and trust and love, and held his cup of water high, "I'd like to toast the birth of Brendan Jacob, may he live up to and inherit the courage and strength in the wearer of both names; toast to the news from Brian and Dani, I am certain their news makes them as happy as it has made all of us;

the successful rescues our young ones accomplished in the past few weeks; Gavin, you have no idea how grateful we are to have you among us, you do indeed work hard enough for three and make it all look so easy; we all celebrate the recovery of our Dave." He tipped a nod in Dave's direction and everyone smiled, agreeing, "And, a toast to our fabulous musicians and singers for the wonderful entertainment; thoughts for our Lily and how much love she gave us, love that was returned by all," he cleared his throat, nervously and said, with a gravity so unlike him, "and another thing that we've been trying to avoid because it makes us sad and I know that they wouldn't want it to continue that way. A toast to our founders, Gwen and Path, wherever they are. I don't know if you believe as I do, but I have to believe that spirits that strong will never die, may they be allowed a lifetime together filled with love and happiness in their next incarnation. They deserve as much, I send my love outward to them, wherever they may be."

The others raised their glasses and their voices in response, "To Gwen and Path, wherever you are!" The stars twinkled as they all looked upward at once, the same stars that had twinkled above their ancestors for many generations. The night sky was beautiful, vast and clear, and the future stretched out ahead, eternally, a canopy of twinkling magic above them. Off in the distance, a wolf howled and that ghostly chorus began. Yellow Feather smiled, hiding tears that came to his eyes as he heard the howls. Gwen's wolves were singing for her, and in good voice.

*

Declan and Melody's son, Brendan Jacob Donnelly, laughed the deep belly laugh that his parents had come to love so very much about him. He was a happy child, full of smiles, his gray eyes taking everything in as he watched his father and mother prepare for his second birthday party. Soon everyone would gather around the community campfire to partake in the festivities and help celebrate the second year of his life. He toddled to where his mother was tuning her violin and sat unceremoniously down on his diapered rump, his chubby little legs sent sprawling as he struggled to keep his balance to not fall backward. He gave her a wrinkled nose grin, showing two teeth on the bottom of his smile and four on the top, and she smiled down at him, softly saying, "Do you want to hear it again?" She let the bow move across the strings and played what seemed to be his favorite tune of the week, "Wild Mountain Thyme", as he clapped his fat hands together awkwardly, as if trying to keep time to the music.

"For the hundredth time?" Declan asked her, smiling as he worked to assemble the little scooter they had found in Denver. It had a seat that would support Brendan so that he could sit inside, yet push with his legs. As he got more confident and skilled, they would be able to remove the harnessing part of the seat and he would have more freedom to scoot around on the little bike.

"It's the favorite song of the week," Melody told him, chucking her little son under the chin, "last week he was far more discriminating and only wanted Mozart and a couple weeks ago, 'Hickory, Dickory, Doc' was the most amazing thing he had ever heard. He danced to that one, remember?" she smiled, "At least he's musical! I can't wait to begin teaching him. He can already play a little on his recorder. It may not be much, but it's a start!"

Constance, one of the youngest of the original Golden children, was frosting cupcakes at the kitchen table with her sister, Crystal. The girls loved spending time with the Donnellys, often spending more time there than with the other children. There were always children coming and going from this cabin, and little Brendan had no shortage of attention and love poured on him from all the residents of Golden. Crystal laughed and added, "He also likes Beatles songs. Brian played him some on his guitar and he wiggled his bottom and danced! It was so funny!"

Brendan sat, rocking slightly back and forth, grinning up at Constance as if he knew he was the subject of their admiration, but he was busy looking around to see what else he could investigate and his attention was now on Declan. Curiosity got the best of him and he worked his way to his feet, putting his hands on the ground and pushing upward. He had been walking for months now, but the standing and stopping was always performed clumsily, as if he just wanted to move too fast and lost patience. He would be running before he mastered the rest, everyone told his parents.

Melody went to answer a light knock at the cabin door and greeted Conner, Shawnee, and Little Moon, who was just slightly older than Brendan by a few months. Brendan squealed with delight to see his playmate and they babbled together in the center of the floor as Little Moon, also known as Tebethto, settled in to play.

Shawnee went to look at the cupcakes Constance was working on, complimenting her work and smiled, sitting down with the two girls to help. Conner stood looking at Declan and Melody, smiling, almost unable to contain himself.

"Something tells me you have something to share, boyo," Declan said, noting how antsy Conner seemed, how he seemed on the verge of bursting at the seams with delight. Declan stopped what he was doing and gave his full attention to the other man. Of all the men in Golden, Conner would come the closest to being what Declan would consider a best friend, although he found himself liking everyone here, come to think of it. He was getting to the point where he could read Conner, knowing when he was troubled or frustrated, when he needed a rest from the responsibility of being the man everyone came to for decisions, or when, like now, he was so filled with joy that he needed to share. This must be something big.

"I know it might be almost too soon, since Tebethto is only two but Shawnee and I are going to be parents again," Conner said, almost all in one single breath.

"Seriously?" Melody squealed, happily, jumping up to embrace Shawnee, then Conner, "When did you find out?"

"We've known for a couple weeks now, but wanted to be sure before telling anyone," Shawnee told her, "But Conner couldn't keep it in another moment, he wanted you two to be the first to know, we're going to announce it at campfire, after little Brendan's party, that is. So," she added, addressing the two little girls, "Can you keep our secret for us until we announce it to the rest?" Crystal and Constance grinned and nodded, happy to feel central to this great news.

Declan was on his feet, congratulating his friends, as happy for them as they were for themselves. Conner and Shawnee were, as everyone expected them to be, excellent parents. They had always been great with the kids they were teaching and patient and kind, everyone expected no less of them as parents. This would make the fourth birth since all the people had gathered in Golden and formed the community they had come to love. Now that Brian's and Dani's little boy had turned one about six months ago, the residents of Golden were growing proud of the new, healthy, happy babies being raised by the "village", under the watchful eye of doctors, nurses, educators, and friends.

Brendan stared up at the happy couples, his parents nearly as thrilled for their friends as they would have been had this been their own news. As he played with Tebethto, he allowed his mind to seek the tiny little spark of life he knew to be inside of Shawnee. For the first time, he used the talents that Travis had taught him as he sent out a thought, "Gwennie?" it was a soft whisper of a thought, hoping not to be too harsh to the tiny little ears forming in the amniotic fluid inside of Shawnee's womb. He could hear a soft, liquid bubble of a response, a whisper seeming to come from many miles away, so faint he had to strain to hear.

"Path? Where are you?" she questioned, wondering how this voice was inside of her head and yet she was not in the *blink* stage, she felt that she was floating in the ocean; a soft and comfortable feeling of shelter and warmth and sustenance and love surrounded her. As tiny as a kidney bean, she moved a stumpy hand in front of her face, looking at the transparency of the skin, the webbing between the fingers. Everything about the being that she was seemed foreign and alien to her, helpless, contained, curled in on herself. And yet she felt good. The pain she had suffered in the *blink* stage after she and Pathogent blazed out of their lives, was gone completely. She was not feeling fear. She felt protected, afloat, and wonderful, as if curled in a dream and happy to have no compulsion to be independent of her environment.

"I've been born, Gwennie," he told her, "as you will soon be as well. You will be delighted when you find out who your parents are. Oh, Gwennie, my dear, we are going to be rewarded with the best life yet, mark my words. Now we know that our energy is limitless and we are strong enough to survive. Do you understand what I'm telling you? That I've been born as a baby and I am the son of Declan and Melody!"

Gwen smiled, listening to the voice so comforting to her, her position drifting against the side of something that was not quite solid, but firm enough to resist her and send her bouncing back slightly to float free again.

"Are you kidding me?" an exuberant and happy male voice chimed in. "Path, is that really YOU? Is Brendan YOU? "

A tiny frown wrinkled the forehead of the toddler and he grunted, then answered the thoughts pouring into his mind, "Travis, please don't let anyone else know. Please let us enjoy a childhood, I'm asking you to remember how important that was to all of you. Give us a new life untainted by reputation or somehow changed by our parents not knowing what to do if they were to find out. You know they'd treat us differently; it would be so strange for them to be raising someone they consider to be an ancestor of theirs. I've tried to think of this from all angles and it really is better if they just think of me as their son, Brendan."

"It's too late," Yellow Feather answered, "I am hearing this, too, and my heart has lifted with joy, my friend, I never dared hope to see you again in this life."

Soon it was obvious that the more talented travelers among the children knew the secret. Path had never learned how to block their thoughts, yet all of them realized how important it was to Pathogent and Gwen that their parents not know. They could relate to this dilemma personally, since it was the same thing they felt about revealing themselves as "travelers" to the camp, for fear that the adults would treat them differently, knowing they were teaching such august company, not just children.

"So, it's only between the five of us," Travis assured Path/Brendan, "you, Gwen, me, Yellow Feather, and Gavin, I don't think any of the other children are quite here yet. We can take them into dreams of others but they can't launch themselves. But if there are, please identify yourself," he said in a general request, then added to

Pathogent, "your secret is safe, my friends, but it does bring me so very much joy to know this."

Gavin inserted his thought, shyly, "And this will finally give me an opportunity to know you. You are a hero to all my newfound friends."

"You knew us quite well back there in Duran, Gavin. Yes, quite intimately. Gwen and I knew that you and Travis had joined us when we were blazing with energy, lending us a much needed boost to defeat Casto's strength. I am glad he wasn't aware of how much magic he was capable of; he was very strong and extremely psychopathic, his mind, no, his entire essence was bent." Brendan was quiet and thoughtful as he sent these messages but still managed to pretend to play as normally as a two-year-old would. What he left unsaid was the fact that Casto, too, could possibly be reborn somewhere and may again be a threat.

"And I don't think that Gwennie is developed enough to retain the significance and understand what we're doing here," Brendan Jacob Donnelly thought, yawning and grinning at Tebethto, his little playmate.

"Be careful with your assessments, smart guy," tiny fetus Gwen warned. "I may be tiny, but I will be out there with you soon enough so you want to be careful what you say," she teased.

"Have you found out yet if Tebethto is a traveler?" Path asked the others, looking into the gray eyes of his playmate and smiling. She was chewing on a leather thong that held a special little medicine bag that hung from her neck, seemingly oblivious to all conversations but the one her parents were having.

"We have communicated with her, and she remembers being in other lives, in other hosts, but so far, none of them has been 'world-renowned', although I would imagine those people were astounding. She is a strong, capable, admirable mind, Path. So, the answer is yes, she's a traveler, we just haven't wanted to push for too much information because we, too, want to allow her to simply be a child again. She's going to be formidable. What else would we expect from the genetics she carries?"

Brendan smiled as he watched his parents and Gwen's "parents-to-be" as they laughed and talked and relaxed with one another. "By the way, has anyone checked little Johnny? Is he a traveler?" He wondered if his mind could hide his concern about Casto's possible "rebirth."

"Yes, Path, we worried about the same thing, little Johnny has been many people in the past, but no evil man like Casto."

"I don't think Casto is going to be reborn here," Travis said, "It seems to me that he would return where he could easily fool people and lead them again. If he even survived what the four of us did to him, he would probably flee as far as possible from our energy."

Brendan turned his attention to the adults, not wanting to consider the possibility that such evil could possibly invade Golden.

"We haven't even thought about a name yet," Shawnee said, replying to a question posed by Declan. "Healthy...that's all I want to think about for now." She smiled as she watched Tebethto and Brendan playing, happy that the three children, which included Brian and Dani Colton's little boy, Johnny Cash Colton, born to the residents of this new village, were happy and thriving and given clean bills of health by their attending physicians.

She laughed, "Every time Gayle plays with "Beth", by the way, since everyone is calling her that, I guess that's her new nickname," she paused, wincing at the fact that even she was calling Tebethto by the Anglicized name, "but, as I was saying about Gayle, she does this sneaky, thorough examination, checking Tebethto over without her even knowing she's being examined. Gayle has got to be one of the most skilled pediatricians I've ever witnessed. She missed her calling by not going into that field. Beth just sits and smiles and plays with Gayle, moving her arms and legs and giggling when Gayle puts pressure here and there. If there were thousands of pediatricians around, as in the times before, I would still choose Gayle for my children."

Melody smiled and agreed, nodding, "I would trust Gayle with any child of mine, for sure. But it's really no different than Lincoln. Don't you feel that every time he's talking with you, he's watching everything about your expressions and gestures, making certain everything's working okay? I think we really lucked out having so many skills among us, including among the "children", who, by the way, are growing fast and some of whom can no longer be considered children...I think there will be several more doctors in the village soon if Lincoln's little acolytes are any indication."

"Speaking of which," Conner interjected at that opportune time, "I keep half expecting another announcement at campfire. I wonder when Gavin and Laurel are going to make it official? Do they think we can't see they're in love? The whole village is happy for them and I have to smile when they would orchestrate moments to be alone, making it look accidental and completely innocent. At least now they publically spend time together, more comfortable with that relationship."

"Husband," Shawnee chastised, "it is not the village's business what they do. They may not want marriage yet and it's not up to us to begin insisting on 'ceremony' where some don't want it."

Conner smiled and caught the stern look in her eyes, yet that look softened when he declared, in front of his friends, "I did. I wanted the whole world to know that I was lucky enough to win you, to have you accept me as your own."

"Wait there just one moment, boyo, aren't I the one branded the incurable romantic around here?" Declan teased. "No, seriously," he continued, taking Melody's hand, "I know what you mean about that, my friend. However, we don't want to begin making others adhere to our own personal beliefs and customs, remember, that greatly contributed to the mess that this country became. They can make their own vows and commitments, whatever that may be, y'know?"

"The village has already voted that others would be free to live the life they saw fit to live, unless that life threatened or affected adversely the lives around them. I would never suggest that anyone should marry. I was simply stating that Gavin and Laurel are being so coy about their relationship. No, it doesn't bother me, it's actually quite charming!" Conner amended.

"And romantic," Melody agreed, "Gavin treats Laurel like she is a treasure that he finds himself unworthy of and he wants to be the best man for her, in her eyes as well as the eyes of the village. He is proving to be such an asset to us all. I love working with him, his energy is endless."

"And such a handsome boy...what a fine form," Shawnee observed.

At Conner's arched brow, she laughed and added, "The fact that my heart is taken is no reason for my eyes not to admire and witness beauty where it exists, husband!" She took a bit of frosting on the tip of her finger and put it on Constance's nose, and smiled.

Melody smiled and agreed. "Yes, I am certain that there are many young girls and older women, as well, who agree that our Laurel is getting a keeper."

"Gavin, can you hear them talking about you?" Brendan asked, inside his head, just curious if this "talent'" allowed them to be passive witness to things he was witnessing.

"I'm not fully witnessing your surroundings, though I could. I didn't want to intrude. Yellow Feather did that when I was in Hades, but I wouldn't like to unless invited, so...no, I'm not. Maybe I don't want to know..." Gavin answered.

"No, lad, it's all good, they are talking about what an asset you are since you've come to Golden. I just wanted you to know how welcome you really are and how you've been worth every effort put forth to bring you here," Brendan told him.

He could feel Gavin take a deep breath and knew that it had been weighing heavy on his mind that three of Golden's original founders were sacrificed for his freedom. "I want you to know that this comes from my heart, Gavin, and Gwen's as well. You were and are a part of us now and you were worth all risk. You gave us an opportunity to rise up as a community and show courage, faith, and love that had not been tested up to that point. You must never allow yourself to feel anything but the love we freely give you, from our hearts. You are a part of Golden now. There is no 'before and after'. You are here because we all wanted you to be here. I am certain that Lily would agree, if she could. You gave her death meaning and purpose. Nothing more could be asked of a soldier's sacrifice."

He could feel the tears Gavin was holding in his heart and almost heard the sigh of relief. It would be so very hard for the three mind travelers to treat Brendan Jacob Donnelly like a small child but they had all pledged to, knowing that they would still be able to communicate like this with one another and that was an additional plus of having Pathogent's calm and considered advice and guidance again. They knew that they would need to consider the little boy simply Brendan, laying aside the name "Pathogent." Tonight at the campfire, they would celebrate as they would, the birthday party of any beloved two-year-old child and they would all keep the secret that they knew Conner and Shawnee held.

Yellow Feather added one last comment before leaving Pathogent's and Gwen's minds. "I am so filled with thanks to know that I will have you both back in my life again, my friends. I know the name I will be suggesting to Shawnee to consider for you, Gwen, my dear friend. She and I always talk to one another in our native Algonquian tongue to keep it in our minds. I think she might like my thoughts on this."

Brendan smiled as he felt his mind freed of their communication, knowing that they would leave him to his privacy. He retained the link to Gwen but realized that she was sleeping, which was something she would be doing a lot of in the months to come. Inside his mind he smiled at the thought of his precious fey angel curled in her slumber. He turned his attention back to Tebethto and they played with blocks, piling them to knock them down over and over. When his father, Declan joined them on the floor to play with them, Brendan gave him his cute wrinkled nose grin, getting a gentle caress on the head in return.

*

Gavin, who had managed to skillfully hold Laurel off, telling her time and again that, although he was not religious, he respected her too much to take her virginity lightly and wanted to pledge special vows to her before they consummated their relationship. There were times, though, that it was so much harder on him than it was for her, although he never let her know that it was. He was becoming used to cold showers. He could see their wedding night play out in his mind and his imagination was vivid as he planned romantic things to make it special and memorable for her.

He did not want their first time together to be sordid or guilt-ridden. He wanted it to be a storybook moment for them both and while she thought it charming and lovely, she had memories of her other lives and loves, and realized that it was often made into too much more than it should be. At least that was how she saw it, the glorification of virginity and the losing of it were nothing more than romanticizing something to make it less painful and awkward. She was far more pragmatic than he lately, not really caring if anyone thought her too young or if they disapproved of the two of them becoming romantically singular with one another so soon after his arrival at Golden.

He was surprised by this, since she had been a poet in so many of her lives, wondering now if past hurts had driven the romantic in her to rethink some of her poetic notions and dreams. When she told him the names of the poets she had been, a few of the most romantic in history, he was actually rather surprised. Had hurts dealt by the hands of others changed her? To add to her frustration, this made him even more determined to idealize their love, to give her a memory that would erase all others. A memory worthy of eternal verse and breathtaking words.

She sat watching him as he was working with Coyote to build the stables for the horses. He was stripped to the waist and covered in a sheen of sweat, as they measured boards, sawed them into the proper lengths and worked together with David and Randy to hammer the boards to the four by four framework they had made. It was impossible not to notice the perfect body of her tall, lean beloved, his muscles developed by hard work long before coming to Golden, shoulders broad, arms well-defined and muscular, and his stomach so flat with obvious musculature of the pectorals her eyes explored that part of him, so sensual and compelling to her that it literally drove her to have to look away, her breath quickening.

She loved the way his shoulder bones stood out as he lifted, the way the cords in his neck sometimes stood out if he strained them, his firm biceps, his forearms and those big hands that held hers so gently as if afraid to break them. His dark hair hanging in wet curls, darkened by the moisture, fell forward into his clear and compelling green eyes. He saw her watching and smiled over at her, a look of apology for becoming so involved in his work that he had nearly forgotten she was there.

She seethed through her teeth at the beauty of the love in the look he gave her, in his genuine and engaging smile, and made herself look at the horses, at Golden's Lily, the beautiful palomino that Coyote had captured and her black colt, that the children had finally decided to name Golden's Galaxy when Coyote let them vote for the favorite name at campfire.

Her mind could not stay long on the distraction. She knew what the other girls and women thought of Gavin, that he was a fine-looking, brawny, powerful young man. What she thought of him was making it impossible to sleep at night. He took her breath away.

Since she had met him, her mind had completely lost its skill to express her feelings poetically and she could not understand how, when she finally found the love of her life, the love of ALL her lives, her muse would desert her so completely. She had attended Conner's poetry classes, hoping to rekindle the poetic fire, trying to get the feelings back that once inspired her to write of forbidden romance, the misery and pain of unrequited love, any number of human emotions and experiences. Even the simply rhythms of writing poetry had completely deserted her.

Conner told her not to worry, that this was only temporary and she would soon be stunning them all again with her talent. She was not so certain. It felt like her muse had deserted her. What she was left with was something so feral and almost shameful that she struggled to understand what was wrong with her. It struck her that, if she couldn't have him soon, this man she wanted more than she'd ever wanted anything, it would completely drive her mad.

He laughed when she tried to tell him these things, blushed at her flirtatiousness and forwardness. He then nodded understandingly, telling her that he wanted her, too, and that he lived for the day they could be together. However, she could not believe that he really did understand, since he was able to work with the others, concentrate on jobs, continue to ply his skills and build friendships, while she felt herself withdrawing into a state of selfish introspection, a one-track mind that made her shake her head and want to hide beneath her bed. She wasn't being a very good friend to her friends anymore. She wasn't being a very good student anymore. She was becoming obsessed, and it wasn't healthy. For her, tomorrow wasn't soon enough. She was like a mooning, lovesick calf and she was embarrassing herself in her preoccupation with her dreams.

As she watched him, she realized that she was going to have to seduce him to save herself, to restore herself. Seduce him or convince him that they could not just talk about a "future honeymoon." It had to be soon. It had to be now. Suddenly it came to her what she could do and she signaled to him that she had something to do, then she ran to find her friends, Christine, Crystal and Cassie, especially, but anyone she could find who would help her and who would love her enough to keep her secret until the time was right to share it and spread the news.

*

Brendan's party was a delightful time for all the children. There was a piñata that Melody had carefully crafted to look like Bella, the sweet camp beagle, one of Brendan's favorite companions. The children had so much fun trying to break it, blindfolded, as Declan made it swoop and soar out of reach time and again. Finally, it was broken by Toby, who was so proud to have been the one to send handmade candies and small toys flying to be gathered by the smallest children.

Cupcakes were enjoyed by all and everyone sang Happy Birthday to Declan and Melody's adorable little boy who was getting sleepy and, though grinning at his well-wishers, cuddled into Declan's shoulder.

Everyone was sitting around the campfire enjoying the night. While he was sitting among his friends, Travis, Yellow Feather, Coyote, Cody, and others, Gavin was nonetheless used to having Laurel by his side and, though he had looked for her before campfire, he had been unable to find her. He didn't think too much about it, since he knew that she had planned to help Melody before and after the birthday party and that was probably what she was doing. He kept expecting her to arrive, noting that friends of hers had slowly filtered their way into the festivities, appearing and disappearing like wraiths. The night was misty, which added even more of an air of mystery and surprise as the faces changed around him, people wandering in and out and around, greeting friends, changing seats, trying to talk to those they wanted to visit with. This was normal, but tonight, with the mist and the way people could move a few steps from the fire and completely disappear made it special and yet, strange, like magic was afoot.

Moving on to other business, there were progress reports from all work teams, gardeners, and all of Golden's business was discussed, every voice needing consideration heard. Shawnee stood and gave her good news to everyone in the encampment, raising more cheers and happy wishes to both her and Conner. Adults fondly played with Brian's and Dani's little son, Johnny, the youngest citizen of Golden, and applauded as he took toddling steps to entertain them and moved from lap to lap happily.

When Conner asked if there was any further business, there was a long pause of silence, then Laurel appeared at the far edge of the campfire, walking out of the mist like a ghost, while someone played a haunting tune on a flute off in the distance. When he saw her, Gavin almost gasped aloud, she was dressed like a creature of magic, an element of the forest: barefoot, with a gauzy white shift of a dress hugging her young, slim figure, her blonde hair curled and dressed with a crown of flowers and ribbons. She was always beautiful, but tonight she was a vision that would inspire his dreams for years to come. She seemed to glow in the firelight. She walked slowly toward the center of the group's clearing and turned to Conner and said, "I have some business I'd like to bring before the village..." she said, softly.

He smiled and nodded, in on this surprise, and she told those gathered, "Lately I've been unable to concentrate enough to write poetry. You are all aware that I've never suffered this affliction before, but, you see," she paused and exhaled a long, thoughtful breath, then continued, "I'm blinded by love right now and simply can't concentrate on anything else." Her eyes locked on Gavin's as she talked, "So, I need instead to perform a poem that I wrote in another life, a poem that outlived me and grew into legend and became so much greater than the sum of my lives; it became a standard for expressing undying love." She moved away from him now, addressing the others, "Tonight I want to recite this poem for the man who makes me feel this poem in my veins like no man has before, I hear it singing in my heart, it pours from every cell of my body..."

She turned to Gavin who was across the clearing from her and began, stepping closer one slow step at a time, as she recited, "**How do I love thee? Let me count the ways. I** love thee to the depth and breadth and height my soul can reach, when feeling out of sight for the ends of being and ideal grace. I love thee to the level of every day's most quiet need, by sun and candle-light."

She smiled as his eyes locked now on hers, he narrowed them and gave her his focused attention, and that look drew her nearer. "I love thee freely, as men strive for right. I love thee purely, as they turn from praise. I love thee with the passion put to use in my old griefs, and with my childhood's faith. I love thee with a love I seemed to lose with my lost saints. I love thee with the breath, smiles, tears, of all my life; and, if God choose, I shall but love thee better ..." she stood close enough to touch now.

He stood and put a finger to her lips to stop her from saying the words, "after death," unable to even bear to think of that concept. He put his hands on her upper arms and looked deep into her eyes, tears shimmering in his eyes from the beauty and spontaneous drama of the moment. She leaned forward and whispered, "Tonight, my love?" He gave her a slow, half-smile, took a deep breath, then looked over her shoulder to Collin and said, with a decided and firm nod to her, "We have some other business tonight."

The entire group of people around the fire had been nearly all holding their collective breaths at Laurel's performance and her recital of a poem familiar to so many of them, and they smiled when they realized where this was leading. She gave the poem a life they rarely saw in the performance of its beauty. Of all the performances they had witnessed at the campfire, she had made this one the most romantic, sensual, and beautiful. Laurel had given them a glimpse into the heart of a poet, of what brings such beauty to lips and page.

Conner's smile was broad and bright and he said, "Well, you know we have more than a few witnesses if what you have in mind is what I think it is? Gavin?"

Gavin gave a little nod, tearing his eyes from hers so briefly, then into Laurel's eyes and raising an eyebrow, "A handfasting?"

She smiled and nodded, holding up the long strip of white cloth she held in her hand. "Our minds are finally in sync."

And there, with the entire village of Golden as witness to their union, Gavin and Laurel were brought forward into the center of the campfire's clearing. Gavin asked Travis and Yellow Feather to stand with him and Yellow Feather made a small cut on their wrists with his blade. Travis then wrapped their arms together as they clasped hands, their blood mingling as the cuts overlapped. Cassie and Crystal moved forward with flowers for Laurel. And the two central figures each pledged their intent and purpose with words heard only by one another and those standing closest to them. The ceremony brief, but beautiful, joined them as one and they moved close to kiss and seal their commitment.

"We have another surprise for you, Gavin," Crystal announced, barely able to contain her excitement, urging him to follow as Laurel pulled him along with her. And holding lanterns, singing and laughing, the children escorted them along the trail as the group led him through the forest to one of the cabins, a special cabin, the tiny one room cabin set apart from the others, one that once belonged to Pathogent and Gwen.

Declan, holding his little boy, was there waiting for them as if he were waiting to bless the union, which was his purpose, "This special cabin contained a love that was so powerful and wonderful it was an inspiration to us all," Declan, brought in on the surprise by Laurel and her friends, announced. "We hope that you will both continue a tradition that began within its walls, a tradition of a love and devotion that proved to be eternal. A love so pure and wonderful that it will last forever, whether on earth or in the stars somewhere." He choked up a little at the end of his speech as thoughts of his long lost friends filled his heart. Brendan seemed concerned by his father's tears and Declan smiled to reassure him that he was okay. He stepped forward and moved Brendan to his other arm, then opened the door to show Gavin the interior of the cabin where a warm and inviting fire was burning, flower petals made a pathway toward a bed that was also covered with more petals and sweet-smelling herbs on the soft, downy, snow white comforter.

Gavin smiled and bent to lift Laurel into his arms and stepped across the threshold with his bride.

"And now we leave you, my friends, may your love continue to grow..." Travis told them, smiling as he pulled the door shut for them.

Little Brendan, in his father's arms, beamed and enjoyed the delight on all the familiar faces as he looked around the group surrounding the cabin. It was wonderful when the entire village was involved in such things as the marriages and celebrations of birth. Today was a three-fold celebration. It was entirely inspirational that Golden was so filled with love and joy. It thrilled him that the cabin, so loved by him and his Gwen, would be a honeymoon cabin for such a wonderful pair of young people. He sent a little message to Gwen, cradled in the womb of Shawnee, "Oh, I wish you could see this, sidhe." As they had moved past him, Gavin's eyes had caught Brendan's and Gavin winked at him and mouthed the words, "Thank you."

Inside the cabin, with Laurel still in his arms, Gavin looked at her and smiled, mischief in his sparkling eyes. "I take this to mean that you no longer wish to be a virgin, my incredibly beautiful lady?"

She smiled a wicked and knowing smile, tossing her curls as she dipped her head in a nod, "I felt you needed a little push, Gavin, and, I did it to save my sanity, because being close to you without being with you was driving me completely insane."

"Well, we can't have that, can we?" he said, putting her carefully and gently on her feet. He cupped her face in his hands and, with lips close to hers whispered, "I've never wanted anything more than I wanted this moment, Laurel. I want you to know that I appreciate your letting me know that you wanted this, too. I know that I seemed to be putting it off..."

"That's the understatement of the year!" she breathed, almost laughing.

"...But," he continued, "I wanted the moment to be perfect, and I wanted to be worthy of the moment," he admitted. He looked around the beautiful cabin. "If you hadn't done this, if you hadn't moved this forward, I might never have felt worthy, because I treasure you more than you'll ever know and I could never conceive that I might be worthy of having you as my bride."

Poetry returned in a surge of emotion as she told him, "You make my heart raise its voice like no earthly sound that was ever born or conceived, I feel my love for you in deeper depths than I knew existed in the confines of the human soul. You are manna to me, my ambrosia, the food of the gods, and I but a starving and unrepentant beggar at your feet. If I could give you more than the pledge of my life, my very being, I would give it without hesitation or consideration. I am yours and I want, more than I've ever wanted, to give myself freely and without hesitation into your hands and heart."

"And you have me, Laurel, I am yours to do with as you wish," he smiled, "and, oh, how I hope you have endless wishes." He raised his face to meet her gaze, his eyes full of mischief and promise, and smiled, then covered her lips with his to kiss her deeply, moving her backward slowly, toward the bed.

*

She awoke in the middle of the night, alone in the bed. Almost too sated and exhausted to want to move, she forced herself to rise to look for Gavin, and noted that the door to the cabin was wide open as if to let her know that he could be found outside. She threw on her shift and, wrapped in a shawl that had belonged to Gwen, stepped carefully to the door, looking for him. She found him lying on a small patch of grass to the side of the cabin, near the trail to the other cabins. He was staring up at the stars. He was dressed only in his pants, his hands clasped behind his head. As she approached, she said, softly, "Gavin?"

He turned onto one elbow and smiled up at her. "Come here, Laurel, lie a while beside me, the stars are a spectacle tonight of all nights, and tonight is the most beautiful night of my life, after all. I want to remember and cherish every single moment. I am as content as a cat right now, I feel like something pent up and denied for years has finally been emotionally sated. I am the veritable picture of contentedness, a Cheshire cat purring."

"I'm sorry I fell asleep on you, Gavin, you...well, you exhausted me," she blushed and grinned. She knelt beside him and he helped her put the blanket under her, then wrapped it around her to keep her warm, pulling her close so that her head was on his shoulder as he lay back and relaxed.

"Before I am much older," he told her, "I want to learn the name and placement of all the constellations so I can teach them to our children. My brother knew them all and he would point them out to me and tell me stories of their namesakes."

"I wish I could have known your brother, "Laurel told him, changing the subject away from the talk of offspring.

"I wish you could have, too. He would have liked you very much. He was both brother and father to me and I loved him more than I loved anyone ever, before you. He always wanted what was best for me and he would have been able to sense that you are what's best for me." He kissed her forehead. "Laurel, I used to look up at the stars back there in Hades and dream of a better life. Now I have that better life and it's more than I ever dreamed possible. I have the world right here in my arms. When I was there, I saw no future, then I met you and it was all I ever wanted, a future with you here in Golden. I never really dreamed I'd ever get this lucky."

She stared up into the night sky and let her mind drift, enjoying the closeness and the warmth of the man she could now call husband. Her mind went over the pleasures of the last few hours and she realized that she, too, felt more fortunate than she'd ever been in any of her lives, more enriched, more satisfied, more secure, more content.

"Gavin, have you ever been able to remember some of the lives you enjoyed before this one?" she asked softly and carefully, knowing that Travis and Yellow Feather had probably asked this of him so often, he might be tired of the question. He had always seemed to evade it even though everyone could sense that he might have more talent and power than any of them.

"I was a farmer once, in Africa, and I narrowly escaped being taken down by a big male lion that took my neighbor's goat instead...only two feet away from me at most. I could feel his heat as he flew past me in his killing leap," he pondered, remembering.

"I'll bet you can still remember the feeling of relief," she sighed, sympathizing.

"No, not really. No time to gloat over being spared, the lioness took me out less than twenty seconds later," he told her. He waited for her reaction and gave her a small smile.

"You're kidding me, right?" she laughed.

"No, I'm not, but it is a funny story to tell in retrospect. Everyone always thinks I made it up and am joking but it really did happen that way. The fact that it was a close call barely had time to register in my brain when her teeth clamped down on my neck. Travis had the exact same reaction you did but it really was true. One second I was a happy village farmer, the next I was lining the bellies of a lioness and her cubs, I guess." He gave her a sidelong glance and his ironic grin, "I know what you're really asking, if there was anyone famous that I can remember having been. I have thought of a few but I didn't want you to be disappointed that I wasn't really someone heroic or political or anything. In one of the more recent lives, I wrote a lot of morbid and twisted, strange tales and I guess that I suffered morose depressions in that life, and that had to have been something ingested or caused by an outside source because it's the only incarnation where I ever suffered morose thoughts, or at least that is what has been written about me, supposedly by those who knew me, can you guess?"

"You were Poe?" she asked, giving him the first thought that came to mind.

"Very good!" he said, smiling, "I don't really think I was as withdrawn and depressed as they try to make it seem. I know I could WRITE about it, but it was just that, me writing about a feeling I knew others felt. I know that I'm nothing like that now, I've never felt clearer and happier and, in this life. I've never really been what you might call 'depressed', even when I was experiencing hopelessness in Hades, I always felt that if I just kept my morale high, good things could come." He paused and thought about the next disclosure, "How do the past life memories come to you, Laurel, do they come piecemeal, little bits at a time, like dreams? That's what is happening with me since I came to Golden. I never really gave it a thought until you and the other kids here in Golden opened my mind to it. Now things are not just coming through; I remember details I could never had gotten any other way but having lived those lives. And, I know that I was considered a strong and mysterious magician in one of my lives, but time-traveling lent me that mystique. I allowed people to think that I was magic by borrowing things from the future that they could not relate to and using science to solve problems, science they had no access to, so they thought me a powerful wizard."

"So you WERE Merlin!" she stated in an "I thought so" tone of voice.

"I don't know. That wasn't really my name at the time, Laurel, it really never was but I think I was the person who CAME to be referred to by that name, perhaps. I was actually given the name Emrys only because I was living at the time in Wales and it was the local form of my name, Ambrose. We lived in Britannia for most of my young life but I was actually born in Rome. I had the same name as my uncle, Ambrosius Aurelianus, a Roman military man in charge of a fort in Britannia. You do know what the name Ambrose means, don't you?" he asked, his face so animated as he talked, she could almost see those ancestors in the set of his jaw, the arch of his brow, the mystery burning in his eyes.

She lifted herself onto one elbow to take him in better. She loved the way the starlight played off the planes of his face and, looking into his eyes, she could tell when he was being serious, or when he was trying to humor her. "No, tell me..." she requested, having never really known that the two names were in any way connected. "I seriously didn't know that 'Ambrose' and 'Emrys' were one and the same."

"Yes, Emrys is Welsh for Ambrose, and Ambrose means 'the immortal'." He tilted his head to let that sink in.

He continued as she took a deep breath at the implications of a meaning, "It's funny that I didn't really remember this until the day I linked with Travis in Gwen and Path and began to remember some of my past lives. Honestly, Laurel, I think at that time, when I was Emrys, my entire family were what we now call 'travelers'; we even traveled together at times. Physically, I walked and traveled the width and breadth of that country, England, Scotland, and Ireland as well. Mentally, I had no boundaries, nor time constraints. And, no, before you ask it, I never knew a British tribal leader named Arthur and there was no sword in the stone in my story," he told her. "Although, I was pretty skilled at swordplay, one had no choice in my family, it was like learning to breathe! It was just a real life on a very big island being invaded by Saxons and my family was drawn into those tribal altercations due to their ranks and positions."

"It would make for a very interesting perspective on that story. Perhaps we should write it all down the way you remember it," she said, smiling. Reaching to take a lock of his hair in her fingers, she moved it back from his forehead, loving the way it curled around her finger. "Oh, Gavin, don't take this the wrong way because many men don't know how to handle this word, but you really are extremely beautiful." She let her finger trail down from his brow, down over his noble nose.

He grinned, "I really don't mind being called beautiful, I'm especially happy to know that you think so, my love. After all, aren't we actually agender?" This caused him to smile as he went on to reveal another memory to her, "In another life, I was a poet," he smiled, knowing this disclosure would intrigue her, "and preferred my words be called beautiful, not my countenance...and I used those words wisely, to seduce, to embrace, to sing the body electric, but, no, I was not Whitman."

"Please don't tell me you were Byron or Shelley...they were such cads," she moaned.

"Of course not, more exotic than that, my love...it was one of my lives as a woman, then here's the hint, as her, I would still have fallen for your beauty and your current, irresistible, desirable form, but more so for your strength and moral fiber." He ran a finger slowly up her arm as he talked.

Laurel smiled slowly and purred, "Oh, I know it now, you were Sappho." She paused, then her eyes widened, "You were Sappho?" Now she realized from where the tremendous amount of skill, patience, uncanny insight, and tenderness had come in his lovemaking and why he was so sensually passionate. She whispered a little segment of Sappho's poetry that she had once memorized and now seemed so appropriate, "Smiling, with your immortal countenance, asked what hurt me, and for what now I cried out..." Memories of earlier in the night came back to her, words whispered against her skin, a touch so magical and soft it felt like silk instead of the hands of a hard-working man, tears she had shed that had not been from pain or sadness but from a great swelling of love and emotion. She closed her eyes and took a deep breath and smiled contentedly at that memory.

"There's that word again, 'immortal', I think we always knew it, then as now, the word for what we really are, Laurel," he observed.

"Why couldn't we be like Gwen and Path, living this over and over again? Think of all the centuries we could have been lovers..." she complained.

"I'm sure that even they had a starting point," he said, raising up onto his elbows, then leaning toward her to kiss her. "This is our starting point. Now we can look for one another for many lives to come. Besides, this has been so intense for me, neither of us had a pre-conceived idea about the other and we're breaking ground. I love you more with each revelation. Think about those future lives we'll lead, knowing what we know about one another in this one."

"I just want to appreciate every moment of this one first. Like your acute and uncanny understanding of anatomy to begin with," she told him. "Come, let's take this back inside, we don't want one of the neighbors to trip over us while we're doing where this is leading..." she urged him, her breath quickening at the strength and urgency in his kiss. He quickly rose to his feet and helped her up, then playfully bent to pick her up and throw her over his shoulder, "Tarzan take his woman to Tarzan's bed, make many little Tarzans."

"You're insatiable!" she laughed with delight as he carried her back to the cabin. While she had spent the last two years pouring her heart and past out to him, he was beginning to really open up to her and put the unpleasantness of Hades behind him. Now he was not only talking about the future, but about future lives together and she was so happy in this moment that she never wanted this night to end. She realized that she had pushed this night upon him. She hoped he would never begin to regret it. She knew deep in her heart that she would never feel regret for taking the lead.

"Don't be silly," he assured, reading her mind, "you have no idea what a gift you've given me."

*

Little Brendan talked to her often over the months she was gestating, letting her know about changes in the village, keeping her up with the growth and expansion. He told her what a wonderful job the younger people were doing of working together, keeping dissension to a minimum by compromise and making improvements constantly to their community's way of life. Soon there would be a power grid, the technicians among them were working toward that end. Colorado was beautiful and the mountains were scenic and breathtaking, but it was cold in the winter and there was no need to suffer the fact when modern conveniences still lived in the memories of many present.

He talked to her often, having learned how to block out even Travis and Gavin, or so he had come to believe, because they never interfered or commented during his conversations with the tiny fetus. He told her that the young ones who knew their secret had promised them a childhood together.

"Think about it, Gwennie, a whole lifetime together, from the very start! It's even better than Harmony and Jacob, since then we were 'borrowing' the bodies and this time it's really us from the start. This is something new for us, birth. It didn't really hurt but I have to tell you, I was contented with being in the womb and really had no way of knowing what it was all about. You have the advantage of knowing where you are heading when the birth begins. I thought I was emerging onto a new plane of existence or something, nothing prepared me for 'birth', that was a strange experience, to be sure. When I looked up and saw familiar faces in the room with me when I was free of the womb, I was overwhelmed. There were Lincoln, Stephanie, Gayle, and, of course, Declan, and Melody. It was a delightful and unbelievable surprise, I have to tell you."

"Oh, Path, now that you've told me, I get to experience something I have assisted in so very many times but from one of the two perspectives denied me. Wouldn't it be wonderful if I get to grow to experience the other as well?"

Brendan laughed aloud, then sent a thought to her, careful that when Melody looked at him to see what he was laughing at, he crawled toward Bella, to make it look like she had done something to amuse him. "Let's just take this one day at a time, my love, and enjoy every single moment."

"So Matchsquathi Tebethto will be my older sister? I wonder if she is a traveler, as well."

"If so, she keeps it very close to the vest, or perhaps, like most of the children here in Golden, she hasn't learned to communicate with the mind and Travis taught only a few. She's a sweet, sweet child, you will really love her, so pleasant, so happy. You have to realize, you'll be so lucky to have the parents you'll have. You will get to witness Conner and Shawnee from another perspective as well."

"How much longer do we have before my due date?" she asked, growing groggy and ready to sleep. A tiny yawn escaped her.

"Three months!" Brendan told her, "And, though that seems like a long time, the past six have gone very quickly, considering. Don't you think? Gwen?" He smiled because he knew that she was, once again, sleeping. The windows of opportunity to speak with her had been very few and far between, she slept so much, using all her energy growing and developing into a viable human infant.

There was a knock at the door and Melody answered to invite Dave inside. Brendan jumped to his feet and toddled as quickly as his diapered rump would allow to wrap his arms around Dave's legs. Dave had made Brendan smile and gurgle since he was in the cradle and Melody and Declan loved the way that Dave lit up with joy over how much Brendan responded to him. He leaned his cane against the wall, bent and lifted the little boy high into the air, "So, partner, how are you today? Now, don't go spitting up on me like you did the last time!"

Melody laughed, "That wasn't really spit-up, he is teething and he drools a lot! Be thankful you didn't smell like sour milk that day, if it had been spit-up, you would really have regretted tossing him in the air."

"He loves it! I'm not one to deny him something he loves this much, a little spittle doesn't hurt anything." Dave tossed Brendan a few inches into the air, rewarded with a deep belly laugh that brought a smile to Dave's face. "That laugh of his, it's just what his life is all about, joy and more joy! I could never have a bad day with this little munchkin around."

Melody smiled, agreeing, then realized that Dave seemed to be looking for someone else, "If you're looking for Declan, Dave, he told me to tell you to meet him down by the new horse barn; he left about twenty minutes ago."

"Oh, okay, Mel, thanks!" Dave nodded, putting Brendan back down on his feet and patting his head. "Can hardly wait for the day this littl'un can follow along with us."

"Oh, I hope that day is a long way off, I want to appreciate every moment of his life, I want the passing of time to slow down so I can appreciate every single stage of his childhood!" Melody said.

"Me too," Brendan thought, "me too, um, Mom." THAT would take some getting used to!

*

Gavin was in deep, REM sleep, a small smile crossing his lips as he walked in his dreamscape. He was in a forest similar to those that surrounded any of them as they went deeper into the Rockies, a part of the forest that seemed familiar, as if perhaps he and Conner or Yellow Feather had walked here on one of their excursions. There were mostly conifers, the bristlecone, lodgepole, and ponderosa pines he had learned to identify in Shawnee's and Mary's botany classes. There were blue spruce, juniper and aspen mixed in this misty forest. It was early morning and the world was just awakening. He could hear the birds beginning to voice up for their morning song, beginning with little chirps and twitters that would soon enough build into the symphony he always enjoyed on his morning walks in the woods. He heard someone softly, faintly, but distinctly calling his name so he hurried toward the sound.

The smile grew broader as he approached a beautiful, secluded glen in the forest to see that Laurel was lying on the soft grass of a clearing in a soft, silky, billowing gown that spread out with many yards of cloth stretching out around her. It caught and fluttered in the wind and actually seemed to be lifting her beautiful body. She looked like a painting by one of the Pre-Raphaelite brotherhood, like a study by John Everett Millais or William Holman Hunt. His spirit soared at her glowing beauty. He stopped to take in her beauty, but faltered as he realized that she was calling out to him in obvious pain and fear.

As he came nearer, running quickly now because she needed him, he was shocked to see her swollen belly as he went to his knees beside her. She was hugely pregnant and obviously in labor, sweat glistening on her face and her teeth clenched in reaction to the contractions moving her body. He took her hand to assure here that he was there for her and, when her eyes met his, he saw the fear and doubt in them. He had to help her, he had to be there for her, he could not bear the doubt in her eyes.

Where was Lincoln? Where indeed was Gayle who always kept such a sharp eye on such things and would never have let Laurel wander away like this, like a wounded animal seeking healing and shelter in the depth of the forest. He looked around him, hoping to see someone, anyone from the camp who could help him or run to get others. He wanted to cry for help but he didn't want Laurel to see that he was afraid for her.

Strange concerns went through his mind, like would the scent of her blood and other fluids draw predators? Would this be a safe place to give birth? Should he not carry her back to the safety of the cabins and the camp? Could he be enough to defend his wife and baby bare-handed if predators approached? He panicked, wondering what he could do but realized that it was far too late for him to move her, the contractions were too close, she was in too much pain.

He had never witnessed birth but had read enough about them to think that he would be able to know what to do. There would be the crowning, then the birth. He would need to sever the umbilical cord after tying it in two places...he began removing a lace from one of his boots, he would cut that into two pieces. Even in the dream, he had his knife. That was good, he thought, as he laid it down near him, on Laurel's gown. He would have to make certain that the cord was not around the baby's neck as it was born. His mind went through everything he had ever read, worrying that he would miss something really important, something essential to the process, then tried to relax as he remembered something that Lincoln had said, "Women have been birthing babies since the dawn of human life on earth, most of it just comes naturally if you learn to relax and not stress about it."

He found it strange that neither he nor Laurel said a word at all. She had only called his name and stopped making any sound once he came to her.

He watched her closely, took off his shirt and put it under her head for a pillow, using the sleeve to wipe her brow. The contractions were so close, it seemed they came in one wave after another with almost no time in between. Could they do this? Could they give their baby a life? He determined not to fail Laurel. He would do everything needed, including fight off predators, if necessary. His conviction built along with her need, her strength needed to push this life into being. She grabbed his arm and pushed, her nails digging into his forearm. He looked between her legs and could see that the baby was coming fast so he moved down to position himself better.

The tiny boy slipped from her after the head and shoulders were pushed out and he caught the little body in one hand, just in time. Having cut off a small piece of Laurel's gown, he then wiped the face with the soft cloth, clearing the mouth and tilting the baby down over his hand, waiting for a sound and was rewarded with a lusty wail.

The baby was still covered with filmy white stuff, he couldn't remember what it was called, was it vermix, something that sounded like it was wormy and gross, while it actually was not either of those things. The baby's skin was a strange dark shade of nearly a blue color but it didn't frighten him; he knew this was normal, somehow. Smiling and satisfied that the impossibly tiny infant was breathing on his own, he put the baby on Laurel's stomach and worked on the umbilical cord, tying it in two places nearly midway between Laurel and the child. After it stopped pulsing, he cut it in between the ties and placed the baby where Laurel could reach to cuddle and clean the baby further as he helped her with the afterbirth. He cut off another portion of Laurel's gown to clean her and then went to her side to share in the bonding process that he wanted to share with her.

She smiled, having wrapped the baby in his shirt for warmth and opened the flap of shirt covering his face to give Gavin a closer look at their newborn son.

There he was, his face and head naked of any hair, including eyebrows and he looked up and said, clearly and distinctly in his southern accent, "I swore I'd git you, boy, and I meant it. I am so going to enjoy turning you on a spit!"

Gavin sat bolt upright in bed, covered in sweat and suppressing a scream as he realized just in time that Laurel was sleeping peacefully in bed beside him and she was his normal newlywed wife, not a silent pregnant woman.

What he had seen in his nightmare was enough to make him cry out, internally, his eyes wide with terror.

"It was just a dream, Gavin, just a dream," Travis' voice assured him.

"You were there?" Gavin asked, inside his mind.

"I felt it, I felt the entire thing, like your mind was reaching out to me, as if you needed me. I almost jumped out of bed to run into the forest. At first I thought you needed me there but when your message was that Laurel was giving birth, well, I was awake enough to realize that Laurel isn't even pregnant. Then it came to me, as I entered your mind, that you were dreaming. Damn, Gavin, that was a hell of a nightmare!" Travis mind-whispered.

"No, seriously, is this a possibility?" Gavin wanted to know, shaken to the core.

"I thought about this when we found out that Path and Gwen were coming back to us but I really thought that there would be no reason for Casto to be born here. He has no connection to this place. He would want someplace where he could build a force against us. There's nothing for him here..."

"Except revenge," Gavin finished, ice water running through his veins. "We, Laurel and I, can't have a baby, we can't take that chance!" He swore, looking down at his beautiful new bride. "How am I going to tell her that?

How am I going to convince her that we can't take that chance?"

"Gavin, it was just a dream, chances are your baby will be ..."

"Chances are the dream was a premonition. Our lives here in Golden can hardly be called normal, Travis, we are a village made up of time-travelers and the descendants of two very specific time-travelers who are being reborn TO four of their descendants. How 'normal' is that? However wonderful it is to us that this happened with them, you can hardly call it normal! You can't say that his being born to Laurel and me is outside the realm of possibilities. It makes sense, he would want revenge against me, that would give him the opportunity because, whoever he might be, Laurel and I would be protective of our child. I've cursed us, Travis! We would be raising my own murderer."

"Stop it!" Travis said, half-heartedly, not really able to disagree with his friend.

Gavin looked at Laurel as she slept. Her hair was a halo around her head, draped over the pillow in silken, golden strands. She looked so happy and peaceful. How would she take the news that they could not risk having children? Then he gasped, what if she was already pregnant? He had used nothing to prevent that possibility. He hadn't even thought to carry any protection, not expecting this marriage to happen so soon. Many women became pregnant resulting from their first unprotected sex. His mind was spinning with fear and disgust as the dream child's face kept coming back into his mind.

"Gavin, consider this, the baby would be a normal baby, not the monster you saw and, even with Casto inside somewhere, you and Laurel would be loving and good parents. Whatever turned him into the monster he was, it would not happen to him here, he would grow with the other children, learn to love and be loved..."

Gavin shook his head, "So, you don't think there's a chance that there are psychopathic sociopaths who can time-travel just like the rest of us and are evil to the bone in every single incarnation? Let me ask you this, did this life here, during this time, change the person inside of you into something you never were before? What if, like me, he just didn't realize what he was and hadn't worked to draw on his past lives properly with no one in Hades who was like him to point them out to him? You know how long it took me before I started to remember my former lives and that was with your help, and Laurel's help."

Travis thought long and hard and had to admit that Gavin had a better argument than his. While nurture might be extremely important to the average human, time-travelers were anything but average, carrying with them so many things they had learned in past lives. If Casto were a time-traveler and not just an anomaly, and Path seemed to think his was magic too strong to have been anything else but a time-traveler, he probably was as evil in each incarnation.

Hadn't Path said that Casto seemed to have been far more powerful than even he had realized about himself and that the additional energy from when he and Gavin joined Gwen and Path helped to defeat him? He sighed, "Do you want my help talking to Laurel about this?"

Gavin closed his eyes, "No, I'll talk to her." There was a long pause, "I just can't figure out what I can say to her. It's as if our future just got ripped away from us. How on earth can I expect her to accept this based on a dream?"

*

She listened, not interrupting, nor interjecting even a sound as if she was holding her breath as he talked. She sat, taking it all in. He knelt before her, holding her hands, then stood and paced as if he were arguing a case before a jury and still she was silent, waiting for him to vent all of it, to get everything out of his system. He told her the dream in great detail and she could picture it all in her mind. All she could think about was how disappointed he seemed, how he seemed to expect her to share that deep sense of disappointment. It seemed as if he were giving her news that she was dying of some exotic and incurable disease, his distress was that deep. She watched his face go through agony after agony as he told her about his dream and about the very real possibility of it coming true.

When he finished, he seemed drained of energy and the spark he always carried with him, the ceaseless and inspirational energy he always displayed that allowed him to work circles around nearly anyone at the camp, with the exception of Randy and Brian who both had worked hard all their lives and also had that seemingly endless energy and stamina. He sat with his head down, letting the thoughts float around in his head, now scrambled and impossible to put into some order to continue their discussion. She hated seeing her happy-go-lucky and optimistic man acting this defeated by a "dream."

When she was certain that he had nothing more to say, she reached toward him and rubbed a finger over the creases in his brow that had been there all morning. She ran that finger down over the side of his face and hooked it under his chin to draw his eyes up to hers. "I have been on birth control for a couple years now and never miss one of my pills, Gavin. Relax, I am not pregnant. I don't want to have children, and I mean that sincerely. I was hoping to have this conversation later, since we never really discussed it before. I should have brought it up but, you see, I spend a lot of time around children, other people's children. The happiest lives I've lived have been when I decided not to have children of my own. I treasure my solitude more than most people realize. I like it when I can send the children back to their mothers and go home to quiet spaces. I had decided that, if it was so important to you that it would hurt 'us', I would have a child with you, but, please don't hate me for this, Gavin, I would only be doing it for you." She was sincere and looking deeply into his eyes as she said this. "Will it hurt you if we don't have children? Will you envy those who do?"

His eyes widened as she talked and then he tilted his head to the side, "Is there some physical reason you can't have children?"

"How would I know that? I have never even wanted to find out," she told him, "What if we found out that there was? Would you love me less?"

He smiled, "There is nothing in this world or any others that could make me love you less. Laurel, I'm sitting here trying to process all of this and what you just told me is such an incredible relief. You have no idea how relieved I truly am. I actually thought that you would insist on having a child, convinced that no child we raised could possibly be 'Casto'. I can't risk this, Laurel, I could never fight against my own child, does that make sense?"

"Of course it does! But, I do have to tell you, now I'm going to be frightened that any woman in this village who does become pregnant might give birth to that abomination." Her eyes grew wide as she thought about that, "What about Shawnee?"

"No," he assured her, "Travis is already in contact with Shawnee's baby, you're going to adore the sweet little thing." He didn't feel that he had the right to reveal what he knew about Conner and Shawnee's baby. That secret must truly stay between him, Travis, Yellow Feather, "Brendan" and the little girl waiting to be born.

Laurel smiled at this news. Already she was seeing Gavin begin to recover from his worry. She was finding the memory of the dream already fading as she realized that this was the longest time since their ceremony that she and Gavin had been awake together without making love. She blushed at this thought, already warming to the idea that the gap had been too long for her liking. She shook her head to chastise herself and looked into his eyes and saw that he just might be thinking the same thing as his smile captivated her heart once again.

*

Christine was one of the oldest of the children who had been found in Denver by Gwen and Pathogent. She had not been with the original five, but a member of a group that had been waiting at the meeting place a few days later when Pathogent and the little boy, David, had gone to Denver for supplies. They had found Christine's group of orphan children standing and waiting for the promise of rescue. The children had been drawn by the posters that Gwen and the other children had left around the city. Only a few of them could read. Christine was one of those who suggested that this might be a trap, so they were extremely cautious when the man and boy approached them. The childlike man, who would become known as Pathogent to them, such a funny name, won them over with his kindness. When they were taken to Golden, Christine became instant friends with Cassie because she could see that Cassie was a real help to Gwen and being close to

Cassie meant that Gwen gave her much needed attention, too.

In many of her former lives, Christine found it nearly impossible living with other people, particularly people who wanted to be close to her, who wanted to invade her personal space. She had often chosen solitude in those other lives, even going so far as to have lived with animals instead of humans. She had been considered a witch, a voodoo woman, a recluse, a throw-away and many other things because of her personality. She could not help it that she was often stronger in conviction and could relate to creatures who didn't babble and brag. How she missed Africa and the beauty of waking to a dawn when she would encounter no humans, only her beloved friends, the gorillas.

Sometimes she just felt so jealous of Cassie because everyone loved her and came to her because she was so protective and sweet, but even more jealous of Laurel, who seemed to always have everything go her way. Laurel was possibly the luckiest girl alive. She was almost too beautiful to be real with her silky, gold hair and her cornflower blue eyes. Christine envied her because her own mousey brown hair and brown eyes never really seemed to draw anyone's attention. She had always seen the way boys looked at Laurel, all the boys, even the younger ones, sometimes even the men. No one ever looked at Christine that way, no one. And now Laurel was married to a god, to the handsomest and kindest male creature ever to exist. It was so unfair. There were times when she angered herself being jealous of such silly, things, she really needed no one.

Shawnee had once gotten frustrated with Christine when she refused to participate in class because she felt the class was "stupid." The truth was that with Cassie and Laurel being so smart they knew all the answers and everyone else was expected to keep up with them. Christine had grown tired of having to live up to their standard. Everything always came so easy to them both, everything. They were the smartest, the prettiest and the adults always talked to them as equals. Nothing came that easy to Christine because she could care less about learning math, or grammar or anything that seemed useless when she had already had many years of education, when the woods was her chosen home, but when she tried to explain why this was unfair, Shawnee called her a word that she had to look up to try to understand why anyone would say this about her.

Shawnee had said, "Oh, Christine, don't be so petulant." Christine never forgot that moment, it hurt her even though she had no idea at the time what the word indicated. She did know that Shawnee was frustrated with her, so being petulant could not be a good thing. Shawnee, being one of her favorite people in the camp, could hurt her with only a word, though Christine had grown thick-skinned with everyone else, little caring what they thought.

A petulant person would become angry because they don't get what they want. Shawnee was so wrong. Couldn't she see how wrong she was? It was different with her because Christine NEVER got what she wanted. What she WANTED was to not be here, to not even need to be here. Laurel had already gotten the only thing Christine wanted or envied for many years, for many lives, that was the truth and Christine was certain of it. Especially now, especially when Laurel had Gavin.

The first time Christine saw Gavin, when he came to the ridge where the village was waiting behind their trucks out there in Duran, she thought her heart would stop beating. He was better looking than any rock star she had ever seen in any of the books in the library, more gorgeous than any movie star. He got off that motorbike, took off his helmet and she gasped at how handsome he was. He wasn't built like a boy, he was built like a man, no, better than a man, he was BUILT. Then he stood there with that cute but shy guy, Travis, and the wind was whipping his hair down across his face and she just wanted to walk over and touch him, just touch him. When she saw Laurel take his hand, her heart fell into her shoes, how on earth did it always end this way, with Laurel getting everything?

Christine couldn't take her eyes off of him the whole time, even when the shots were fired and Lily was killed, even when Gwen and Path caused the flames and killed the leader of that other group, still she watched Gavin as if mesmerized. She made certain to be in the same truck as he and Travis and Laurel when they returned to Golden so that she could steal glances at him, hardly believing that someone as beautiful as this was real.

The curse of all of her lifetimes was that she had always been passionate and had a weakness for strong, capable men. There was that photographer back in Rwanda who had, for a short time, made her life so very much more interesting.

She watched him from afar, even though he was seldom far from Laurel. Laurel monopolized him from the start. It was hard to be able to catch him without her, but Laurel didn't like climbing with Conner, so Christine found an opening and learned to climb. She had spent so many lives using physical exertion to explore and survive.

When she went climbing with Conner and Shawnee, Yellow Feather and Gavin often went along. Gavin loved climbing, so Christine became a passionate climber, ready to try to scale anything. Conner was so impressed with her he called her fearless and she was getting closer to him and Shawnee than she had ever been because they were both happy to see her take such an interest in something. Yellow Feather and Gavin were also impressed and told her so. They would often belay for her, coaxing her along a difficult rock wall, but she really was becoming very impressive on the rocks and needed little coaxing.

It made her heart sing when she could hear Gavin's voice telling her she was doing an amazing job, or commenting to Conner, "Look at her go, she's finding handholds where

I don't even see them!" Hearing him address her, "Christine, you're making this look far too easy!" made her blush with pleasure. Her name on his tongue, imagine how thrilling that would have to be!

It began as a way to be near him, but it became so much more to her, the cliffs made her feel invincible and strong and she was getting muscles in great places and was looking better than she had ever looked. She had never been so fit. It felt wonderful being this strong. Sometimes she felt she could free-climb but that was something Conner and Shawnee both frowned upon, both of them refusing to sanction it. Sometimes she even went to the rocks by herself. With no one to belay her, she would free-climb. What Conner and Shawnee didn't know couldn't hurt them, she thought.

The magician watched her, hoping that his ploy would work. This was almost too easy since he had seen Gavin prepare for his woodland walk just moments ago and he was actually heading in the same direction as Christine. When he had been "in limbo", he found himself visiting the minds in Golden, searching for opportunities to seek the revenge he desired, no, the revenge he NEEDED. He would spend time in one of the villager's minds while it was dreaming, then switch to another; there were times when he felt like he had been inside the mind of every single dreamer in Golden! He got to know them intimately, their hopes and desires, who was happy to be where they were, who was a discontent. He avoided the strong ones, the Native American boy who seemed the physical leader of the young ones, the Native American woman who was almost strong enough to be a shaman herself, the young one who had ejected him from his mind before, Travis was his name, wasn't it? He could never resist occasionally trying to enter Gavin's mind. Gavin, however, was growing strong enough to reject him, though never strong enough to reject magic. Besides, he would need to do little to Gavin but affect what he saw; the magic would be directed toward the girl, Christine. She would be enough.

Casto smiled, released from limbo (what Pathogent and Gwen had referred to as "the Fade") by the very power of his mind. He had something very close to a physical presence in the here and now. He smiled grimly, this "between world" must be where people saw things like ghosts, and perhaps fairies. Now this golden opportunity had presented itself to him, the tableau almost too perfect, as if written by one of the romantic writers of the past. He had read many tales in other lives, tales of fairies crossing into the lives around them, causing havoc and miscommunication. He had read the story of King Arthur and how his sister, Morgan Le Fay (or was it Morgause, the other sister?), he could never understand if they were meant to be the same person or if they were distinct sisters in the tale, had duped Arthur into fathering his own son with her. He had loved that twisted tale of incest and deceit and planned to borrow elements from it today. Sometimes he astounded himself with his own cleverness.

Gavin would come across his own beloved Laurel in the woods. Not even questioning why she was there, he would find her responsive and willing. This was almost too precious to consider possible but he was certain that he could make it work. He used all of his concentration to change the girl, not much more was needed but to make certain that Gavin saw Laurel when he looked at Christine. Christine would most certainly, if her dreams were any indication, do the rest for him. Gavin might be too strong to resist a mind invasion by Casto, but he would never dream of trying to resist an invasion by something so microscopically tiny as a sperm. Casto congratulated himself for his own brilliance. Now he need only sit back and watch the show and what an entertaining show it would be.

Gavin heard a sound off to his left and, curious to see if it might be an animal they had not spotted yet, headed toward the sound, hoping for an elk, or maybe something even more elusive. The morning was perfect, now that Laurel had eased his mind about the baby thing, he felt his old self again, worries set aside for another day. He found himself headed toward a place where he had been many times with his friends, one of their favorite climbing cliffs, a place where the handholds were almost perfect and made climbing the rocky precipice a great exercise, if not the most challenging, the most perpendicular of the cliffs they were discovering, a challenging climb when gravity worked against you.

As he drew near to the cliff, he smiled. Laurel was there for some reason. Perhaps she had known that he might go there; it was one of the closer cliffs to the camp, so it made sense if she thought of finding him climbing. However, this morning's walk was simply meant to be a walk, he hadn't brought any equipment. But then he noticed that she had. Her hands were covered with chalk, preparing for the climb.

"What are you doing here?" he asked her, grinning with obvious pleasure.

She looked up and smiled, blushing when she saw him, "Don't tell anyone, I was just thinking of trying to see how far I could get..."

"Without a belay? Honey, you should never try such a thing without a belay. Promise me you'll never do this without me from now on." He moved closer, concerned that she would try so hard to do something she didn't enjoy just to please him. "You didn't tell me you were going out this morning or I would have joined you."

She looked at him in surprise, "You would have?"

"Of course, why would I not?" He reached a hand forward and ran the back of it over the beautiful familiar face. "My morning walk just got a whole lot better, better than I could dream."

She gasped as he touched her, how could this be possible? How could this dream of hers finally be coming true? This was too much for her, her breath quickened at his touch and he was looking at her with love and desire in his eyes. He was standing so close, close enough to touch, close enough to drive her nearly crazy. She put a hand against his strong chest, expecting him to move away and reject her but he sighed and smiled instead, taking a deep breath, expanding that amazing chest. When he reacted that way, she puzzled over this, he had never been anything but kind before, treating her with respect, like a friend. What on earth could have changed? Was it that he finally realized that she was learning to climb to win his admiration and perhaps more?

He looked around at the aspens and pine and realized, perhaps for the first time, how cathedral-like this clearing actually was. In times past, here with Conner and the others, it was just the climbing they were concentrating on, looking upward, not outward, not taking in how beautiful this spot really was, how secluded and secret, the trees protecting the cliff from casual view. A person would only find it to climb if they knew it was there, otherwise, it was camouflaged by trees until it rose above them. "This is a pretty place for a rendezvous." He grinned and moved even closer. Christine could actually feel his breath on her hair. She held her breath. Was she dreaming? Oh, how she wished he would pinch her so she could know.

He took his wife gently into his arms and kissed her deeply. She pushed him away, just slightly. It surprised him. He had never realized how strong she was, how muscular her arms until this moment. Was she angry with him?

He looked into her blue eyes and smiled, "Want to talk about it first? Did I do something wrong?"

"Oh, no, you're doing everything right! I just wasn't prepared for this. I wasn't ready for it. I just never allowed myself to dream..." she said, standing on tiptoe to kiss him, wrapping strong arms around his neck. He lifted her into the kiss. When did she ever seem this small to him? It was as if she were inches shorter and much more wiry and taut, her softness and curves concealed, perhaps by the fact that she was stretching to reach up to him. He bent and put an arm behind her knees to lift her into his arms, still kissing her, not taking his lips from hers. Again, she gasped with pleasure. Carrying her to a soft pile of pine needles and molting leaves, he laid her gently on the ground.

As they made love he marveled at her newfound strength. His first thrust seemed to hurt her and he drew back, wondering whether they had been perhaps doing this too frequently and she needed time to heal. He had no idea that this was his second deflowering in a two days' time. She shook her head and drew him down to her and whispered to him, "Oh, don't stop, please, harder, harder." He was a little taken back by the fact that she wanted him to be rougher than usual. Weren't they both a little sore and tender? He was caught up in it so strongly that he felt a buzzing in his ears, he lost himself in the moment and rode the waves of pleasure with the scent of the forest filling him up, his release so strong that it shook him that every single time this happened, it could make him feel so weakened, so depleted.

The wicked magician embodied in a tiny sperm had succeeded in implanting himself in the microscopic, now fertile, egg deep within Christine's body. He wanted to shout for joy, he wanted to let the boy know how badly he had been duped, he wanted to parade his triumph, so he swiftly and completely removed the chimera he had cast on the girl's countenance to exact his revenge. How he wanted to see the look of shock on his enemy's face.

When Gavin looked down to see Christine beneath him instead of Laurel, the shock went through his body like a lightning bolt. He recoiled in horror, falling back from her in dismay and disgust so deep that he was certain she could see it on his face.

"Gavin?" she asked, innocent of having played any part in the deception. The look on his face said it all: he was ashamed for what he had done and repulsed by it. She was confused and hurt by his reaction. She had done nothing to "arrange" this opportunity. She had done nothing wrong but to love him. Yes, it was true that they were both cheating on Laurel, but hadn't Laurel always had all the advantages, was it fair that she always won? It shook her when a strange and unwelcome voice used her lips to say, "I swore I'd git you, boy, and I meant it. I am so going to enjoy turning you on a spit!" She gasped and covered her mouth in horror. What on EARTH had just happened to her?

"No, NOoooooo." Gavin shouted, then launched himself at Christine speaking with Casto's voice, putting both of his huge hands around her throat. Her eyes went wide with fright and she struggled hard against him, trying to breathe, kicking and fighting for her life. Her face was turning from healthy and vigorous pink to a vein-filled purple and her body was going limp. When he realized what he was doing, he pushed back from her, looking down at his hands in terror at what they had nearly succeeded in doing. She struggled to take a breath, it wheezed back into her slowly as her throat tried hard to reopen. She pushed back away from him and tried to regain her consciousness, she had been only a breath away from passing out. She was choking and coughing trying to breathe into her emptied lungs.

She saw him there, standing where they had been lying in pleasure only seconds ago, and sobbing, looking down at his hands as if not recognizing them. She choked with anguish and emotional pain to know that he had gone so quickly from making love to her body to trying to kill her. What was happening? What had gone so very wrong? She pushed against the ground to gain her feet, kicking herself backward until she was trapped against the rocks of the cliff.

He looked up, slowly. "Christine, I..." he struggled to find something to say, anything to say to her. He started to move toward her, still on his knees.

"Don't!" She threw up her hand to fend him off, holding her shirt closed with the other hand. She moved several steps to the side, keeping her back against the cliff and watching him carefully. Where had that voice come from? What had it said? What was happening to her?

"Christine, please, we need to talk. Please. I didn't mean to hurt you, I didn't mean, I ..." he faltered, "I didn't mean any of it. I don't know how this could have happened. I thought you were Laurel. I - I am so sorry I hurt you, I am so sorry for all of it, any and every part of it. Christine, you can't - oh, God, how do I tell you this? You can't have a baby. Oh, God, I am so ashamed. Please believe me, you can't be pregnant. We have to go see Lincoln or Gayle or somebody to make certain." He stepped forward thinking, "How will I tell this to Laurel? How can I make the rest of the village believe me?" Aloud, he added, "Christine, if you are pregnant, you'll be giving birth to a monster, we have to go to Lincoln...maybe Gayle."

"Don't you touch me!" she shouted, "Don't you come near me! No. No. I mean it, stop or I'll scream." He stopped. She tried to clear her head to think. "I don't know what is going on here, but you just tried to kill me. Don't ever come close to me again."

"Christine..." he tried to reason with her.

It went through her head like another voice was speaking to her, that no one would believe her against "Wonder Boy", that the whole village would turn on her and think her a liar, or even worse, a seducer of married men. The voice told her that she would be seen as worse than "petulant", that she would become a pariah, a fallen woman. Something in her mind said to her, "I know where you could go where you would be worshiped and adored, I know a place where you would be the 'Queen Bee' and we would live like royalty." She didn't think to question who "we" might be. "He wants to take your baby away from you, a baby that you will love and adore, don't let him do this to you."

When he didn't seem to be getting through to her, Casto tried another tack, "God wants you to save your baby from him, Gavin wants you to abort it so his wife doesn't find out that he cheated. You have to get away from him. You have to save this precious life inside of you." Her parents had been very religious and had taught her to live a holy life. In all of her lives, she had been deeply and completely dedicated to God. Believing now that this was some kind of sign, trusting that God would soon reveal this confusing and frightening mission to her, she turned on her heel and ran.

He followed, floundering, but she put a lot of distance between them, running in fear for her life. She did not run toward the village, but toward Denver instead. Her mind was concocting a plan. She had to save this baby and go where the baby could grow to become the leader he was meant to be. The voice inside of her was telling her this, to go find a bicycle, better yet, a car and drive south toward El Paso. She was sure this was the right thing to do. He told her that she would be welcomed when she got there because the baby she was carrying was meant to go back there to rule.

Gavin tried to catch up with Christine but he soon realized that she had lost him. Though she might be hiding somewhere in the forest, he was unable to find a sign of her. He stopped and leaned against a tree, his mind spinning in dismay, his ears listening to even the slightest rustle of leaves. Everything that had been so good this morning had suddenly turned so very bad. How was he going to face Laurel again? How could he make this horrible crime up to Christine, willing or not, she did not realize that he had been fooled by Casto into thinking she was Laurel somehow. He felt so dirty, so wrong. Somehow Casto had contrived this entire thing but would Laurel believe that. Even if she believed it, how would it make her feel to know that another woman might be carrying a baby that they had just discussed keeping themselves from having.

He slumped to the ground, not knowing where to go or what to do. His life, so nearly perfect just a few hours ago, now seemed so bleak and damaged.

*

Her disappearance might have been suspicious and Gavin might have had even more explaining to do, had Randy and Dave not been in Denver, working near the New Hope meeting place, when Christine arrived on a bicycle she had found. She asked them to jump a car battery and make certain she had plenty of gas. When they asked where she was going, she told them that she had needed a vacation and was ready for a road trip on her own, hoping to see the wild horses. For some strange reason, they believed her. Whether or not it had anything to do with Casto and magic, no one would ever know but they made certain she had plenty of supplies for her trip. She loaded the car with food and spare gas and joked and talked with the two men as she always did, since they were her genuine friends. However, now she saw them as "Gavin fans" and wanted to put distance between them and her vulnerable baby. The last they saw of her, she was headed south through Denver. When they got back to Golden, they had forgotten all about their encounter with Christine until the search was in full swing. Only then would they reveal all they knew, only then would the village suspect her destination.

Gavin gathered himself together and went home to tell Laurel everything. He was determined not to start their marriage with secrets and lies so he sat down on a chair while she sat on the bed. He gave her room to run, throw things, leave if she wanted, knowing that he had no right to expect her to forgive him but hoped that she would understand when he told her everything. She sat and listened, not really moving at all, not showing any real emotion until the tears started from her eyes and then it was as if a spring had opened up inside her and they fell down from her eyes with a steady and horrible flow. It was killing him to watch those tears fall.

He felt hopeless to help her, not knowing whether to touch her or to just allow her to cry it out. She listened to every word he said and when he felt drained at the end, she asked him only one thing, to tell it to her again from the beginning. The pain he felt from her tears was bad enough but he was helplessly sickened by the hurt in her voice. He repeated the entire story, careful not to leave out a single sordid detail, including how Christine's responses seemed so right, had fit with what he would have expected Laurel to say, so matched to what he said to her.

When he finished, he sat, waiting for a word from her, waiting for the screaming, the battle, whatever might come he felt he deserved that and more. They sat for a moment in silence, then she said, "Nothing will ever be normal for us. I know that most 'normal' people would not understand what happened to you, but, I've been there, inside your head. I've been through all this with you and I know that you want me to believe that Casto survived that cataclysm with Gwen and Pathogent, but..."

"But he did, Laurel! He did! It wasn't just my dream, there are other reasons that I have for believing that he is out there and he intends vengeance against me. Remember what he was capable of, what Yellow Feather told us about the coyote and how he was certain that Casto had possessed the poor thing to spy on us?" He sighed, feeling more defeated that he had in his entire life.

"If I lose you over this, Laurel, I will understand. But it will be the worst thing that has ever happened to me, and you well know that I have had some really terrible things happen to me. Losing you would be more than I can bear. I love you, truly and deeply. I am indefensible if you don't believe that it was Casto's magic and nothing more. I've never wanted anyone else but you, how I wish you would believe that."

Her eyes shimmered with tears, "I'm either the stupidest and most gullible girl on the planet or I just love you too damned much, but I do believe you, Gavin, I really do."

He sobbed and went to his knees in front of her, immeasurable relief washing through his body, "Where do we go from here, Laurel? Can you love me again exactly as you did before I left this cabin this morning? Can we erase what has been done to us? This is only the second day of our marriage and already..."

"I don't know, Gavin, all I know is that I won't allow myself to lose you. I know I'll need time and you will have to give me that. I will have to find a way to forgive this and even believe you, although the entire story is so crazy. What are you going to do about Christine? What will it be like every time you see her?"

"I followed her for a mile or so but she was so fast, I couldn't catch her, I don't know where she is, but she is too afraid of me now for me to even begin to apologize to her, to try to make amends with her."

"Send your mind out to her, or have Travis help you reach her, let her know that we don't hold her responsible for this, that she is a victim, just like you." Laurel closed her eyes, unable to believe that these words were coming from her own heart, that she was able to believe the unbelievable, that she was going to someday get over this mountain thrown into their path.

"Gavin, we are never going to have 'normal' lives. We are not 'normal', we have the sum total of many, many lives between us and both of us know that things can and do happen beyond our control. I have made the mistake of jumping to conclusions too many times in too many lives. I am not going to allow anything to ruin this chance for happiness. I know that it is YOU that I want to spend my life with, only you. We will get through this together, but we must trust some of our friends to help. If Christine is out there with that monster growing inside of her, we have to find her and bring her home; this is not her fault, she is nothing more than a host to a parasite. She won't see it that way, she may already aware that she needs to protect her 'baby' from us. But we have to try to reach her. I know that you don't expect me to say this, but I knew she had a crush on you and I feel very sorry for her because, if I were not the one you love, I would still love you strongly, so I can and actually DO identify with her."

He was on his knees before her, reaching up to wipe the tears from her face as his own fell without ceasing. "You are beyond belief, Laurel, how could I possibly tell you how incredibly unique and wonderful you are? With you by my side, there is nothing I won't face. If the village wants to judge me, I am ready, I can take their contempt but I would die inside if I lost you."

*

The voice inside her head spoke to her soothingly. "When you get there, stand your ground and demand to speak to Pit Bull, he will be the person in command now. I will do the rest. Prepare to be loved and worshipped...mother. You are strong and capable, Mother, they will see that, don't bend your knee to them, you were meant to lead them."

Christine wondered if she was hallucinating the voice, if she was hearing it because she was so weary, having driven non-stop since Denver, stopping only to eat, vomit, and put gas from one of the cans in the trunk into the gas tank of the car. She would have to stop soon. She was not only exhausted from driving, but the trauma of the day was catching up with her. Countless times she had heard Gavin and Travis calling to her inside of her head, they begged her to come back to camp, they told her that she was being used and that they wanted to talk to her, to assure her that Gavin owed her more than an apology. He told her that he begged her forgiveness and wanted her to see how sincere he was. They told her that she was innocent of any wrongdoing and asked why she was running away when her friends wanted only to help her.

She listened, but ignored, just as the voice inside of her told her to do. Even when she got a lump in her throat when Gavin told her how sorry he was. Even though he sounded so sincere that he hated that he hurt her in any way. Even though she wanted to see his face when he told her those words. Even when her heart wanted to turn the car around, to face Laurel and Gavin and to see them tell her that they knew that she was innocent of everything but being a sweet, trusting girl, she drove on, letting the inner voice guide her toward a place where her baby would not only be welcome, but would be treated like a king. She knew that she would be strong enough to survive. He promised her a place where she would no longer play second fiddle to the pretty, popular girls, where she would be feared and worshipped.

"You don't ever need to hear yourself called 'petulant' again, you will never cease to get what you want, you'll have everything you want, I'll see to it personally. The men there, they are like the apes you loved," he crooned, reading through her mind like a book, " they need us to protect them, they are so vulnerable, struggling to survive in this harsh world. They need you, Christine, I need you, Mother."

He worked hard to keep up his soothing commentary, trying to block the other voices trying to reach her. His life depended upon it.

The End

About The Author

Jeanette Appel Cave, a native of Ohio, lives in Sacramento, CA, and is an advocate for peace, the environment, endangered species, and efforts to protect the good. She wrote "The Helix Blink" in which many of the characters here in this sequel were introduced and led incredible entwined lives throughout centuries. Her next novel, dedicated to her heroes, Jane Goodall and Dian Fossey, was "Dark Continents: Survival Instincts", another post-apocalyptic, multi-generational web of stories in which survivors try to save gorillas and other apes, after almost all species, including most of the human race, were destroyed. That book was followed by a romantic adventure and mystery set in the San Francisco area, where "second sight" in a Romani family brings together a successful young lawyer and a young mother and her son. All of Cave's fiction is driven by her passion to reveal evil and protect the good. Her books are available online and as e-books.

The author may be reached at jennycave49@gmail.com

Made in the USA
Middletown, DE
21 May 2023

30765514R00166